THE LAD AND THE RING

PART ONE

The Lad of the Rings: Book 2 - Part 1

By: Johann Balthasar Knörtzer

The Lad and the Ring – Part 1

For more information, visit:
https://www.mythicbookspublications.com/johann

Book and Cover design by
Johann Knörtzer and MythicBooks

Paperback ISBN: 978-1-954948-03-7
E-book ISBN: 978-1-954948-04-4

First Edition:

10 9 8 7 6 5 4 3 2

V.3

Dedication

For my son and daughter, who may read this book if I give them five bucks;

for my wife, who continues forcing me to keep writing this stuff and helps to edit and tie it all together;

and for my friend and cousin, Eddockelino Meriodon Knörtzer, who aided in bringing the original version of this tale to life.

Many thanks to my friends over at Mythic Books, who've helped to propel sales of 'The Gabbin' into nearly triple digits, then took over the massive task of formatting and publishing this book and hopefully many more to come.

A special thanks to my Beta Reader, who was able to point out issues my tired old peep-spheres couldn't manage noticing.

Finally, a hugely appreciative thank-you to my followers, supporters, friends, family, acquaintances, and anyone else who's taken time out of their day to look over the nonsense I've typed up with a keyboard. I hope you enjoy this book and further content coming in the future of this series.

Table of Contents

Prologue:
Pre-Story Writings

If you must know... the lad is a young boy/thing living in the land of Skiddle Earth in the year 9999 SY (Skiddle Years). The particular place in which he dwells is named Hometown; a semi-cozy little village that lies to the west of Vim Valley and bordering just north of the nearby river of Crim Creek. The lad is the only son of the dad and his wife... or at least he *was*. For at one point, the young lad was forced to move in with his unclecousin when he was somewhere between the ages of zero and eight after the mysterious disappearance of those parents.

Now, being fifteen to twenty-seven years old, he lives alone in a quaint cottage-house that his dear unclecousin built (or more likely paid someone else to build) for his parents twenty or some odd years before. Some of the long-time friends he's acquired over the years include, but are possibly not limited to: his best pal, BombirThin; the skilled and crafty Bowman Slim; and of course, Sally Kim, who isn't a guy. The lad is at least way less than six feet tall, and has blackish-red, super-straight, squared-off hair that always looks like it's just been trimmed. One might say its shape is akin to a long half-melon with a rectangle cut out for the eyes. He also frequently wears clothes, but likely not the style you'd think.

He loves oranges with an extreme passion, to the point of all his meals being somehow orange related in nature. It should definitely be noted that he possesses one of the most powerful weapons ever seen in Skiddle Earth: The Super-Deluxo-Saber. No one is really sure how the heck he got his grubby hands on it, yet some say he accidentally made it while trying to forge an orange peeler out of a meteor that crashed into his toolshed. At this early point, the odds are slim he is fully aware of the sword's true might.

YOU may think this could be the part where the lad's name is revealed to you. It is not. Nor will there ever be such a time. The lad is what he is, and *who* he is. He is 'a lad' surely, yet also he is 'the lad'; a title and a name in one, never a capital, ever two words. One thing he is not, however, is '*the* lad'. Such an honorable designation could never have been bestowed upon one of such lowly birth. But alas, he cared not—to him, riches and nobility were ridiculous notions deserving of nothing more than passing scoffery. The lad craved only adventure, citrus, and good times.

He can often be found in an apple tree down the street in his ignorant neighbor's backyard. The tree being the source of the majority of oranges he consumed, and unknown to him to be the perfect, ancient, magical, sacred Aplornge tree planted by someone in the distant long-ago. He also didn't know—that soon a simple voyage with his friends would change his little lad life forever.

So—providing you haven't already thrown the book out the least furthest window to you yet—believe it or not, the following pages you are about to read have quite a bit to do with this aforementioned young fellow and his various doings. Let's take a look then, shall we?

Chapter 1:
The Evil Neighbor

This one time, a young lad was sitting in an apple tree eating oranges when he heard a knock at his door only six blocks away. The lad rushed to see who was knocking. He jumped out of the apple tree, threw down his orange, and sprinted across a few dozen yards. All along the way he was dodging trees, ducking under hanging laundry, and jumping over flower beds—as well as sliding through three wet freshly poured concrete patios. Grabbing a long stick while running, he jabbed it into the ground, pole-vaulting over the last fence bordering his own backyard.

After executing a flawless roll upon contacting his unkempt lawn, he sprung to his feet, quickly taking several long strides to his back door. He unlocked it with haste and ran through the house to reach the inner side of his front door. Allowing himself approximately four seconds to catch his breath, he calmly opened it with a grin.

There on his front step stood an elder-aged woman in a mauve robe with a stack of hair like a haphazard tower of playing cards and a frown that could unscramble an omelet.

"Rudolph?" asked the lad in bewilderment.

"*NO!*" yelled the woman. "*I* am your downstreet *neighbor*. You know... *Whilma*? The one that *owns* the *tree* that you can't seem to *stay* out of? What in the flippin' *blazes* do you think you're *doing* up there anyway?!"

The lad, fairly annoyed by all her yelling and overuse of emphasis, just nodded and replied, "What else would I be doing in an apple tree?! I was eating an orange, stupid!"

With a burning anger, Whilma screamed, "Why, you little fruit-sucking thug! I'll teach *you* a lesson you shan't *soon* forget!"

With that spoken, she backhanded him across the face, sending spit and orange fragments flying through the air, splattering his walls and doorframe. The lad was wide-eyed and in shock, but Whilma wasn't done yet. A small box lay to her right side on the step. An ugly, sinister half-grin briefly passed her puffy, protruding lips, and her eyes narrowed as she looked upon the label with the words 'the' and 'lad' written upon it. She then raised her boney knee high, and brought it down swiftly, her steel-toed, high-heeled, slipper-boot striking the box's upper portions with a mighty force. The lad's blankened stare snapped down to the wreckage.

That was the thing he'd been waiting for. The reason he had run home so quickly. He had thought it was the mailman knocking—there to bring him the item he'd sent away for in his catalogue: a jar of the finest and most exquisite freeze-dried powdered orange for seasoning... well... everything.

Now it was *his* turn to be angry. He met Whilma's gaze—fury in his eyes, cruelty in hers.

The lad then spoke in a grave tone. "Lady, if you'd be so kind... take your ancient, repulsive, wrinkly, stinking carcass off my front step."

Then, slowly smiling again, he unsheathed his Super-Deluxo-Saber, and smote Whilma with it whilst he ate an orange with the other hand. Of course, that's what he kind-of *imagined* doing. In reality, he spun fast and whacked his front door with the hilt of the sword. The door slammed closed so hard that when he calmed down enough to go out and grab his ruined box, he had to use a pry bar to get it open. As he stooped to collect his package, he suffered a glance toward the road.

Across the street, that old bag Whilma was at someone else's house harassing *them* about something now. The lad shook his head and went back inside, not realizing that Whilma was in fact tightly pasted to the door across the street from the shockwave blast of his own door slamming. She scraped herself off later and slowly hobbled back home, vowing all sorts of revenge.

The lad brought his box into his living room and set it on his coffee table. Then, he sat down on his favorite spot on the couch: near the far-left side, sunk between two cushions that badly needed more filling inside. The backs of his tender fleshy leg-tops could feel the couch frame in its entirety through the paper-thin sitting squares, but the lad didn't mind, for it was time to see if his prize made it through the outrageous footwear assault.

He carefully sawed at the string with his absurdly large sword, flipped back the flaps, and beheld a thing miraculous. The jar was intact and uncracked. The lad rejoiced at the quality of the glass. He reached in and lifted high the life-changing food additive. Suddenly, his smile fell, his eyes went wide, and he yanked the jar closer for inspection.

With veins bulging and teeth gritting, he loudly shouted, "Frigging SUN-DRIED GRAPE SHAVINGS?!?"

He stood, jumped in the air, and on his way back down, he threw the jar into the floor as hard as he'd ever thrown anything.

'SMASH!!!'

The glass shattered into hundreds of pieces. Then the lad proceeded to rapidly stomp the shards into *thousands* of pieces. He cast himself back onto his couch, cursing the shop that had sent him these blasphemous, unwanted turd-circle flakes.

After a half hour or so of grumbling, he finally got up to get a broom, some bandages for his foot, and some glue to fix the jar so he could send it back. This was just not his day.

He needed to get out of the house for a while; a few days away from the stresses of being an unemployed adolescent freeloader. Tomorrow would be better. He had plans he'd put off for far too long. He would go find some of his friends and take a vacation from this miserable place.

After eating a dinner of pan-fried orange slices and toast spheres, he brushed his teeth with orange-mint toothpaste and was soon fast asleep.

Chapter 2:
Thin Permissions

Early the following morn, the lad awoke to the sound of loud, constant banging in his backyard. He already knew what was making the sound and wasn't bothered by it in the least. He was still working out the details in his head of where exactly he would be adventuring to while he packed a few small bags and stuffed as many useful items as he possibly could in his multitude of oversized pants pockets. He bathed well, combed out his round hair, put on his most rugged outdoorsy outfit, and was off to the kitchen to eat and pack food.

I'm sure I don't even have to tell you what most of the food was, though he did bring a good deal of cheese as well. For cheeses of various kinds were always a close second choice to you-know-what. At last, he was ready. The lad grabbed the Super-Deluxo-Saber and slid it smoothly into the leather sheath on his back. He then locked his house up, exiting out the rear door.

A person stood in the center of the yard in the hazy, dim morning light, facing away from the house. In their hands, they held a wide, flat shovel high over their stout physique. Before the lad could speak, the person spun toward him and brought the shovel down with immense speed.

'WHAM!'

The tool struck the ground hard, flattening the grass at the lad's feet. Immediately, the lad stepped forward, quickly drawing back his right hand.

He cast the hand forth, aiming right for the shovel-having trespasser, who instantly responded with their own right-hand thrust.

The two flattened palms clashed, creating a loud 'CRACK!' that echoed throughout the entire yard.

The hands were drawn back by each of them, only to come back for another strike again and again. They both eventually dropped their hands to their sides, and all went silent.

"Good work," said the lad.

"No problem," replied the shovelbearer. "Figured I'd get done early today is all."

The mystery person was, in fact, the lad's best friend, BombirThin. You see, the lad heavily disliked the doing of chores, so when his lawn grew too tall, he paid Bombir in crisp high-fives to smack the grass down flat with a shovel. He *did* possess a small pile of actual currency from various inheritances, but he needed that to last the rest of his life so he could pay for food and buy neat stuff. The lad's greenish-gray eyes flashed a twinkly gleam as he prepared to make his friend join his ludicrous adventure.

"Bom," stated the lad. "I'm finally doing it. I'm getting

the heck outta this town—at least for a while. Don't know where I'm even going, but I'm ready for some adventuring, and I can't say I would hate it if you'd be so good as to accompany me."

BombirThin slicked back his greasy golden mop of hair and sighed. "Sure, I'd certainly... like to... the lad. But I'll have to see if the folks approve first. I know *you'll* be eighteen in a few months, although you haven't had to answer to anyone in a long while. But I'm a year behind you, and you know how strict my pappy is. He thinks you to be quite the troublemaker anyhow."

The lad looked thoughtfully to the far distant mountains for a moment, then said, "Tell them it'll be a group outing. We'll get everyone to go! I mean crap, Bowman's in like his twenties or something. There's your adult supervision."

Bombir tried to raise an eyebrow, but wasn't good at it.

"Bowman? You think he'd go? He's probably too busy doing cool adult stuff to hang out with us anymore. What should I say to my parents that we're going to be *doing* anyway? Fishing, hiking, camping?"

The lad put his hands on his hips and looked downward, still thinking. Just then, a breeze lightly blew, kicking up a bashed-up piece of grass from underfoot. It fluttered around the lad, and he followed it with his eyes. It landed gently on the edge of a nearly full rain barrel at the back of the house, teetered back and forth, then began see-sawing violently fast.

Finally, it tipped too far, and fell off the outside toward

the ground. THEN, another quick gust of wind kicked it right back up, flipping it end over end. It stopped in midair, still rotating slightly. Gravity overcame it, and back down once more it went, this time landing in the water of the barrel. Slowly, it drifted across the surface toward the other side. The lad approached and watched carefully. He leaned in close to the green blade and imagined a tiny little Bombir and the lad standing on it and waving to him.

"I've got it..." said the lad.

***

The lad and BombirThin strolled down the lane to the Thin residence to seek out some adventuring permissions. The whole way there, the lad non-stop ran his mouth about how they were going to sail a boat up Crim Creek.

"Where are we supposed to get a boat exactly?" asked Bombir.

"That's the fun," said the lad, still smiling like a goob, "we'll build it ourselves!"

Bombir pretended to scratch the right side of his face so the lad wouldn't see him roll his eyes, then replied, "Out of what? We have no supplies or materials! You gonna craft it out of mud?"

The lad swiftly produced a large sack that had been tied to his belt, opened the top wide, and let his friend observe the contents within. Nails, hundreds or more, lined the innards of the bag.

"Pried these out of my house a few weeks ago. Seems to stay up just fine with half of 'em left... possibly a quarter.

I was gonna try building an orange silo with these if I found some extra wood, but I think I go through them dang fruits too fast for that much storage anyhow. Now we just need some of that lumber I could never seem to find. I've heard there's a few abandoned houses down near the creek, and plenty of trees obviously."

BombirThin shook his head. "Got it all figured out, huh?" he said, still trying to raise that one eyebrow. Then a thought struck him. "Not to get ahead of myself, but I *do* know a fellow from whom we might obtain some tools. Old Wally somethin-or-other, out east of town. Practically on the way to the creek."

The lad was relieved to be hearing something showing him Bombir was really on board.

"Oh yeah, I've heard of that guy. Related to Sally, I think... has some sort of hunting store. He's kinda odd if I remember right—a real 'William-of-the-Hills' type character."

BombirThin began to answer but was suddenly knocked on his face by an unseen force behind him. The lad quickly spun around to see two menacing boys. He knew them well, though he hadn't seen them in some time. It was the town bully, SkyScraper Ned, and his sickly looking, yet nearly as horribly mannered sidekick, SteepleCranium Hubert.

The former got his name from being exceptionally gifted in height—at least when compared to everyone else in this part of the world—and his lofty, upward explosion of fiery red hair made his towering stature all the more conspicuous. The latter of the two was of normal tallness, though in body only. His head, however, was lengthy and conical, giving him a creative alias of his own. He hadn't much hair to speak of, but he wore a miniature dark brown cowboy hat upon his dome's peak.

"Looky what we've got here, Steeps," boomed Ned. "Couple of dumb little babies out for a walky!"

The lad gave his most unwelcoming stone-cold stare to the jerk as he pulled Bombir up from the ground.

"Beat it, Scrapes," said the lad. "*We're* going on a grand adventure across the world while you stay here with nothing to do but fart the back of your pants out!"

Ned's smug face faded into what could have very well been unhappiness at that moment. He squeezed his hand into a giant fist and took a step toward the lad.

"Look out, the lad! He's got a fist!" cried Bombir.

But it was too late. The blow came—right at the lad's tender belly. He was lifted upward and thrown several feet onto his back. BombirThin drew his shovel, waving it at Ned, but Hubert dove at him and wrestled the dirt-scooper away. He laughed as he twirled the landscaping tool around and tossed it to Ned, who bit the handle in half and crushed its flat blade into a ball.

He then discarded the pieces by tossing them far off in separate directions. Bombir started wildly swinging fists at the bullies, but Hubert easily held him back with an outstretched hand against the forehead. The lad was having no more of this nonsense; he sprung to his feet, fuming with wrath.

"Just so you crapheads know, I'm packing heat. So unless you want to be looking up at your own butts in the next five seconds, I suggest you back off!"

Ned's unpleasant smile returned, and he pulled a quite oversized sword from his side. He held it out for all to descry.

"This baby is named 'The Long Farewell'. I suppose even you two weenie-babies can understand its meaning. You want to threaten me, the lad? Let's see what you've got!"

Ned drew back the sword, then took a huge, bounding step toward the lad. The massive blade swung around from his side, aiming downward and straight for the lad's left shoulder. In one lightning-fast motion, the lad side-stepped to the right, yanked the Super-Deluxo-Saber from its sheath on his back, and rotated it around for an upward-left swing to meet the incoming strike.

The lad's superior blade prevailed, for it was forged with iron from the heavens. But SkyScraper Ned's sword, though ominous it looked, was nothing more than a cheap, slapped-together, novelty display piece. The Super-Deluxo-Saber effortlessly tore The Long Farewell clean in two, with the now-detached blade flipping and spiraling over the lad's head and into the distant weeds. The lad raised the tip of the Saber to Ned's crooked nose.

The dumbstruck fool just stared for a moment, holding up the stump of his ruined sword for inspection. He stuck the shortened thing back in its sheath, but it fell out onto the ground embarrassingly. Ned snapped out of it and forced the smugness back to his face.

"Come on, Steeps, these diaperboys can't take a joke," he said with a very fake laugh. Then he raised his voice a bit. "We've got a lot of really *cool* stuff to do anyway! No point in wasting our time goofing around with these cheese-brains! Seeya, chumps!"

And with that, the two jerks turned around and walked off, but not before Hubert looked back and stuck his tongue out at them like an infant. The lad stepped toward them, still holding his sword, and their pace quickened to near double.

After Bombir and the lad watched to make sure the two miscreants were truly gone, they dusted themselves off and turned once again to their destination. It was but a few more minutes' walk before reaching Bombir's house, and the pair said little the rest of the way. They did their best to conceal any signs of struggle upon them; the Thins would never let their son go if they knew he just got beat up without even leaving town yet.

Bombir opened the front door and proceeded inside with the lad close behind. There on the living room couch sat Bombir's parents: his bald, round, bearded, spectacled father, PlumborThin, and his surprisingly fit and fair, blonde-haired mother, KandleThin. The couple was eating breakfast on little fold-out tables in front of them and staring expectantly at a large empty spot on the wall directly ahead, as if some form of entertainment should be found there.

"There's some extra sausage and eggs on the stove for you and your friend, Bombir," said Kandle, noticing the boys looming in the doorway.

So, they went and grabbed some plates to load up. The lad passed on the eggs, nearly hurling when he saw them as a matter of fact. He had eaten a big bad egg once when he was very young, never again giving them another chance. He made up for it by swiping some extra toast spheres and pulling a shiny orange from one of his bags. He had, of course, already eaten breakfast, but there was never any harm in having another.

"Think I'll foist some extra scraps for the road," he said to himself, stuffing more food into the last spaces of his pockets.

The two joined Bombir's parents in the living room and began to discuss and negotiate the planned trip.

"How long exactly?" asked Kandle.

"No more than a few days, I'm sure," Bombir answered.

"I don't like this one!" yelled Plumbor, motioning toward the lad. "He's quite the troublemaker anyhow!"

"It's going to be a group though," Bombir stated. "Bowman Slim and some others are coming. Please? PLEASE?! Please-please-please-please-please—"

"Just friggin GO! Sheesh!!" screamed Bombir's dad.

Bombir smiled wide and ran to his room to pack his bags. When finished, he came back down to say goodbye to his parents. Just as he went to walk out the door with the lad, a small girl-person appeared from the shadows.

"I'm coming too, you fat nerds!" cried the girl.

It was Bombir's eight-year-old sister, HendraThin.

"You're too young and dumb, Hendra!" responded Bombir. "It ain't happening."

She drew back one of her pink, wooden, princess play-shoes and swiftly cracked Bombir's shin with the pointy toe. Bombir grabbed her up quick, spun in a half-circle, and threw her across the living room. Without ever looking away from his wall, Plumbor caught her by the back of the pants with one hand, setting her down to her feet and shooing her off. The lad walked out the front door, with Bombir limping behind him.

Chapter 3:
Gettin' Outta Town

The two boys headed east now, Bombir still complaining about how annoying his sister was. They turned from the main road, walking several hundred feet down a long, dusty driveway that led to the home of one Sally Kim. They were in hopes she would join them on their trip. The lad knocked on the door of the aging farmhouse, and not six moments passed before someone opened up.

"Hey there, boys, what can I do for ya?" It was Sally's dad, Guston-Van, hunching on a pair of crutches in the entryway.

"Good day, Mister... uh... Van... sir," said the lad, inexplicably intimidated. "We were wondering if Sally wanted... and... *could*—or perhaps was rather *allowed*—to come with us on a little few-day sailing trip—if she wants to—and certainly only if it's okay with you and Mrs. Van?"

Guston stared at the lad uncomfortably, yet not menacingly.

"Let me talk to Easell for a moment," he replied, softly closing the door.

He came back about twenty minutes later and nearly

caught the lad scratching his rear end.

"Well, we talked," said Guston. "We know you've all been friends a long time, and we kinda trust you. Just make sure she stays safe, and nothing gets *weird*."

"Oh, yeah, for sure!" the lad almost yelled. "Is she... coming out soon? Or should I come in and help her pack?"

Guston cleared his throat. "She isn't here. Went to her uncle's for the weekend, just down the road there. She'll probably have plenty enough packed already."

"Alright, thanks, Mr. Van." said the lad, waving as he rejoined Bombir and headed back to the main road.

A few more houses down was the home of another friend of theirs. Bombir and the lad approached and knocked upon the front door, both of them at the same time. A boy around their age peeked out, then opened the door.

"Y-y-yes?" squeaked the timid fellow.

"Furnitch Klebzmin!" cried the lad. "It's been a while. We were heading out to Crim Creek for some sailing adventures. You interested in coming with?"

Furnitch pushed up his glasses, smoothed out his brown, book-shaped hair, and straightened his sweater vest.

"I'm... uh... pretty busy, the lad. Maybe another time," he replied.

The lad raised an eyebrow effortlessly. "What exactly are you busy with?" Furnitch suddenly looked confused and began to sweat. "You *aren't* busy, *are* you?!" the lad accused.

"NO! I just don't like going outside, walking, boats, or YOU GUYS! Poop off!!"

Furnitch then slammed the door in their faces and ran deep into the house to hide while loudly whining.

"Can't win 'em all," said Bombir. "He's probably still upset about the time when we were kids and he accidentally hit you with a stick. Then I convinced him he killed you and that he was going to jail."

The two had a good laugh at the memory and left the house behind, passing a misspelled sign that said, 'Leeving Hometown'.

It was just about noon; the sun was high and hot. Bombir and the lad had walked for miles since their failed attempt at another companion. Now they came to a large run-down shack with the giant words, 'Deer-Slayin Wally's Wilderness Outfitter and Hunting Supply Emporium', sloppily painted across the face of the second floor. All was quiet, and no one seemed to be around outside, so the boys went in.

A bell jingled as they pushed their way through the creaking screen door. There were shelves surrounding them on all sides, stocked full with just about anything a hunter or survivalist could ever want. The lad's eyes went wide as he examined some of the nearby merchandise.

"I don't think they take high-fives here," mumbled Bombir. Then he pointed out the unoccupied front counter on the right side of the store.

The lad stepped toward it and smacked a little silver bell to call for assistance. They waited a few minutes, but nobody came. The lad then noticed a soft gurgling noise coming from behind the counter, so he walked around to the side, pushing open a short swinging door and ignoring the 'Employees Only' sign. To the lad's shock and horror, Sally Kim lay there on the floor in a mangled mess. Her dark brown hair was stuck to her face, her body was twisted at the waist, both arms were crossed underneath her, and one leg was elevated, shoe caught on a cabinet handle.

"SALLY!" cried the lad as he dropped to one knee, shaking her shoulder.

Bombir jumped on the counter to peer over.

"Whaaaat..." a groaning, muffled voice replied.

Sally slowly straightened her limbs out, then stretched. Sitting up, she rubbed her eyes and wiped drool from the corner of her mouth. She pushed back her matted hair, blinked a few times, then screamed, "AHHHH!!!"

The lad stumbled back and flipped over the swinging door behind him.

He quickly stood, gasping for breath, and asked, "Sally? You alright? What happened here?!"

Sally stood, still rubbing one eye and breathing heavily. "Oh, uhh... hey, the lad. Haven't seen you in a while. My uncle asked me to watch the register while he did— whatever it is you do to make jerky in the back. Nobody's been by all morning. I guess I got bored and dozed off."

"Oh, thank cheese," said the lad with heavy exhalation. "We thought you'd been murdered up."

At the word *'we'*, Sally glanced to her left to see BombirThin awkwardly waving after climbing back off the counter.

"Well... this is embarrassing," she said. "What are you guys all the way out here for?"

The lad grinned a little. "We're going on a sailing adventure! Gonna build a boat and take it up the creek. We asked your mom and pop earlier if they minded you joining us, and they were surprisingly okay with it."

Sally, still waking up, replied, "Yeah, of course. That sounds interesting. Let me go upstairs and grab my stuff, maybe wash my hair right quick. Then I just have to let my uncle Wally know."

She ran up the steps, and the two boys kicked back to wait.

A while later, a back door flew open, revealing a tall, muscular man wearing a tan leather outfit and a small round hat with antlers sticking out the sides. His humongous reddish-brown beard bounced up and down as he walked toward Bombir and the lad. He eyed them suspiciously, gripping a long spear that clung to his back.

"Where's my niece?" he inquired scratchily. "I left her here to tend the register."

"We're her friends—just waiting for her to get her stuff and come down."

Wally didn't believe a word. He yanked the spear from its resting place, pointing the sharp tip to the lad's nose.

"Hey, man!" cried the lad, "I'm telling the truth! We got permission from her parents, and as soon as she comes down, we're foisting outta here."

Just then, Sally began descending the stairs with her bags.

"Uncle Wally, stop! These are my friends, the lad and BombirThin. Please don't skewer them. I'm gonna be going with them on a boating trip."

Wally quickly flipped his spear back in place. "Whoops, sorry, guys," said the Deer-Slayer. "Can't be too careful. Since you're my niece's pals and all, how's about I get you set up with some extra supplies on the house? It's the most I could do. Or is it least? Anyway, take whatever you need. I'll even grab you a fresh batch of my semi-famous deer jerky."

"That'd be awesome!" said the lad.

So, the group geared up, now with extra food that would stay unspoiled far longer, and some various tools. Items such as: fishing supplies, a fire-starting kit, bug repellant, mini fold-out tents, ropes, and a slingshot for Sally. She already carried a long, curved knife for protection, but her uncle figured she could do with a ranged weapon as well. They all thanked Wally and said their goodbyes, then the three of them started up the last leg of the journey to Bowman Slim's house and the creek just beyond.

***

Not much happened in the hours walking past the infrequent farmhouses and sprawling wheat fields on the way to Bowman's cottage. They caught up with current goings-on in their lives, which wasn't a whole lot. Then the lad and Bombir told Sally of the incredible showdown between them and the town bullies, much to her fascination.

At one point, they stopped under the shade of a large tree to sit for a while and eat a late lunch. Sally practiced hitting distant trees with her new slingshot, missing consistently.

"Have you heard any news of your unclecousin?" she asked, while studying the slingshot's craftsmanship.

Bombir winced slightly at the question, but the lad replied, "Nah, it's been almost a year now. His house—if you wanna call it that—was boarded up recently and a little memorial thing was placed out front. I think he was starting to lose it. He was taking a lot of trips out of town toward the end—nobody really knows why."

"This trip have anything to do with him?"

"Maybe a tiny bit," answered the lad once more. "I mostly *did* just want to get out of town. But I believe he may have been coming out this way, so it's possible that I might find out something about his reasons for it. As far as finding him—I doubt he's still alive. A couple months back, some fishermen found remains near the slopes of the mountains and brought them back to town. I saw them myself. They were his clothes for sure, though tattered and worn, and several bones were found along with them. I'm kinda used to people vanishing and never finding them again, so at least there was something to bury this time."

"I'm sorry," said Sally. "I've been helping at the store a lot and spent the winter at my grandma's place up north in Eldenhall. I woulda been there for the funeral if I'd known."

The lad just shrugged and nodded while drawing shapes in the dirt with a stick. Then they all sat in awkward silence for a time until the lad got up and stretched, telling the others it was time to keep moving. A goofy smirk formed on his ladly face once more as they packed up to go.

"I meant to ask," the lad said to Sally as they began to walk down the road. "What happened to your dad? I noticed he was using crutches."

Sally laughed and shook her head. "It's a long story."

"We've got plenty of time," said Bombir.

"Okay then," she replied. "You're not gonna believe this."

Chapter 4:
Slim Chances

Miles more the trio traveled, down the well-worn path under ever-thickening trees. The woods were not dense here, but the trees were large and wide, casting forth long branches that overflowed with sun-shielding leafery. The boughs eventually met from each side of the road, crossing and intertwining to form an enormous green tunnel from there on until the creek.

The three friends were talking and laughing, when all of a sudden, a shiny metal object passed the lad's nose by less than an inch, lodging itself deep into a tree on their far left. It was a throwing-knife, one meant to find a home within the lad's skull. The lad snapped his attention to the area in which the knife had come, where a person stood a half-step out from behind a tree.

He recognized the assailant at once due to his outfit: a tight fitting, layered, dark purple garb with a hood, mask, and gloves, whole body covered save for the eyes. Upon the chest, painted in a yellowish color, was an image of a crowned horse-headed person in a full sprint, a sack of cash slung over one shoulder and a few loose bills fluttering in the breeze behind.

This was a member of the Royal Steallions, a bandit group that prowled all over the surrounding countryside. Only the one singular member was visible at the moment, but they never traveled alone. There would be a dozen or more in the immediate area.

"Shoot the tree!" yelled the lad to Sally.

Without questioning the lad, she quickly chambered a stone into her slingshot and fired at the target. It missed the tree, but struck the bandit in the throat, knocking him to the ground for a few minutes.

"Come on!" cried the lad, and the three ran for their lives down the road.

Eerie neighing sounds echoed through the woods around them, coordinating an imminent attack.

"Keep running! But get ready to fight!" the lad screamed out, while narrowly dodging another throwing-knife from behind.

For nearly a mile they ran on like this, but eventually, due to fatigue and other factors, the bandits seized the opportunity to close in. Five of the hooded ruffians darted out from the trees ahead, blocking the way. The lad, Sally, and BombirThin came to a halt, and upon hearing more of them behind, put their backs together to keep all sides in check.

Five more bandits rushed out to span the path behind, followed by another five to the left side. Finally, a line of seven filed in on the right.

All at once, they threw back their heads and roared in

unison, "NEEIIIIGGGHHH!!!"

Then, each one pulled out a pair of items. It was unclear what they were, but as the bandits began banging them together, they made the distinct sound of a horse's hooves. It started slow: 'clip----clop, clip----clop', increasing in speed every few cycles. It kept on like this for almost two agonizing minutes, reaching an almost applause-like crescendo:

'CLIPCLOP-CLIPCLOP-CLIPCLOP!!!'

Suddenly, all went to complete silence as every bandit froze in a weird reared-up position simultaneously. There was a rustling from above, and soon after, a final member of the group dropped down from the branches, landing on a knee and rising in front of the lad. The image on this one's chest displayed a horse-headed person wearing *three* crowns, obviously signifying leadership.

"C'mon, dude, what do you want with us?!" shouted the lad impatiently.

"Ain't no dude, *dude*," replied the bandit leader, pulling away the hood and mask to reveal a girl that couldn't be more than twenty.

She shook her head and let fall her long, wavy, blonde hair. Then she stepped toward the lad, staring him down with bright, fiery, blue eyes. For a seemingly half-crazed, nasty, murderous, thieving, steaming pile of cow dung bandit leader—she was, surprisingly, quite the looker.

"And what we want," she continued, "is you three dead, and all of your possessions in our pockets. We'd normally just rob you, but this was a special request."

Before the lad could do anything, the wretched lady-bandit put a knife to his neck. Her eyes bulged and her mouth twisted into a deranged smile.

"Have fun being a corpse!" she shouted maniacally before breaking into a disturbing cackle.

The lad felt his shoulders drop from hands pressing into them, then he fell to his knees as Sally Kim vaulted backwards over him, kicking the bandit leader in the face and causing her to stumble back. Sally turned to face her, knife drawn, but a look of shock overcame her when she realized she knew this girl.

"Aramel... Stannifer?" asked Sally.

"It's Stab-knifer," hissed the bandit. "How do you know me?"

"We went to Girlycamp together for a few summers... years ago. After you stopped coming, I heard you ended up being sent away to a place for jerk kids."

"So what?! I *was* a jerk kid. Now, I'm a jerk adult! I steal stuff and do pretty well for myself. I don't give a flying turd that you remember me from idiot-camp—you're dying today, and I'll make sure it's *much* more painful now for kicking me in the face!"

Aramel swung her dagger, and a loud ringing sound filled the air as Sally knocked it away with her knife. Now consumed with rage, Aramel went on full attack. Sally dodged or countered nearly every strike, getting some jabs in of her own, but taking a few cuts to the forearms and one to her left side.

In a flash, Sally tossed the knife from her right to her left hand and brought the right hand down as if it still contained a weapon. Aramel swung upward to meet it, but Sally simply moved her arm past it. At the same time, she threw her knife down from her left hand. The blade sank into Aramel's right thigh, and she crumpled to the ground on her backside, yelling in anger and pain.

Sally then lunged on top of the girl nonetheless, holding her down and punching the everliving snot out of her face repeatedly. All of this happened so quickly that the lad and Bombir were just now coming to their senses, but it was too late. Unseen to Sally, Aramel gave a quick wave of her hand toward the two boys, and they were promptly detained by the two extra bandits from the right side of the road.

One was very tall, and the other just had a tall head. They pulled away their face coverings to reveal themselves as they held the lad and Bombir tight, knives to their throats. It was SkyScraper Ned and SteepleCranium Hubert. Ned whistled loudly, then Sally stood, turning to face them with blood dripping from her knuckles. Aramel was sprawled out flat on her back, all but unconscious at this point.

Sally was unarmed, save for a slingshot that would take time to load and was likely to miss despite being only eight or so paces away from them.

"Time to watch your stupid little boyfriends get what they deserve!" yelled Ned. "Maybe if they'd known we were certified Steallions, they would have thought twice before crossing us!"

"You attacked us first, you giant buttwad!" choked the lad.

Ned punched him in the side of his head and pressed the knife closer. Sally knew there was nothing she could do, but she wouldn't just stand there. Before she could begin to charge at them however, she was quickly grabbed by bandits on either side of her.

Ned laughed, his face overflowing with that trademark smugness as he started a slow countdown. "Five... four... three... two...."

No more words came. The knife slipped and fell from his hand. He wheezed and gasped, then he looked down with eyes wide at his chest, where an arrow was firmly planted.

"What... the..." Ned croaked, as he loosed his grip on the lad and sunk toward the ground.

In half a moment, the very same happened to Hubert, then another bandit, and another. They were dropping left and right, one every second it seemed. The remaining eight to ten began to scatter and run into the surrounding woods, two of them dragging away their still-unresponsive leader. Sally ran toward them and yanked her knife free before she lost her chance.

"Should've stayed in Girlycamp, you stinking dirtloaf!" Sally shouted.

There was no reaction from Aramel, but the other

bandits continued dragging until they disappeared amongst the trees. Bombir was frozen with fear, and the lad drew his Saber, preparing to attack whoever was left—but none were still standing. Ten or twelve lay motionless on the ground, arrows protruding from various places. One of them was Ned, he looked to be... something that rhymed with his name.

Hubert, however, had run off, leaving behind a snapped arrow and a trail of redness. The three friends turned now to look for the one who had saved them. They walked down the path beyond the wreckage of bandits, and only a minute later did a shadowy person nimbly take four strides down the branches of a tree ahead. He dropped silently into the road and saluted them, putting two fingers to his forehead under a pointy, gray, feathered hat.

"Bowman friggin Slim..." sighed the lad in relief.

"Been a long time, guys," said Bowman Slim. "Good thing I happened to be this far out. I was low on seasnins, and I thought I saw a seasnin bush around here last week."

"Yeah, thanks for that," the lad replied. "Was the town bullies, Scrapes and Steeps, if you remember those morons. Me and Bom had a run-in with them early this morning. Didn't know they were part of an actual gang, but I guess they wanted revenge after we made 'em look stupid."

"Sounds like you've had quite the day already," Bowman said, stroking his shiny black goatee. "At least 'Mr. Wonderful' wasn't with them—heard he got locked up a while back. Anyway, I assume you'll be coming back to the cottage with me. Before we head there, let's go check the area and remove any weapons left behind. That group of thugs is bound to come back eventually."

Bombir didn't say much, but the lad told Bowman the rest of the story with Ned and Hubert while they all gathered up stray knives and other weaponry, then shoved the fallen bandits off the road. To their surprise, SkyScraper Ned's body was nowhere to be found. Perhaps he hadn't eaten the cheese after all. They continued scanning the surrounding area for a little while, but the bandits seemed to be long gone.

So, the companions—now four of them if you weren't paying attention—moved on once more. Bowman's cottage was still about twenty minutes away, and they all had much catching-up to do. Aside from a brief visit at the lad's unclecousin's funeral, it had been half a year or so since any of them had seen Bowman.

"Guess you're getting better with that thing," said the lad, motioning toward Bowman's bow. "I mean I *hope* those arrows that passed me and Bombir's heads by a couple inches was all from skill."

"You got it," Bowman replied with a nod. "Been practicing eight to ten hours a day for months. I told myself I needed to be in top form in case you-know-who comes back... if he's even still among the living.... That aside, bowmanship is always a good thing to have at one's disposal, especially with a name like mine... *and* when I live alone way out here with a group of bandits led by a crazy ex to worry about."

Sally Kim's look of wonder was no doubt about to burst

into endless questions, so he answered before she had a chance.

"It was years back, and she wasn't looney then. Well, not *as*. We got along fine for a good while, but eventually things got ugly. You see, we both loved to eat hard-boiled eggs. I liked mine plain, maybe a little salt once in a while if I was feeling adventurous. But this woman, if you can call her that, put *lemon pepper* on them. Not just hers either. She'd always put it on mine as well, no matter how much I pleaded for her not to. She couldn't understand me not liking the vile powder and I refused to consume it any longer—so we finally broke up one day. Then, it took me a couple *more* days to realize my wallet was gone. Not much more to say about it really—other than I think that girl really needs to be sent off for an extended stay at Thortimer's or something. Until then, I'm hoping the little display I just gave will keep her and the rest of them well away from here for a good while. And, of course, we can't forget *your* contribution Sally—looked like you smashed in that adorable little nose of hers pretty good."

Sally blushed. "Well, they *did* teach a decent self-defense class in the last year of camp."

The lad could not have cared less about Bowman's failed romance story—especially the part about eating eggs—he was too busy trying to think of ways to strike up a conversation about the sailing trip.

The group soon crossed into Bowman's property, his cottage just ahead and Crim Creek barely visible in the distance beyond. He and his mother had moved out here around five years earlier after his father left, and Bowman inherited the property two years later upon his mother's sudden passing.

"Come on in and make yourselves at home. I started up some food earlier that should be ready by now—there's probably plenty if you can stand my cooking," Bowman said, leading the group across a large front deck to the entryway. "Mind the tripwires as well," he added without explanation.

He threw open the door after unlocking a few locks, and the overwhelming scent of fried stew and thrice-baked fiddlebiscuits filled the air. BombirThin had been fairly quiet and shaken up since the bandit encounter, but he seemed to quickly forget about all the recent horror and bloodshed, happily gulping down food before anyone else even took their shoes off.

The rest came, filling bowls, plates, and cups, then they all sat down together around the impressively large dining table. While they ate, the lad made his move.

"Sooo, Bowman," he started, "I noticed you never asked why we're out this way."

The lad stared at Bowman, and Bowman stared at the lad.

Clearing his throat, the lad continued. "We came out here to go on a sailing trip up the creek. Before you say anything, no, we don't have a boat. We were planning to build one with the tools and supplies we brought and any materials we can foist from around the area..." he trailed off in thought for a moment. "You know... Sally and Bom's parents would probably slap the heck out of me for even thinking of going any further after what happened on the road.... But we're fine now and they don't need to know about that, right? Anyway, what *I* would like to know, is would you... be interested in joining along? Unless you think it's dumb of course. You don't have to."

"Sure," said Bowman. "I've got nothing else to do. Maybe I can get in some advanced target practice out there. It'll be getting dark soon though, so it'd be best to start in the morning. I'll go ahead and throw together some places for you all to sleep."

The lad gave a low thumbs-up and did a quick, serious nod, trying his best to look like a cool guy. All the while he was giggling like a childish fool inside.

Chapter 5:
The Night Adventure

Later that night, the lad went out alone and completed the boat in an incredibly short time. He was going to go back and get some sleep for the voyage the next day, but the others must have heard him working. They were dressed in their sleep attire still, and they boarded the large vessel with looks of amazement at the progress the lad had made.

"This is unbelievable!" yelled Sally. "How did you complete it so fast?"

The lad smiled and replied, "I taught myself a bit of craftsmanship over the years, just for a hobby really."

He began to show them around. The wood was stained a deep red and sealed with a glossy finish; railings, posts and control pieces for the ship were intricately carved by hand. A moment later, Bowman and Bombir were spotted coming up the ramp again—the lad hadn't even noticed they had left. The two were pushing a huge cart filled with all their supplies. So, everyone quickly unloaded everything to its proper place.

"Ready to shove off, Captain!" said Bowman.

"Now? It's like three in the morning."

"Of course," added Bombir. "Why wait until it's all bright and hot out?"

"Well okay, if you guys are cool with it, I guess I'm awake enough. Let's go!"

The anchor was raised, the ramp pulled in. BombirThin let loose the sails, which unfurled to display the name 'The S.S. Ark-Orange'. The lad took the helm, and the ship jolted quickly away from shore. It picked up a massive amount of speed unexpectedly, but the lad was quite alright with it. He swerved back and forth, throwing huge waves this way and that. He looked over to Sally, who was wearing a white top hat with dozens of flowers sticking out of it.

"Isn't this great?!" cried the lad, pretty confident he'd seen her wear that hat before.

"Huh?" Sally replied, not looking at him.

Bombir came to the upper deck soon after; he was juggling six or seven watermelons and singing a weird song.

'Melon over here,
lemons outside,
stick 'em in my ear till I curl up and die!
Salad in my shoe,
steppin' on pie,
feed it on a spoon to a hairy old guy!
Metal underwear,
flyin' in the sky,
pants don't fit cuz my bum's too wide!'

The lad stopped listening after the third line, he was

busy fighting against the increasingly rough waters. One colossal wave came, and the lad steered into it. The ship rose rapidly, but before it reached the top, Bowman's grip on the center mast was lost and he was thrown violently from the ship.

"Bowman!" cried the lad in vain.

He then looked to Sally, but she was gone. Bombir was just singing and juggling those darned melons, not helping at all.

Suddenly, Bombir slipped on the decking as the ship pounded against the churning, rolling wave. He fell against the side rail and flipped overboard, the words of that blasted song that he couldn't seem to stop singing soon faded into the sounds of the rushing water.

Finally, the ship crested the top of the wave. It looked to be thousands of feet over the creek. Of how this could be happening, the lad had no idea. The wave fell away, disappearing into mist below. But the ship did not follow. It continued forward, as if some magical force held it aloft. The lad was sailing through the clouds high over Skiddle Earth.

There were mountains slowly becoming visible ahead as the sun rose over the horizon. He went to turn the ship, but a big slippery squid was now covering the wheel and holding it tight. Disgusted and confused, he quickly ran to tie up the sails. Nearly halfway there, he suddenly fell through a hole in the deck, tumbled through the dark, and landed in something wet.

When he sat up, he was in a tub holding a rubber duck

in one hand. The room looked very much like his own bathroom at home, but he didn't remember building anything like this below deck. On the other side of the room, a big weasel was eating from a pile of his oranges. He jumped out of the water-filled tub, dry as a whistle, and swung the duck—which was now a wooden rake—at the weasel. Though the animal never moved, the lad's strikes missed again and again.

He was starting to get frustrated, so he turned to grab something else. He didn't find anything, but when he looked back to the weasel, it had vanished, and the corner of the bathroom was a wide-open archway that led out into BombirThin's backyard. He walked through the opening and saw Bombir's father smacking grass down with a shovel—except it wasn't a shovel. It was a four-foot spatula with a pancake on top that flipped every time he lifted it.

The lad spun around once more to look at the bathroom. All that could be seen now was a patch of thick, dark woods. A person stepped around a tree, flashing a golden knife in their hand. They were wearing a purple bandit outfit; one of the Royal Steallions no doubt. The hood was cast back. It was Bombir's sister, HendraThin. She raised the knife, and it turned into a banana.

She cast it forcefully at the lad. He tried to dodge, but he was stuck in place, unable to move any part of his body. The banana hit him straight between the eyes and bounced back off with a squeaking sound. Hendra was gone, but the lad was now dressed in a formal suit and had a blue glowing flute in his hands. Though he tried to play it, all that came out were pink bubbles that made butt noises when they popped.

He attempted to throw it down, but it just wouldn't come out of his hand. Soon after, a large cucumber with arms and legs fell in front of him from out of the sky. It grabbed the lad by the hand, and they danced and danced for what seemed like hours.

Then, he ascended the waves again, sailing across dark rivers, entering ancient mists.

Chapter 6:
A Floater Is Born

Just before the sun rose the next day, Bowman Slim provided his guests with a grand breakfast: skillet-seared ovalpastries with cream, fresh picked purpaberries, mounds of bacon, and eggs cooked sunny-side up. He even broke out some of his infamously delicious, deep-fried, breaded buttertubes.

The lad and Bombir were seated at the table, laughing, discussing their plans, and stuffing their faces. Sally came out of her room late, yawning and rubbing her eyes. She entered the dining area, bent at the waist and dragging her feet, then fell onto a bench opposite the lad and Bombir.

"Did you manage to take a good look at the final sentence of that last chapter?" the lad asked her.

"What'd you just say?" she replied while squinting hard in confusion.

The lad slid closer and repeated himself a bit more loudly this time. "I said... did you manage to get a good rest in that room last night?"

"Uh... yeah, I guess so," she answered, bobbling her head around and yawning once more.

Just then, Bowman came over from the kitchen area and scooped the last bit of food from a pan onto a large platter. After he removed his apron and a tall white hat, he seated himself in the chair at the head of the table. The four of them talked about old times a while, then switched back to the matter at hand: building a boat, ship, or sailing craft of some kind for their adventurous voyage. Bowman confirmed the lad's suspicions of abandoned houses further up the creek. No one owned them, and nobody would be moving into those run-down places. It was likely there'd be a good amount of usable, already-cut lumber to be found there.

Upon finishing breakfast and getting cleaned up, they gathered all the useful items they could find and loaded them into a cart that had to be pushed by hand, for Bowman had no working animals of any kind there. They took turns, two at a time, pushing the heavy thing down the seldom-used trail that ran parallel to Crim Creek. It was over half a dozen miles to the shacks, but to their relief, they passed all the way there in good time without any hindrances.

Three sagging, crooked shacks there were, and the remnants of a fourth. No sign of any recent use was to be found in the hollowed-out interiors—not that their skeletal frames would offer much safety or comfort against the outside. The group got to work right away, prying, sawing, hacking, and grabbing every morsel of salvageable wood. The lad unleashed his secret stash of nails and began hammering things together. Bowman applied some kind of sticky tar from a large container between each of the boards as they were nailed. It looked like he might know what he was doing, so the lad said nothing.

Within several hours, a flat, floating raft was bobbing around in the water a few feet from the bank. They tied it down of course, then began building up the sides of the vessel. BombirThin chopped down several massive trees for masts, and it soon became clear that some sort of mechanism or system of pulleys would be needed to haul up the heavier parts to the main and upper decks.

They turned their attention now to this task—Sally Kim being fairly handy with ropes, gears, and wheels from her days at camp. Not to mention her own father worked with machines that could lift objects of substantial weight. She rarely came to work with him but had seen some of it in action and knew of a few crude designs. By the time they had built something to hoist up the masts, it had already grown dark.

Tents were set up, dinner was consumed around a campfire, and all went to bed for an early start the next day. Bowman slept well; it certainly wasn't his first time spending the night outdoors. Sally was also used to it due to—well, you know the story. The lad never really had many concerns about his well-being, or put much thought into danger, so he drifted off easily too. BombirThin, however, was curled up tight with a blanket over his head, shivering and listening to every little noise. He gripped the handle of his shortsword, imagining terrible things stalking the outside of their tents—bears, wolves, or worse. Hours passed, but eventually he succumbed to his weariness.

The Lad and the Ring

The next day brought more building. Large parts were set in place, and it was beginning to look somewhat like a boat. Unfortunately, the project was taking much longer than initially anticipated. The day passed by quickly, yet much more work needed to be done. So, they took turns, two of them at a time for safety, traveling back to Bowman's cottage for more food and supplies. They did this a few times over a period of four days before the boat was almost complete.

All it needed now was a sail of some kind. Though no cloth or material for such a thing was available to them. They thought of stringing leaves together, or maybe just trying to row the thing, but that was nonsense.

After half a day trying to come up with something, Bowman discovered an item of interest deep in the woods behind the now-dismantled shacks. It was huge and square in shape, most of it buried beneath mounds of leaves, dirt, and fallen trees. It appeared to be an old door, roof, or covering of sorts. The weight of the object was obscene, for of solid iron it was made, nearly three inches in thickness. It was in good shape, somehow free of any corrosion or cracks.

The group got together, putting all their skills forth to free the prize from its place of rest. They spent hours dragging the enormous iron square to the shoreline with ropes and pulleys. Once there, it was realized the tremendous thing was not a single piece as first thought. Instead, there were four smaller strips, two on each side of a larger central one, that swung on hinges and could be locked in place by sliding bolts. This way, the whole thing could be folded up when not in use. Miraculously, the strange mechanism happened to be exactly what was needed; nothing more perfectly appropriate for the specific function could've been dreamed of. It was slowly hoisted into place with Sally's makeshift crane against the large center mast, then roped and bolted tight with only a few concerning noises coming from the wood that held it.

The supplies were loaded onto the boat, and everything was checked once more. It was finally time to set sail. The lad was overjoyed. This was the moment he'd been dreaming of, as long as it wasn't like his dream from several nights before....

"Make ready to cut the tether lines!" cried the lad, as he unsheathed the Saber.

"Wait!" yelled Sally. "Aren't we going to name this thing? All sailing vessels need names. I heard they'll almost certainly explode if they don't have one."

"How about 'The Water Arrow'?" asked Bowman.

The lad shook his head in virtually undetectable disgust.

BombirThin threw in his two cents as well. "What about like, 'The Floating... Thing'—I don't know." He put his hands on his hips and looked away in embarrassment.

"'Shacks Reborn', or maybe, 'The Creek Traverser'," added Sally while swiping a hand through the air with each proposed name.

"'The Buoyant Bowstring'," said Bowman, unable to

think outside of archery terms.

More names were thrown in and thrown right back out by the lad's disapproving gestures.

"I have it," whispered the lad with a grin. "'The S.S. Ark-Orange'!"

Bombir turned back around and hastily replied, "You named a boat that already! Maybe even two. You remember that summer we carved that log out enough to sit in and float around the pond behind your unclecousin's place? You scratched those very words into the side! If you're going to name it after food, which I do not disagree with, that one's been crossed off. Try the next thing down the list. Maybe toast or bacon perhaps?"

"Alright then," the lad shot back, "I know exactly what it'll be called. This vessel upon which we now stand, will be known now and forever as... 'The S.S. Ark-Cheese'!"

Nods and cheers of agreement all around. It was a fitting name, especially since they had used hundreds of pounds of cheese to fill in cracks on the upper parts of the boat when they ran out of Bowman's special tar. Sally went over to the rail and sat on it, leaning out far enough that she was almost upside down, and wrote the name on the side of the boat with some paint she happened to have. She gave the other side the same treatment soon after.

Then the lad ran down the length of the deck, slicing the ropes away that tethered the vessel to the shore. The anchor was lifted as well, and the boat drifted slowly out to the center of the creek. The iron sail was majestically unfurled, and the wind swept them away up the creek at last with the lad at the helm.

Chapter 7:
The Amazing Voyage

The wind wisped through the lad's hair; the smell of muddy banks and the scent of the wrong end of fishes were pungent. It was late afternoon on a perfect spring day as the S.S. Ark-Cheese cut across the waters of Crim Creek like a sharpened frozen pickle through three-month-old, hot, runny, steaming, mayonnaise-flavored gelatin. That's not to say that the creek water was dirty mind you, it was quite clean and clear.

BombirThin's gut was being pushed in uncomfortably as he leaned over the railing, peering down at various aquatic creatures darting to and fro under the surface. Sally Kim was sitting right on the bow of the boat, looking ahead to these new lands unseen to her—or the rest of them for that matter—until now. Even Bowman hadn't been much more than a few miles up the creek, and they had already passed that point close to an hour earlier. He had mentioned something about, 'if he sailed one more water-square forward, it'd be the least close to his house he'd previously found himself located at any point in his existence'.

Now, he was perched on the top of the center mast,

forty feet high and on the lookout for assailants or treacherous obstacles in their liquidy path. But it was all smooth sailing for many a mile, and their boat was holding up splendidly even as it maintained a steady thirty knots or so in speed. The creek grew wider the further upstream they traveled. When they had departed, the width was around thirty feet; now it was pushing fifty and another hundred. The land on either side remained obscured due to thick woods, aside from several feet of sandy driftwood-littered banks.

Eventually, the sun sank below the hills of the higher land that lay far in front of them. They wouldn't go on much longer this day for fear of tearing the hull open on rocks that poked their jagged heads out from the creek bed like angry rabid bathing grandpas in the more shallow areas.

Night came quickly, followed by clouds that blocked any hope of starlight. The boat's anchor was dropped, the sail folded tight, and the crew gathered on the main deck where a fire awaited them for dinner and merriment. The world beyond the side railings and masts above, the last things the light from the cooking fire fell upon, was thick with mist and darkness. They heeded it not, and their conversations went on until the wee hours.

"I know it kind of makes you uncomfortable," said Bowman to the lad whilst chewing the last bits of a deer jerky stick, "but what exactly was your unclecousin looking for out here?"

The lad stared into the fire for a moment in thought.

"It's cool, but honestly, I'm not sure. When I was young, he'd sometimes tell me stories of places he traveled to a long time ago, but I assumed he was making it up. He spoke of a crazy old man that came to town. The man and some of his friends—or henchman maybe—dragged him off one day. They traveled far across the world, battling beasts and meeting strange folk from foreign lands. He never went into much detail, really."

Bombir and Sally slid in closer; they had heard some of this in the past, but the lad didn't speak of it often.

"Do you remember the old man's name?" asked Sally.

"I... I *believe*," said the lad, trying to remember, "his name was Rudolph. With a P H at the end, not an F like you'd think. His henchmen had weird rhyming names too, like 'Clacker and Slacker' or some such nonsense. It's weird though, now that I think of it... my unclecousin mentioned another thing one time—reluciously, it felt like—and seemed to trail off, never really bringing it up again."

Staying silent and assuming he meant 'reluctantly', the rest of the crew leaned in; eyes wide with anticipation at this newly remembered information. The lad's mouth opened, but his eyes darted to the distance beyond the confines of the boat.

"What is it?" asked Bombir in a concerned whisper.

The lad did not answer, but stood to his feet, striding over to the rail for a better look. The others slowly got up and followed, gathering in close behind.

"I saw a dim light," said the lad in a hushed tone. "It was

only for a quick moment, like someone put it out. I'm not sure if it was over in the woods or closer... maybe right there on the water."

"I don't see squat," said Bowman. "Perhaps you're just tired. You *have* been steering the boat all day. Maybe we should get some sleep."

The lad nodded and turned from the side of the boat, making his way back to the fire to extinguish it for the night. Before he could reach it, he stopped in his tracks. This time, he saw something for sure. Where the rail on the other side of the boat met with the rising wall of the upper deck, a dirty hand rested, gripping the top of the railing. A barely visible face lay just behind, peering around the wall straight at them.

'BANG!' A wide plank of wood slammed down hard on the rail further toward the front of the boat from out of the darkness. It rattled violently as a dozen or more ungentlemanly looking fellows tramped across the board to the Ark-Cheese. From the generous abundance of peg-legs; shiny black brass-buckled shoes; hooks and eyepatches; gold teeth and earrings; bandanas and square shoulder pads covered in parrot droppings; unkempt beards; giant feathery hats, and large, fancy, stabbing utensils... these were almost certainly folk who were up to no good.

"Foist the anchor!" cried the lad.

Bowman and Bombir saw to it quickly, and the lad rushed to the plank, cutting through it cleanly in a single sword swipe. Two or three of the ruffians clung to the side of the boat, but the rest plummeted into the dark waters of the creek. The lad shouted for Sally to take the controls as Bowman came running back from the anchor to activate the sail.

"This vessel are now belongs to The Dread Pirate John!" loudly croaked one of the attackers that was now climbing onto the deck.

"Ye'll roll the day ye watered the sails of this land," another said.

"What?!" replied the lad in confusion. "Are you guys saying real sentences?"

They just growled and ran at him, swinging their ornate weaponry wildly. The attacks came so fast from the two at once, that the lad was only able to deflect the blows. A third tried circling him but was tackled by BombirThin. Bombir knocked the sword out of the pirate's hand, swiftly kicking it overboard. Then, for the first time on this journey, he drew forth his own sword. The sword was passed down from Thin to Thin for generations; a symbol of protection and valor of his family that had kept them safe for hundreds of years. Out it came, aiming straight at the grinning face of the filthy seafaring yokel.

But wait, why was he smiling in the presence of cold, gleaming death? Bombir looked upon his outstretched sword and his heart sank, for it was no sword at all that he carried. In the reckless haste of leaving his parent's house, he had evidently grabbed the toilet plunger by mistake. Nonetheless, he slapped the well-used, rubbery end across the face of the pirate, which likely made him cleaner than he was previously.

Then, Bombir seized him up in his dazed stupor and cast him over the rail into the water. The Ark-Cheese began picking up speed, allegedly pulling away from the unseen pirate vessel. Bombir and Bowman joined the lad, and together they gave the remaining two goons a serious thrashing that ended with them being tossed overboard as well.

The three boys thoroughly scanned the boat inside and out for more pirates as Sally blindly steered at top speed through the hazardous dark. There was no sign of any more attackers on board, so the lad took over the controls while Bombir hung over the bow with a lantern to warn the lad of rocks and debris. They kept at it throughout the night, only one of them at any given time taking short naps. A feeling of hope returned when the first hazy light of dawn shone down the creek from behind them. However, the sky remained cloudy and became more overcast as the day went on.

By noon, the clouds had grown darker; rain was likely on its way. The Ark-Cheese was anchored around this time, the group rowing a small raft to shore for lunch and of course a break from the endless movement of the boat. The fact that they had been recently pursued had apparently escaped their minds. After laying out a blanket, they all grabbed their respective packed meals and chowed down.

The lad ate a sandwich of orange slices and cheese. So much did he enjoy it, that he refused to allow anyone to speak to him until it was finished and his fingers were licked clean. Bombir had a bacon sub which consisted of nothing more than a pound and a half of the crispy pig products between two-foot-long halves of a narrow, elongated roll. Butter may have been involved in some way as well. Sally brought an egg sandwich, much to the lad's dismay. He slid his butt a few cheek-paces away upon smelling the fart-scented food. Bowman packed no such bread-encased edibles; he simply snacked on more deer jerky and a bag of peanuts.

When their lunch was complete, the group had a quick look around the immediate area. Nothing of any interest was to be found, just more woods with no end in sight. A deep rumble was heard in the distance, so they made quick work gathering up their things and rowing back to the boat.

They took their places once again, with the lad shouting, "Alright lady and gents! Get that anchor foisted and prepare to set sail! The foothills of Some Mountains will be upon us within the tri-hour!

Chapter 8:
Thunder on the Creek

The lad's giant smile fell a bit as the inevitable gentle drizzle came, but he was still having the time of his life and wouldn't let a little weather get him down. The others, however, weren't so tolerant. The lad leaned over the upper deck railing with fingertips still on the wheel to see what they were doing down below. He hadn't heard a peep from them in a while. The lad shook his head in annoyance at their lack of commitment.

Then, he got an idea: he would scare their pants backward with two simple words.

"HELP!! PIRATES!!!" the lad screamed, so hard that his voice cracked. He waited, but no one came.

Getting frustrated, he stomped hard on the floor—which was also the ceiling of the main deck bedrooms—and cried out again, "OHH MYY GAAHHSSHH!! THE PIRATES! THEY'RE BACK! THEY'RE GOING TO STAB MY BOOTY!!!"

The lad could not remember a time in his life when he had yelled so hard. He was dizzy and seeing stars from the effort. This attempt paid off though, for the lad heard the door below him quickly fly open, and BombirThin's face soon popped up from the stairway, looking all around.

"You okay?! Where's the pirates?!"

Sally and Bowman then came up as well.

"There *are* none! What on Skiddle Earth are you goobs doing in there?!" asked the lad sternly.

"It's raining out, the lad, and besides we thought we heard you come in and lie down in your room. Didn't you notice the sails were tied and the anchor was down? We did that like an hour ago!"

Now that he thought of it, the lad *had* been feeling like they weren't traveling very fast.

"Look, Bom, we need to keep moving. I didn't know how far we'd make it up this creek, but we're far enough now that we might actually be able to take the Ark-Cheese out on the lake."

"PimWimQuim?" asked Bowman.

"Exactly," the lad replied. "I've heard folks talk about it before and it sounds like an incredible place. But we'll never get there before we run out of supplies if we stop every time a few droplets fall from the sky!"

The rest of the crew grumbled a little but nonetheless returned to their posts after folding out the sail and lifting the anchor once again. The boat was hardly moving yet when the lad glanced over his shoulder to the left. There beside them sailed another boat—or perhaps a ship it could be called—for it was nearly twice the size of the S.S. Ark-Cheese.

Upon the rotting, barnacle-covered side was written the name: 'The P.S.S. StealYaGold'.

"PIRATES! PIIIRATESSS!!!" yelled the lad, his voice hoarse from his previous shouting.

The others didn't bother looking at him, and only Sally responded, "Suuuure, and I bet there's a great big squid monster too!"

She continued staring ahead with a frown on her face and a flat hand over her head in a vain attempt to keep her hair dry. The fools wouldn't listen, and it was too late now.

Five of the pirates were already swinging from ropes over to the Ark-Cheese. The lad cut the wheel hard to the right, causing them to miss and fall into the water. The turn also got the attention of his crew, who were picking themselves up from the deck after the sudden maneuver.

Now that they saw the danger, they readied their weapons. The idiotic pirates somehow fell for the same swerving trick three times, with around twelve going in the drink before they resorted to other tactics. Small square windows opened on the side of the ship, and from out of those holes poked long metal barrels of what looked to be cannons.

"Take cover!" the lad squawked.

A deafening 'BOOM!' filled the air, followed by two more in succession. The lad and crew watched in horror as parts of the Ark-Cheese erupted into splinters. One of the cannonballs missed Bombir's head by less than half a foot after taking an upward path through the deck from the boat's side. Bowman did his best trying to fire arrows at the pirates up top, hitting a few of them; at his current angle though, he could not reach the ones below who were operating the cannons.

In a panic, the lad turned hard again, this time towards the pirate ship. The Ark-Cheese smashed violently into the side of the StealYaGold, sending everyone aboard both vessels flying. The lad himself was thrown over the rail and into the rigging of the other ship. He tumbled this way and that, falling downward until he landed on the pirate ship's main deck. Sally Kim ran to take control of the Ark-Cheese, yanking it free from the tangled mess before both vessels were dragged down to oblivion.

Several pirates had also been thrown onto the Ark-Cheese as well, prompting Bombir and Bowman to scramble to the base of the upper-deck stairway to fight them off and keep them away from taking over their boat. A flash of white lightning split the darkening sky, striking a tree on the nearby shore. Then the rain picked up heavily. The lad stood to find himself in the presence of two pirates—ones that looked very familiar. For they were none other than SkyScraper Ned and SteepleCranium Hubert.

"So, we meet again!" barked Ned. "Try striking me down with an arrow, will you? Should have thought about that before you messed with a crew member of the infamous Crim Creek Pirates!"

Hubert just nodded and chuckled in agreement.

"I should've taken you out while I had the chance..."

said the lad, still catching his breath from the fall.

Ned and Hubert drew their swords. The lad reached for the Super-Deluxo-Saber, but all he felt was the back of his rain-soaked shirt. He looked up to see the sword still caught in ropes high above. He grabbed whatever was closest for protection, which happened to be a plain wooden plank. There *was* a rusty nail sticking out of the far end, so that was a bonus.

He swung it at the two bully thief pirates, missing repeatedly as they hacked the wood apart with their swords. The lad then threw the plank in the air, did a backward roll, planted his feet against the ship's side rail and shoved off, springing back at them on his belly across the slick surface just in time to grab the falling board and smack that rusty nail straight into Hubert's foot, pinning it to the deck.

Hubert cried out in pain, "AHHH!! I'll kill you for that!!"

The lad was sure Steeps was already planning on doing so either way. But he took this chance to get away from the two jerks and get his weapon back.

He rolled onto his side, then jumped to his feet, running around one of the masts looking for a way to climb up. He spied a rope hanging from the backside of the mighty wooden post and threw himself at it with all his strength just as Ned's sword lodged into the mast, mere inches under his feet. The rope's end was grabbed, and the lad planted his soggy shoes against the mast, beginning the climb up to his lost weapon.

Ned started up after him, able to easily reach the rope with a small hop. The lad pulled himself up onto the first horizontal beam but saw that his sword was still well above him, so he took hold of another rope and moved up to stand on the next level. Ned was just behind, about to grab him by the ankle.

Not a moment too soon, the lad jumped off the mast toward the Saber and began flailing his arms in an attempt to catch onto something. He stopped suddenly, gripping a length of wet rope a few feet from his sword. He shimmied closer to the chaotic mass of rigging and began trying to wrest the blade from its ropey prison.

Some of the ropes snapped, and the sword loosened, but the lad couldn't tell whether he would fall if too many were cut. A drop to the deck from this height would likely break his legs at least, and he certainly didn't need that.

Back on the mast, Ned had climbed to the next beam above the one the lad previously jumped from. He planned to cut the ropes that hung from it, sending the lad down to a world of pain and suffering. Ned couldn't quite reach the ropes though; they were hung too far out from the topmost cross-beam. For fear of losing his chance at vanquishing the lad, he jumped high and swung his sword hard at the beam. It broke somewhat, but not in two. The long piece of cracked wood drooped down to a forty-five-degree angle, lowering the lad several feet as well.

He wasn't out of danger from a fall, but he *was* closer to the mast now. The lad held the rope above him with his left hand, and with his right, he yanked with everything he had—once, twice, twelve times until the Saber finally pulled free, causing the tangled ropes to unravel. Ned jumped again, this time cutting the beam all the way through. As it fell, so did the lad, but he managed to quickly swing the Saber at the mast. The sword sunk into the substantially damp wood, shaving off a thick outer layer and slowing his descent until his feet softly touched down on the main deck. The large beam of wood came next, crashing straight through the deck mere feet away, shattering boards and leaving behind a huge hole as it landed deep below.

Hubert had pulled the nail from his foot, then rushed the lad in a rage. The two clashed and began trading sword strikes, the Saber leaving notches in Hubert's far inferior blade. While this was going on, Ned climbed back down the mast to aid his tall-headed friend.

Then, something else happened—black smoke started pouring out from the hole in the deck. It wasn't long until flames began to rise, spreading rapidly throughout the ship. What was left of the crew tried desperately to put out the fire, but Ned and Hubert still focused on ending the lad for good. The lad moved around and put the main ship mast to his back, waiting for Hubert to strike once more. The swing came right for the lad's neck.

The lad lifted his still-straightened legs out in front of him, letting himself fall to a sitting position as the sword stuck into the mast above. As Hubert pulled like a madman trying to free it, the lad stabbed him in his knee with his pocketknife. Hubert clapped both hands over the spot immediately, howling in anguish. The lad stood quickly, kicking him in his side and causing him to stumble, fall, then roll over to the railing of the ship.

By this time, Ned had reached the bottom of the mast. He pulled Hubert's sword free, then approached the lad in dual-wielding fashion. The lad turned to face him.

"Time for your death, laddy-boy!" said Ned in a dead-serious tone.

"That ain't my name and you know it, SkyCrapper Den..." replied the lad.

No decent end could come now that insults such as these had been uttered. Ned gritted his teeth and prepared for attack. The lad felt the heat from the ever-growing fire and braced himself, then gripped tight the hilt of his Saber, holding it outstretched toward his foe. Ned let out a piercing holler, and just as he pushed off to charge the lad... he stopped. The metal tip of a golden blade thrust forth suddenly from Ned's gut, then a large hand rested upon his shoulder.

"Captain?" asked Ned shakily.

The hand grabbed Ned's shoulder hard and easily cast the large fellow to the side of the ship. There, he collided with Hubert who was in the process of standing back up, sending the two flipping over the rail and into the churning waters of Crim Creek. Between their wounds, the storm, and their distance from shore, it was doubtful they would survive. The lad actually pitied them somewhat, but they had brought it upon themselves.

Now, the lad was faced with a new and seemingly much more dangerous threat: The Dread Pirate John... or so he assumed by those very words being embroidered in gold on the giant man's puffy black shirt.

"What've ye done to me ship?!" cried John.

"*You* started this, Fartbeard!" the lad screamed back. "This is what you get!"

The huge pirate issued out a deep, rumbling laugh.

"This be *MY* creek. Ye trespass upon the waters of The Dread Pirate John. Yer vessel was forfeit the moment ye set sail here! Now ye'll feel cold death from The Fortune Filleter fer setting this ship aflame," he growled in reference to his quite valuable-looking weapon hanging loosely in his grasp.

Lightning flashed, as if putting emphasis on his words. It was an intimidating scene, even for the lad who was so often fearless. John pulled low the brim of his extra-wide black hat, out of the top of which protruded a large red feather. His dark, sunken eyes reflected the fire his crew still worked to put out. The jet-black beard that hung down to his multiple oversized belt buckles at his waist was soaked from the rain and swaying sideways in the wind.

The pirate raised aloft his lengthy sword, wiping Ned's blood from the blade with a black handkerchief as he took a few board-creaking steps toward the lad.

"You want a fight? You got one, fatty!" yelled the lad as he ran at John, knowing his time was limited.

He slid across the deck and brought the Saber upward at John's face, who quickly deflected the blow with a reflex much faster than the lad anticipated.

Then, the two really went at it. John's golden sword was no ordinary weapon, and it kept up with the Super-Deluxo-Saber well. The two blades rang out in a symphony of metallic clatterings that echoed across the surrounding water. Several minutes of the most forceful onslaught the lad could muster had passed, and he was growing tired. John showed no signs of slowing and seemed to barely even be exerting himself. It wasn't looking good, and the lad was beginning to think he might soon lose. He tried some fancy footwork, then dodging and rolling, but John's strikes were always right on him.

In the lad's exhaustion, he tripped over a rope that sent him tumbling to the deck like a sack full of coconut pie. John went to bring his sword down for a killing blow, but an arrow came out of nowhere, piercing him in his right shoulder. The big pirate was thrown off and slammed the sword down into the deck where it stuck fast. He snapped off the arrow, and as he pulled the blade from the deck board, the lad ran at him from the side, slicing at his head.

Alas, he too was knocked off balance as the ship hit something in the water. The Saber missed John's head, but cut his big, feathered hat clean in two. It slid off each side of the pirate's dome and the pieces fluttered away in the wind. John snapped toward the lad with hatred burning in his eyes, his appearance growing somehow even more menacing, despite the now-revealed, bad comb-over that frayed out in various directions from his cranium.

"Ye'll pay fer that!" he bellowed. "Do ye have *ANY* idear what I paid fer that piece of headwear?! It was on sale as well! Ye can't get it fer that price any longer!! Ye've took me most prized possession from me. Now... I will hold back me full wrath no longer."

Just then, a loud crunching sound was heard, and the ship shuddered hard, throwing flaming debris everywhere. Waves spilled over the rails and the foremast snapped at the base, sending it crashing into the water.

John now stared past the lad, a look of concern filling his face at what he saw.

"In all me days..." he muttered.

The lad thought it might've been a trick, but he suffered a glance anyhow. Lightning was striking frequently, revealing a deep whirlpool in the center of the creek between the two sailing crafts—as if something were draining the water away.

Suddenly, several incredibly large tentacles thrust upward from the depths, each one a hundred feet in length at least. One of them came down and swept across the top of the StealYaGold, taking out the remaining masts. The lad threw his free arm over his head and ducked under several flying chunks of wood, then looked on in horror as another tentacle slapped away at the Ark-Cheese in the distance. He could just barely see Bowman firing arrows at it, and Bombir throwing various objects.

The lad remembered his foe, dodging quickly before John's sword could take his arm off. If the lad stayed on this ship, he'd be killed for sure; he had to find a way off. There was nothing to do but try and swim for it.

He circled John and kicked some flaming wood up in

the pirate's face. As expected, John swiped it away effortlessly, but the lad seized that moment of distraction to run as fast as possible to the side of the ship. John somehow caught up and grabbed his leg, preventing him from going over. The bearded lunatic raised his sword one final time, booming with crazed laughter.

Another tentacle came around from behind and smashed into the stern, sending the bow of the ship high and tossing both adversaries in the air. John came down and landed on his back in the middle of the stairway to the upper deck, breaking a few of the steps beneath him. The lad fell belly-first on the rail next to John, knocking the wind out of him and causing a loud, awkward, involuntary 'HOO!' sound to escape his mouth upon impact. The Saber came down right after, and thanks to some quick thinking, the lad snatched it up and stuffed it in its sheath.

"I'LL KILL YE!!!" roared John.

"Get in line, buddy," replied the lad casually.

Then, he simply let go of the railing and splashed into the creek. He bobbed up and down, gasping for air periodically as he tried to navigate his way through the rushing waves in the extremely normally-temperatured waters.

He heard someone yell from the increasingly distant pirate ship, "Cappin! The fire has reached the gunpowder barrels! We need to abandon ship!!"

"Never! No one is to leave! Now get this vessel back under control before we're dragged down to Danney Joe's Pantry! Aarrrrgg!!!" cried The Dread Pirate John as he struggled to free himself from the hole in the stairs.

As the lad continued trying to keep his head above water, he caught sight of what was creating the whirlpool: the open mouth of the creature to which the tentacles belonged. It was a hideous, silvery, greenish gray, with giant, beady, black eyes and row after row of teeth the size of swords in its gaping pie-hole. Without any doubt, this creature was certainly the Unmerciful Sea Monster; a foul beast from the wretched depths believed to be nothing more than a fairytale. The lad was being drawn toward its mouth, and he could not escape the current.

He looked to the Ark-Cheese to see that it had cut low, passing by the head of the monster and following the curve of the whirlpool to come back for him. A chunk of wood landed in the water near him with a rope tied around it. He grabbed hold as Bombir and Bowman reeled him in. At last, he climbed back aboard the Ark-Cheese as Sally steered back around the sea monster and headed on up the creek. The lad ran to the upper deck and leaned over the stern to get a look at the carnage shrinking away behind them.

The StealYaGold veered sharply away from the Unmerciful Sea Monster but was grabbed and pulled back to the mouth by multiple tentacles. The tremendous creature bit down on the pirate ship—just as its stock of gunpowder erupted in a massive explosion.

"Hold on!!" cried the lad as he bore witness to the approaching shockwave.

So powerful was the force of it that the lad was knocked

on his back and the Ark-Cheese was boosted up to fifty knots for almost half a minute. The rain of burning, splintered boards and chunky globs of monster flesh signified that an end had come for The Dread Pirate John of The Crim Creek Pirates, and the Unmerciful Sea Monster, Terror of the Deep.

Chapter 9:
Guardian of the Gate

Pretty much immediately after the explosion, the storm passed, the rain stopped, and the clouds parted. The setting sun burned a deep red, and the crew of the S.S. Ark-Cheese was thankful for their miraculous escape, ready to put it out of their minds like it never happened and continue their journey.

Soon, the hills began on either side of the narrowing creek, rising sharply into more mountainous terrain. Aside from getting the iron sail stuck in a giant sequoia bush that hung too far over the water and having to cut it away, they were incident-free for many miles. Another stop was made for some much-needed sleep, but they were off again at first light the following day.

The mountain cliffs grew ever steeper the further they sailed, becoming almost perfectly vertical in their rise from under the water and up through the clouds above. They were walls of white stone, with only the occasional plant struggling to hold tight to the smooth, featureless surface. So straight were they in fact, that it seemed impossible to believe that this enormous fissure through the mountains was made by any natural process.

The lad tried clearing an odd lump in his throat and motioned off the port side. "It was probably a little farther back since this is getting so unwalkably steep, but this is likely the area where the hunters found the remains."

"Oh, right," replied Bowman, "you were telling us before of something strange your unclecousin said, but you never finished, thanks to those darned pirates. What was it again?"

The lad worked the wheel, following a long, sweeping, blind, curved chasm between the towering walls that seemed to always be closing in on them.

"He told me he found an item that may have had some kind of 'special properties'—whatever that means. A piece of jewelry like a bracelet or a crown.... Probably not a crown. Anyway, all I know is, he made it sound as if he'd somehow misplaced it on the way home from one of his journeys. I'm wondering if that's why he kept coming out here. Maybe he was still trying to find it. I can't imagine how it could've been that important though. He always seemed to have plenty of cash."

With that said, the boat finished rounding the curve.

"Drop anchor and sails—full stop!" cried BombirThin.

There ahead of them—was a dead end. The creek somehow halted at a flat wall with no visible alternate route. The Ark-Cheese came to rest with around fifty feet equally to each side wall, as well as the wall ahead. All of them appeared to be several thousand feet in height.

"What the HECK?!" yelled the lad. "How is this even

possible?!"

"The wall in front of us isn't made of stone like the sides," said Sally. "It looks to be some sort of dull metal."

The lad and Sally took to the raft and paddled to the forward wall for closer inspection. Upon reaching it, the lad smacked it hard with his oar, and a shrill, hollow, metallic 'DUNG!' reverberated through the deep canyon. Sally was correct; of metal it was surely made.

***

After the raft was brought back to the boat, the crew sat and talked about what to do next.

"I guess we just head back," said Bombir. "There's clearly no way through."

"The water obviously has to be flowing from that area," Bowman chimed in. "Maybe it's open underneath and we can swim it."

"You're certainly welcome to go look," said the lad in slight irritation.

Bowman didn't even bother with the raft. He sprinted to the bow and did a front flip into the water, swimming all the way to the metal wall. When he reached it, he rested a moment before diving below. About a minute later, he popped back up, already halfway back to the boat. Sally threw him a rope, and he climbed aboard.

"No good," he said, wiping his dripping face with a conveniently placed towel. "The wall ends a few feet below the surface, but after that, thick iron bars extend down another twenty feet within an inch or so of the solid stone creek bed. The bars go all the way across too and are only about six inches apart."

The lad yelled in frustration, "Well crap darn it! If we can't *sail* the lake, I'd at least like to see it. We came all this way after all."

"Okay, the lad, and how exactly are we supposed to do that?" asked Bombir. "The walls have nothing to hold on to. They're perfectly smooth and almost look like someone comes out here and waxes them down semiannually."

The lad's face curled into a smirk; he had a clever thought cooking up no doubt. He got up and ran below deck, coming back moments later holding a toilet plunger from the bathroom.

"Don't you have another one of these?" he asked.

Bombir unsheathed his own plunger from his side, having no idea why he hadn't removed it yet.

"I know what you're thinking," said Bowman, "and it's really dumb."

"Yeah, I know," said the lad. "Now let's go do it."

***

The crew stood on the raft that was tethered against the metal wall. All were strapped somewhat safely into harnesses made from a large portion of the Ark-Cheese's rigging. Bowman leaned back and fired a single toilet plunger as high as he could, putting a physics-defying twist on it at the last moment so that it suctioned to the wall. Several hard yanks were made to prove its adherence. A rope had been fastened to the handle, running all the way down and attaching to each one of the crew's harnesses in succession. First to start climbing was Bowman, followed by the lad, then Sally. At the bottom of the line was Bombir, who had the job of sticking his own plunger to the wall every few feet in case the upper one gave out.

"If this actually works and we don't die, I'll eat my own friggin hat," said Bowman, his confidence ever-dwindling from the small amount he'd started with.

"Can't wait to see that," the lad replied. "We'll even let you put some salt on it!"

"I don't know, the lad," said Sally, "maybe we should've backtracked and hiked the mountains or something. This *is* kinda nuts."

"Awe c'mon! I thought you two were all about adventure. Besides, we're already like a hundredth of the way up—right, Bom?"

Bombir simply shook his head continuously, staring straight at the wall and operating his plunger.

The group continued climbing until they reached the first plunger, then Bombir handed his up the line to Bowman who suctioned it next to the other one, looping some of the rope above him around it. Bowman removed the first plunger and fired it from his bow once more. When it planted into the wall again, he took hold of the newly stretched rope to test it, then untied the knot from around the other plunger, handing it back down to Bombir. This simple and realistic process took only about twenty-seven repetitions before the crew finally reached the top of the wall.

After pulling themselves up, they each removed their harnesses and began to move toward the far side to have a look. They could now see that the wall was around fifteen feet thick, but before the view of the lake could be taken in, Bombir noticed something else.

"We aren't alone up here," he whispered, nodding his head to his left.

There, a couple dozen feet down the wall top, was a chair. In that chair sat a thin and lengthy figure dressed in dark armor with a ridiculously tall helmet upon its head which obscured a face of any kind. The dark figure slowly turned its head toward the crew, then silently stood to its feet.

"Hey, we don't want any trouble, Mister!" the lad called out.

But the figure approached without a word, stopping several paces away. It finally spoke in a rough, gurgly voice.

"I am the Crimson Pim—guardian of the gate to lake PimWimQuim. I will allow none to pass here."

The sound of the Crimson Pim's voice made the lad want to cough, and he did. Then, he replied, "Look, man, what do we need to do? Buy tickets? Show some ID?"

As he spoke, the lad examined the weird man—if that's what he was. He found that the armor was made of multiple thick layers of black jellybeans, which would keep almost anyone from wanting to come near. The helmet, about four feet in height, was crafted entirely of used toothpicks—judging by the chew marks on each one. They were tightly and expertly glued together, diverging into different pointed lengths at the top, making the helmet look more like a tall, jagged, wooden crown.

"Nay," replied Pim. "This gate belongs to—hmmm... it matters not. None from either side are permitted to cross, under penalty of death."

"We aren't *crossing*," Sally protested. "We're just checking out the view. We'll be heading back the way we came after we take a look. So, calm down a bit, would ya?"

The Crimson Pim stepped forth again, drawing his sword from his side.

"There is no turning back. You violate the decree even now as you stand upon the gate's uppermost regions. Your sentence shall be carried out immediately."

The moment the sword was raised, Bowman fired three arrows, striking the gate guardian in the chest. Alas, the shafts were turned away or shattered upon the foul armor of black licorice. Bombir was still basically unarmed and didn't dare try approaching the Crimson Pim with a toilet plunger. Sally joined the lad on his left, and Bowman to his right—knife and daggers now drawn and ready to take the guardian down.

The lad unsheathed the Super-Deluxo-Saber, deflecting a few blows from Pim right away. Bowman and Sally repeatedly tried going in for quick jabs, but inside that suit of armor, the Crimson Pim was seemingly invincible. The smell of the jellybeans was intense from this distance, and the three of them could scarcely take a breath without gagging. To make matters worse, the close-quarters fight was causing the lad to nearly kill his allies quite often.

After Bowman getting his arm nicked twice and Sally's eye coming close to being stabbed out, the two moved back and let the lad have some room.

"You cannot win," boomed Pim, "for this weapon I have in my possession is the strongest in the lands. 'Spit: The Sword of Doom' it has been called through the ages. I alone have attained the strength and willpower to tame and wield it."

The lad sucked his teeth at the remark.

"Pfft! You must not get out much then, pal. The Super-Deluxo-Saber can outmatch any blade. Your guarding days are over, Crimbo!"

The two swords slammed together, holding tight.

"Arrogant child! I have watched over this gate for nearly a century. I am not about to be taken down by a loudmouth brat with melon-shaped hair, carrying a crudely forged, glorified potato peeler!"

The lad quickly drew the Saber back and swung again in anger, connecting with Spit once more.

"It's an ORANGE peeler, you ugly, reeking, brainless fossil!!"

The Saber was strong, as was Spit, but The Crimson Pim was exceptionally robust, and the combat proficiency gained through unusual longevity gave him the upper hand. The weapons were locked against each other, with the wielders' faces almost as close. The lad found he was sliding backwards now and could not stop himself. The Crimson Pim was going to push him over the edge. BombirThin ran and slammed into the guardian's side, knocking him slightly off balance. It did little, and Bombir was met with a swift kick to the face which brought him down hard. Bowman fired a couple more arrows. One stuck into the helmet of toothpicks, but it had no effect, and Pim pushed on.

The lad dropped to a lower position, changing the force against him into a downward direction to keep from being pushed back any further. Regardless, he was growing weary. He spun the Saber sideways and placed his left hand flat on the side of the blade, still trying to hold Spit back. Pim stomped on one of the lad's legs, sending him fully to the ground and causing him to drop his sword. Then, Pim lifted Spit for the killing blow, and the blade began to radiate a reddish light reminiscent of low-burning coals. Sally had seen enough. She sprinted forth, ran up the Crimson Pim's back, and clung to him tightly with arms around his neck. He shook and thrashed wildly, trying to throw her.

Eventually, he grabbed her, peeling her off and holding her high by her shirt collar. Pim slammed her down and immediately brought his blade down upon her. She rolled out of the way just in time for it to hit the metal floor with a 'CLANG'. He raised the weapon for another strike, but the lad was back on his feet and charging him. Spit fell from Pim's hand as the Super-Deluxo-Saber rammed through three layers of black licorice jellybeans and into the evil guardian's fleshy sideparts.

The big man turned his head to look at the lad, both armored hands now clenching the Saber's blade. The lad gripped the hilt and twisted the Saber with all his might, then yanked five times before it came free.

"Give up yet?!" asked the lad.

The Crimson Pim did not answer. He simply growled through his pain, then quickly stooped to retrieve his weapon. As soon as he grasped the handle, the lad jumped forward, body-slamming him and sending him stumbling sideways. Pim tried to steady himself, but it was for naught. His foot met with open air, and the force of gravity soon overtook the rest of him.

He cried out at the lad, "You! You!!" But in his distress, he could think of no insults.

His anger turned to panic and horrid screams issued forth from his accursed mouth. The crew of the S.S. Ark-Cheese listened... as his cries faded and were drowned out by the wind until they were no more. The lad wiped sweat from his brow and mustered the strength to bring back his goofy smirk.

"Well, that's that, I guess," he said, sheathing his sword.

He started to walk over and help Sally up, but something was seriously wrong. Yet, to what that thing was, he was blissfully unaware. Bowman's keen eyes were the first to spy the problem: a lengthy, loosened, left shoelace lay outstretched on the floor of the walltop. Pressing firmly down on the lace, was the lad's right shoe.

In the meantime, the left shoe was rising upward in the beginning stages of a long stride. Bowman called out to warn of this tragic revelation, but he wasn't quick enough.

"The lad!" was all the archer managed to utter before disaster struck.

The lace snapped taught, bringing the left shoe to an instant halt. This unexpected cease to motion threw the lad's balance off dramatically.

"No!" cried Sally, as she watched the lad's body lean sharply to one side.

Bombir dashed toward his best pal as fast as his stubby legs would take him.

"Whoooops!" said the lad, just as he fell passed the point of being horizontal.

Bombir dove and slid on his belly up to the edge of the wall, swiping at a flailing hand as the lad flipped over. Their fingertips brushed past each other, but it was too late.

"THE LAAAAD!!" Bombir howled as he watched his friend tumble uncontrollably toward the water... thousands of feet below.

Chapter 10:
Lake of Legend

The lad managed to hastily straighten himself out as he fell. There wasn't much time, and if he wanted to survive this, he'd have to do a perfect pencil-dive into the water. He passed the halfway point and figured there was around ten seconds left to impact.

Nine seconds left now; he tried tilting vertically.

Eight; he failed.

Seven; he tucked in his legs.

Six; he grabbed those legs.

Five; he lifted his head.

Four; he thrust his head down.

Three; he began rapidly spinning headfirst, rolled up like a ball.

Two; he readied himself, trying to make sure the timing was perfect.

One; he snapped his entire body straight, facing directly down, then brought his hands around and clapped them together. The lad held himself as rigid as possible, then, at terminal velocity, he slipped smoothly, silently, and without the slightest ripple, through the surface of the lake.

Thankfully, he'd fallen far enough out that the water was much deeper than directly under the wall—if Bowman's measurements were to be believed. The lad's speed sent him very low indeed, enough that he still collided with the muddy floor of the lake despite his efforts to somehow turn away from it.

After a quick recovery from the impact, he wrestled his way through sunken debris and tangling seaweed, trying to figure out which way was up. Two minutes passed before he freed himself and swam up toward the surface. His lungs burned and his mind was going into freak-out mode. He forced himself to relax and keep swimming upward—until he was jolted to a stop. His ankle was caught, inescapably wrapped by some unseen plant or old rope. He reached down and fumbled with the slippery shackle, pulling and tearing at it to no avail.

A voice in his head cried out for him to find air immediately. He resisted the urge to suck in, knowing that only murky liquid would enter. Dizziness then came, and he felt he would soon pass out. Even if he were to break loose now, he'd never make it to the surface in time.

***

High above the lake, still atop the wall, Bowman, Bombir, and Sally planned their descent to recover the lad's undoubtedly mangled, waterlogged corpse. The ropes they had used to climb up had been knocked off in the commotion from earlier, falling down the side where the

Ark-Cheese still floated. They had but one single plunger to use now, and none of them could think of any practical way of using it to get down.

"We can't just dive in," said Bowman. "We'd just die like the lad. It's hard to see from this high up, but nothing's moved down there since he went under several minutes ago."

"It could take days traversing the mountains to get to the water," added Sally. "Looks like sheer cliffs on either side that go on for miles. I can't even see a safe place to climb down. We'd have to take a several-mile swim after that without a boat and still might never find the lad's body." She turned away from the others as her own words sunk in.

Bombir then thought of something, cutting off Bowman who was about to follow up with more hopeless, depressing details. "Remember what the Crimson Pim kept saying?" The others stared at him without a clue, so he continued. "He kept using the word 'gate', not 'wall'. Maybe this gigantic thing opens somehow. Let's see if there's some sort of switch around here."

Bowman checked the rocky cliffs on the south end, while Bombir had a look around the north. Sally just checked under Pim's fold-out chair. There was nothing there.

"Aha!" yelled Bombir. "A worn path up this hill to a little hidden shack! This must be where he lived."

Sure enough, when Sally and Bowman joined him, they beheld a small building covered in camouflaging branches.

These were pushed away to reveal a door. The door was locked, but easily kicked open. Inside was a smelly old bed, a dresser that contained seventeen left shoes, a jar of moldy creamed corn, and a broken wooden doorknob. The tall, thin, final object of note was covered in a sheet. Under this covering was found a metal lever.

"I'll bet this opens the gate!" exclaimed Bombir.

"Worth a try, I suppose," answered Bowman.

Bombir pulled on it, but it would not budge an inch. So, all three gripped the end and gave it all they had at once. Still no movement. Bombir just stared at the thing, scratching his head. After a while, an idea came to Sally. She went back to the dresser and pulled out the wooden doorknob, then brought it to the lever. Upon a thorough search, a hole was found on the floor nearby.

"I think this is a key," said Sally.

While holding the knob, she inserted the jagged shaft on its other side into the floor hole. It slid in perfectly, then turned with a loud 'CLEENKT!'. Bombir took hold of the lever once more, and it smoothly pulled to the far position without issue.

'BOOOOM!!!'

A furious rumbling shook the little building, knocking boards and shingles to the ground. The group ran outside to see the gate had separated at an invisible seam down the center, and two doors were swinging slowly open toward the creek.

"Oh crap!" cried Bombir. "The Ark-Cheese!"

The three of them continued out across the top of the still-moving door, looking down to see if their boat would be smashed against the cliffs. Relief came as they spotted it anchored in place and untouched by the colossal rectangles of swinging metal. The doors finally came to a halt within an inch of the mountain walls, never coming in contact. Bowman walked to the edge of the door and looked straight down its side.

"Well, ain't that a thing of beauty," he said, pointing downward. "Now *this* is something we can use."

The sides of the doors meshed together when they were closed. One side had tabs sticking out, around two feet or so apart all the way down. The other—their side— contained slots for those tabs to slide into. It was like a perfect ladder, and they couldn't have asked for a much more fortunate turn of events. There was nothing left to do now but start the terribly long climb back down to the water.

***

The lad was still alive, yet still underwater. Rather than fumble around for his sword or a pocketknife with which to cut his bonds, he reached for something quite different: his water canteen, featuring a no-leak, screw-on cap. He had forgotten to refill it that morning, and for that, he was thankful. He felt its buoyant, upward pull, making sure to keep the strap wrapped safely around his arm as he put the side of the lid to his lips. He twisted the cap, drinking in the cool, clear, refreshing, and life-saving oxygen. Only a little was inhaled—since he had no idea how long it would take to get himself out of this mess.

With renewed strength of body and mind, the lad was able to get a better idea of what held him. A rope it surely was, but no ordinary sort. It was crafted of solid wood and would not break easily. The people that inhabited the shores of the lake long ago—'The Lakers' some called them—learned how to make these wooden ropes. Alas, the secret was never passed to outsiders, and was lost when the tribes moved on or died out. Nobody was really bothered though, as the Elves made better ropes anyway.

Of course, the lad knew none of this and did not care in the slightest. All he wanted was to get away from it. He hacked at the darned thing repeatedly with his sword, but the cumbersome blade moved far too slowly through the water to do any serious damage. He then tried sawing at it with the jagged backside of his two-inch pocketknife, every once in a while taking sips of air from his bottle. After about eighty-one minutes, the wooden rope broke away; the lad's ankle was finally free. He gulped down the last few drops of air he had and made for the surface.

The moment his waterlogged, yet still melon-shaped hair breached from out of the depths, the lad had to quickly dodge to one side, for the front of the S.S. Ark-Cheese was coming right at his face.

"Hey!!" yelled the lad.

"There he is! Down there!" cried Bombir.

Bowman threw on the brakes and Sally cast a rope for the lad to climb up.

"I can't believe it!" exclaimed Sally as she helped him onto the deck. "We were sure you wouldn't survive that fall."

"Yeah, me too," he answered, wrapping himself in a blanket Bombir handed him. "I managed to do a flawless dive. Still bashed up my face a little when I hit the bottom, but I'll live."

"We were watching the area constantly and didn't see you surface till now," said Bombir. "Were you somehow underwater this whole time?"

"Yeah, I was actually," the lad responded. "My leg got caught on some stinking ancient rope made out of wood and it took forever to cut through. Luckily, my bottle was filled with air, which kept me alive just long enough to make it back up to the land of the breathing."

Sally was so overjoyed that she gave the lad a firm handshake. Right after, Bombir approached the lad, looking to be suspiciously concealing an item behind him.

"Check out what I found lodged in the Ark-Cheese's deck," he said.

Then, from behind his back, he produced a sword. The sword... of the Crimson Pim.

"No trace of Pim," he continued. "I think he's gone for good. You were the one who took that maniac down though, so this blade is rightfully yours."

The lad took it in his hands and studied it. The handle was a glossy black with blood red, masterfully carved inlays, and letters that formed the name 'Spit'. The long, thin, slightly curved blade was the color of ash, yet it glistened with an immaculate sheen. After finishing the inspection, the lad made a few decision-making pooty mouth sounds. He then looked back up to his friend and held the prize out to him.

"Thanks, Bom, but we all know that I already own an incredibly awesome sword. *You*, however, are still wielding a toilet plunger. You're the only one of us without a proper weapon. Keep it."

Bombir grinned tremendously as he quickly took it back. "Oh, I was hoping you'd say that!" he shouted.

"Remember to be careful, Bom," added the lad. "That Pim guy said that it contains some sort of power or curse... but that probably isn't true, so forget I said anything."

Bombir wasn't listening anyway.

"The helm is yours, the lad," said Bowman, "kept it warm for you."

"You know, I think I'm just going to sit and enjoy breathing oxygen for a bit longer," the lad replied. "How about you take us straight ahead, nice and slow, and maybe I'll come up and grab the wheel in a bit if that's cool with you."

"Sure thing, Cap," said Bowman, heading back up the stairs.

"Hey, Bowman," the lad called out.

"Yeah?" he turned and replied.

"Why is your hat on your head and not in your stomach?"

Bowman pursed his lips and half-rolled his narrowed

eyes. "Yeah, that ain't happening," he answered before turning back around.

The lad just shrugged, then walked to the side of the boat to lean on the rail for a bit.

After a while, as the others continued the preparations to set sail, he spied a wonderful perch for his back end: a bench sitting against the cabin wall. He hobbled over to it, aching immensely from his previous strenuities. He spun around and planted his hindquarters forcefully into the seat. Upon contact, he stifled a cry and jumped up, back arching from a sudden sharp pain in his righthand secret-cheek.

"What the—" he muttered under his breath.

It was something in his back pocket. He reached inside and pulled out none other than the small, spiky, pinkish-colored shell of a lake mollusk. Frustrated, he ran to the rail, winding it up for a long throw back to the watery depths from whence it came. He stopped himself right before releasing, thinking maybe one of his nerdy friends might find it interesting. So, he stuffed it into a side pocket, sat back down on the bench, and soon after, drifted off to sleep.

***

The lad awoke to a starry night sky, the sound of small waves gently lapping up against the anchored boat, and his companions sitting down to dinner around the fire pit on the main deck.

"Finally awake I see," Bowman called out, seeing the

lad stirring. "Just in time for some eats. Come have a bite."

Bombir passed a plate of orange slices and cheese cubes to the lad as he came over to sit with them. Roast pork sandwiches and salty potato cylinders were there for the taking as well, being kept warm on a platter near the fire in the midst of the crew. They talked a bit, but the lad was still worn out. He figured he'd be up for more adventure once he got a full night's sleep in an actual bed. Way out here on the dark open lake they'd most likely be safe from any sort of attacks. So, the fire was doused, and all of them decided to retire to their own little rooms in the cabin area at the same time, a first since they'd set sail.

Later, as the lad was lying on his bed, he was viciously stabbed in his thigh. "Darned shell," he mumbled. "I meant to show this to the others.... Whatever, I'll do it tomorrow."

He pulled it out of his pocket and set it on his tiny nightstand, then promptly conked out.

***

The next morning brought a bright, warm, cloudless day. There was a slight cool breeze, and the water was fairly still. The lad was ready for his dreams to come true. He washed up, put on some clean clothes and grabbed that shell off the nightstand. Except... his hands were still wet from getting cleaned up, so the shell shot out from his grasp and across the room, where it met a wall and shattered to pieces.

"Oh well," said the lad to himself.

He turned to walk out the door, but something caught

his attention. In the wreckage of shell fragments, a thing was shining really good. He walked over and stooped to examine the shiny object, and found it was rounded, had a hole in the middle, and was polished to a mirror finish. He picked it up and looked closer. It was a ring, shiny and round—but aside from that, it was quite plain.

All of the sudden, thoughts and memories flooded his mind.

"It can't be," he whispered.

"What?" a voice passing by outside his door yelled.

"Uhh... nothing," he replied.

He kept his speech inside his head after that.

"Stupid memory!" he thought. *"It was a ring, not a bracelet or some such. Could this really be HIS ring though? What are the chances of that happening? After a single flop in the drink—accidentally coming across this and not even knowing until I'm back on the boat?! Only one way to find out, I guess. It supposedly has some kind of magical powers, so I'll try it on and see."*

With hands lightly trembling, the lad slid the gleaming circle onto his left pointer finger and... nothing happened.

"Psh!! I knew it wasn't possible!" said the lad. "Time to get back to sailing."

With that, he shoved the ring in his pocket and exited his room, greeting his crew and taking his place at the controls once again.

"Foist the anchor! Foist the sail! It's time to ship out and catch the gale!" he cried.

"Aye-aye, Cappin!" responded the crew.

Well, all but Bombir, who said 'Right-o' or something.

The iron sail unfurled, sending the Ark-Cheese drifting across the lake like a magnificent stick of butter on a hot frying pan. The lad sailed for hours, enjoying every minute of the experience. The boat was still holding up strong, faring far better than anyone would've originally guessed—especially with what it had been through.

The holes from the creek battle were patched up, though all were mainly higher up and did not pose any threats of hull breaching or leakage. The rigging used to scale the gate was restored in place as well, after the ropes were miraculously found piled in a heap on the boat along with the Sword of Doom. The lad was certainly going to miss this place when they left.

Earlier, he and the crew had agreed to stay for the rest of the day, spend another night on the lake, and begin the trip back home in the morning. There was still a decent amount of supplies, but it would be foolish to cut it close. Besides, those of them who had family would soon be missed, for the journey had already passed the 'few day' mark that was previously stated. The lad tried to put it out of his mind for now.

Instead, he focused on scent of the lakey air; the sights of the endless, ripply, sparkling water that cast back the brilliant blue of the infinite sky above; and the sound of the lakegulls passing overhead, crying out with a whispery 'Pssst!'. Whispery 'Pssst'? That couldn't be right. The lad looked around, thinking someone must be trying to get his attention, or maybe prank him into looking like a goober.

"PSSST!!" he heard again.

It was coming from... his pants.

"Dumb noisy pants!" he grumbled, as he punched them a few times.

His last punch was to the pocket, where his knuckles felt the bite of metallic punishment in the form of a small, circular artifact. He sucked at the back of the reddened hand for relief, then reached in his pocket to pull out the ring. He gave it another look, then slipped it on yet again. He let out a sigh, disappointed once more that no effect could be felt. The sound of footsteps was suddenly heard coming up the steps to the upper deck. He couldn't be seen wearing jewelry, it would likely undo his years of hard work trying to become a certified cool guy. The head of Sally Kim appeared over the rail—no time to take it off. He slung the arm around to his back, pretending to scratch it as Sally began to tell him something.

"Hey, Bom's just about to have lunch ready if you—the lad?"

She stared right at him, or even *through* him rather, as if he wasn't there. A look of concern washed over her.

"Huh?" replied the lad simply.

Sally immediately jumped, eyes darting all around.

"The lad, where the heck are you?"

"What are you, six?" asked the lad somewhat rudely,

yet more polite than he would've been to the others. "I think you should practice on the jokes a bit, we're nearly adults now you know."

"THE LAD!!" she yelled. "I *CAN'T* see you! You're the one playing the childish prank."

Tired of her games, the lad reached up and poked her in the forehead, making her blink hard and stumble back in shock.

"See me *now*, Sally?" the lad asked sarcastically.

Then, he remembered the unmanly ring on the very finger that did the poking. He stuffed the hand in his pocket and quickly flicked the ring off with an adjacent free finger. Sally gasped in horror, covering her mouth and staring straight at him now with eyes wide and knees shaking.

"You—you just—" she stammered.

"*What*?" replied the lad impatiently.

"Do you not realize that you... somehow... just became... visible?"

The connection slapped the lad upside the brain like a bag of lightning. It was the ring; it had to be. He was waiting for a feeling, or a vision—he never noticed that he couldn't be seen.

"Hold on, Sally. I think I have an explanation for this."

He drew forth the ring, holding it out in his palm for her to see. Then, he put it back on his finger, less worried about his coolness rating now that he knew the ring was magic. Sally threw her hands up and rested them on her head, still unable to accept what she was witnessing. The lad left it on for only a moment, then removed it again, regaining the ability of seeableness.

"I can't believe it," said the lad in excitement. "This is it, Sally. *THIS*, is the mythical, magic ring... of Bobill Gabbin."

Chapter 11:
Guests of a Cave Man

During lunch, the group of sailors sat and discussed the item the lad had found, passing it around and trying it on with wonder and amazement. After a little while, it began to make the lad somewhat uncomfortable.

"Alright guys," he said, "let's not get carried away and use up all its magic juice or whatever."

Bombir really wanted to look at it a bit longer, but reluctantly handed it back to the lad, who stuffed it deep into an inner, double-zipping, secret pocket.

"The entire existence of this thing should be kept between just us for now," said the lad. "Something this special is bound to be wanted by a lot of people, especially ones with ill intent."

The others agreed. The lad prepared to take his place at the wheel again, but something quite unexpected happened then.

"Help-help!" a distant voice cried.

The lad ran to the railing in the direction of the sound, scanning the waters whilst shielding his eyes from the sun with his hand. The others followed, and Bowman's keen archer eyes spotted the source first.

"There!" he called, pointing to a specific area in the unending blueness.

"Someone's drowning! We need to get over there!"

The lad thought this was a bit suspicious, but he ran to the life raft anyway. He and Sally shoved off from the Ark-Cheese, paddling as fast as they could toward the unfortunate soul.

After getting closer though, they noticed he was not drowning at all. On the contrary, he was rapidly approaching them, swimming like a gold medal swymnast. The lad let the raft drift to a stop as the swimmer grew ever closer. He watched the stranger carefully, ready to draw the Saber if he tried anything funny.

At last, the person reached the raft, stopping to tread water as easily and naturally as breaking wind. It was a young man, possibly around the lad's own age. His dark brown, significantly curly hair was soaked to the bone for obvious reasons, as was his equally colored, short, thick beard.

"What's the prob, water dude?" asked the lad.

"Me need"—the wet man stopped and looked down at his mouth in frustration—"I-I mean... *I*... need help."

"I am called Jim... Cave-Man Jim. I live on the shore over yonder." He waved his hand, gesturing off to the distant horizon, then continued. "Have you seen anyone else out here? A man. He would have been on a small canoe."

Sally answered, "You're the only person or thing we've seen since entering the lake... besides water and some birds."

Cave-Man Jim nodded and lifted a submerged arm, bringing a large chunk of ham out of the water that he'd apparently been carrying the whole time, then took a huge bite out of it. His other hand brought up a lidded cup with a flip-capped straw in its top, through which he drank of an unknown beverage. The lad gave a look of confusion, and Jim noticed.

"It is a milkshake—flamingo flavored," he said.

"What the heck does that even mean?" asked the lad, now more confused.

"I have no idea," answered Jim. "Anyway, I know it is a lot to ask of you, but the man I seek is my father. I need help finding him. We had picked clean the ham trees on our side of the lake, so he left to find more on another side, though I do not know where, for the lake is vast."

"What's your father's name?" Sally asked.

"His name is Cave-Man Cozwaltin, but some call him by the name Papa-San."

Sally's mouth hung open in disbelief.

"My father spoke to me of living over the mountains as a boy," she said. "He told me he ran away because he was tired of living there, but his twin brother stayed behind. He said his brother's name was Papa-San, which I always thought was odd. Never mentioned anything about being a cave man though."

"Cave-Man Therguson?" Jim inquired.

"Yes, his real name is Therguson, although no one calls him that except for my mom sometimes. He goes by Guston-Van, which I just realized kinda rhymes with Papa-San, actually. Not that it means anything."

"If this is true, it makes us cave-cousins!" stated Jim.

"Just 'cousins' is fine, I think," said Sally.

The lad butted in. "It's settled then, we'll help find Papa. Come back to the boat with us, Jim, and the lake will be given a thorough lookover. No wave or shore will be left unturned."

The lad truly wanted to help. Not only because this fellow was a relative of his least unattractive friend, but the whole affair sounded reasonably adventurous, and he definitely wasn't going to turn down a chance at more sailing. Jim climbed onto the raft, and the three headed back to the Ark-Cheese.

***

After many hours of search through dozens of circular miles of open lake without a single trace of an old cave guy, the sun began to set. The lad steered toward the direction of where Jim claimed to live, then ran the boat down the southern shore to scope out a few miles of beach before arriving. The light was too far gone to find anything now; they'd have to look again in the morning.

"My home is open to you," said Jim. "You have my thanks for the help. I do not expect you to continue to go out of your way for me. The least I can do is let you stay in my house for the night and serve you some dinner."

"Think nothing of it," said Bowman. "We're glad to help a relation of Sally's. I'm just sorry we didn't find anything."

"We'll try again at first light!" said the lad.

Bombir then whispered behind him, "But I thought—"

He was cut off by the lad swinging a foot backwards into his shin.

"Drop anchor here, mates!" cried the lad.

Some supplies were gathered, everyone crammed onto the raft, and they paddled over to the shore near Jim's home. To the crew's surprise, Cave-Man Jim lived in a cave. The entrance was set into the side of a small grassy hill just inside the boundary of the forest—around fifty feet or so across the sandy beach that sloped down to the water. The crew had to quickly avert their eyes as Jim casually flung off his animal skin loincloth, which he hung on one side of a long, two-pronged stick in the ground near the cave's opening. From the other side of the stick, he retrieved a dry, tan, leather outfit and strung it up over his obscenity with reckless haste.

When the crew realized it was safe to uncover their eyes, Jim led them through a rickety slab of wood that served as a door, though it was not attached to the surrounding stone. They traveled down a tight, winding, dark corridor, which finally opened up into one big, dank room. To the right was a kitchen area, which was comprised of nothing more than a pot over a small fire pit next to a hollowed-out stump that seemed to serve as a pantry. Down the left wall were two large slabs of stone about fifteen feet apart. They each had a small pillow-shaped stone on one end, and the rest was completely covered by an impossibly thin, rectangular sheet of stone somewhat resembling a blanket. Doubtless to the crew, they must have been the beds of cave men.

Smack in the center of the room sat a massive stone with smaller ones all around it. Of course, this was the dining room table. The crew pretended not to be bothered, but it smelled like absolute doo-doo inside. The mud floor was wet and squishy, and the ceiling dripped droplets of brown upon their heads. The lad himself was raised in a mudhole for a number of years, but that one was clean and tidy, and the mud was dry. The reek of *this* puke-den was making his eyes water, and it was everything he could do to not run out screaming.

Jim stopped and motioned to the center stone. "Welcome to my cave-home. Have a seat at the table and I will bring you all food."

The crew obeyed, and soon Jim came back from the kitchen holding a rusty metal bucket—it possibly being the most technologically advanced thing in the cave by far. The bucket was placed in the center of the table, then Jim made another trip to the pantry and came back with five stone bowls and a matching number of wooden spoons. The level of the eatware's cleanliness was questionable at best. Jim carefully poured a bit of the pot's contents into each bowl, saving his own for last. It had the look of raw sewage, which was actually somehow more appealing than the way it smelled. The dark green sludge bubbled and frothed in their bowls, and the crew could've sworn that the very vapors emanating from within were green as well.

Jim held his spoon high, proclaiming, "To new friends, and relatives reunited! Let us dig in!"

He began shoveling the foul, stenchious concoction into his mouth with a look of satisfaction. When he glanced up at the rest, who had not so much as lifted their spoons yet, he motioned for them to eat while he continued slurping away.

"You know what?" said Sally. "I'm actually on a diet. Sorry for the mix-up." She gently slid her bowl away.

BombirThin and the lad exchanged glances; they could not think of any excuse. They both lifted their utensils, taking scoops of the unearthly substance.

"Who knows, maybe it'll be tolerable," thought the lad to himself.

"Always good to keep an open mind for new eats," Bombir said in his own mind. *"Perhaps I'll like it, despite the scent."*

Bowman picked up his spoon, stirring the stuff around a bit, then said, "Looks great, though I'm afraid I failed to mention that I have a few food allergies. Could you tell me the ingredients of this soup?"

Jim swallowed a mouthful and dabbed his green-stained lips with a nearby rock, preparing to answer. At the same time, the lad and Bombir were taking their first sampling. If the sight was bad, and the smell was worse... the taste was something else entirely. It went beyond anything that spoken language could properly convey. But if one tried... it was as if the most abhorrent putrification across all space and time merged together into a singularity, consumed every last particle of unspeakable filth imaginable, then vomited the partially digested remains forth, only to partake of it again and again for a hundred thousand years until it finally turned itself inside out in a single, last, disgusting spew into the very container that was set on the table before them. That, however, may be putting it a bit mildly.

Jim began sobbing as he answered Bowman, "It is ham soup, okay?! I cannot cook and my father has been gone. This crud started to spoil a week ago! I am sorry! I was just trying to be hospitable!!" Then, he hocked a big green spit-wad back into the metal bucket, sickened with horror.

Bombir and the lad had tears streaming down their faces as they heard this, mouths still full. Bowman simply pushed back his bowl. Bombir spit his out in the bucket, but the lad was stuck in mouthal combat. He couldn't seem to spit nor swallow. The sludge took over and made the decision for him. It began to slowly inch its way down his throat. The lad pounded the table, crying out with muffled screams.

"MmmmMMMM-HM-HMM!!!" he whined.

BombirThin turned and slapped his back. No good. Then he slapped the lad right in the throat. The gag reflex was temporarily bypassed, and the chunky, cold liquid oozed on down.

"AAAHHHH!!!" the lad shrieked. His stomach immediately went on a rampage, and he yelled to Jim,

"Where's your bathroom!?!"

Jim pointed to the bucket in the middle of the table. The lad swiped it away in the blink of an eye and ran out the front door.

***

The lad emerged from the deep woods behind the cave two hours later. He was exhausted after having to fight off multiple wild animals while trying to do his business. His innards still protested, furious at him for the foolish mistake he'd made in an attempt to be polite. He saw then that tents had been set up on the beach, and the rest of the crew sat around a fire nearby.

"Got your tent all set up for ya," said Bombir, seeing him approaching.

The lad turned and threw the toilet/stew pot at the cave entrance, then sat down with his friends. Cave-Man Jim was not among them.

"Where's Jim?" asked the lad.

"Oh, he's staying inside," replied Bowman. "We told him we'd sleep out here so we wouldn't crowd him. I had to insist."

"I feel sorry for him," said Sally. "He *was* just trying to be nice. You think you'll still try to help him after he poisoned you?"

The lad sighed and looked down at the sand.

"I dunno, I guess I'll decide that in the morning... if I manage to get any rest tonight."

Leftover food sat on a stone next to the fire. The crew had cooked and eaten while the lad was away. He wanted to eat, but the thought of ingesting anything made his head spin and his stomach twist. So, before he felt the need to run back into the woods again, he figured he'd better just try to get some sleep. He said goodnight to the rest of the crew and slipped into his tent.

That night, he dreamt that he was a great warrior. He single-handedly cut down enemy armies, then slayed a mighty dragon. When all had been vanquished before him, he put on his ring. The ring turned black, grew large, sprouted arms and legs, then jumped off his finger. It snatched away his sword and threw it into some lava, laughing at the lad as he cried out for his beloved weapon. The ring loomed over him, then pulled out a huge hammer and started smashing him over the head with it. The lad couldn't move; he was tied up by chains now. The ring pulled out a large bag next, and inside the bag were hundreds of eggs. It began stuffing them in the lad's mouth, one by one. There was nothing he could do but let out an egg-muffled scream.

***

Screams came from the lad's tent in the early morning on the shore of lake PimWimQuim. BombirThin rushed to the opening, peeking his head inside.

"You alright, the lad?!"

The lad quickly sat up, sweat pouring down his face. His mouth was nearly filled with sand, and both of his hands contained more sand, compressed into the shape of eggs. He choked, coughed, and spat the beach-dirt to the ground, quickly taking a few gulps of water from his bottle to rinse.

"Uhh, yeah I... umm..." he answered, then shrugged and shook his head. "A dumb dream I guess."

"Oookay," said Bombir. "We're packing our stuff now, so I'll let you finish waking up."

Bombir went back to the rest of the crew to finish tearing down the camp. The lad emerged from his tent several minutes later and began to take it down as well. Sally came up behind him and asked how he was holding up, and as to what his intentions for the day were.

"He feels really bad about last night," she said. "He apologized like four times already. You saw, he can't do much for himself. We have to help him somehow. He *is* my cave-cousin after all—" She winced. "I can't believe I just said that.... Anyway, we going to keep searching today or what?"

The lad looked at her for only a moment, then replied, "You know what? Yeah. I said I'd look for Papa, and that's what we're gonna do. After today though... we'll have to figure something else out. Is he still asleep?"

Sally pointed out to the lake, where the lad could see Jim swimming in the distance.

"He's been out there for the past hour—the guy is like a findol."

"A findol?" asked the lad.

"Yeah, you know, those big gray fish that breath

through the little hole in the top of their heads."

"Ah, yeah, I guess I forgot about those," the lad said as he gathered his folded tent under his arm to take to the raft.

After setting it down, Jim walked up to him.

"Listen lad—"

"It's THE lad, actually...."

"Yes, right. Well, I wanted to—"

"Don't worry about it, man, I know you didn't mean to almost kill me. We can put it behind us. It's time we head out and find your father."

Jim nodded, and the two shook hands. Then they joined the others in boarding the raft to begin paddling back to the S.S. Ark-Cheese.

Chapter 12:
The Jungle Encounter

Cave-Man Jim suggested they sail to the eastern shore, the farthest point on the lake from the entrance gate. Breakfast was eaten on the fly as they made their way there. It was shaping up to be another fine day, aside from some extra wind. The sails took full advantage and sent the Ark-Cheese flying across the lake at record speeds.

After two hours had passed, the shoreline came into clear view. Another half an hour later and the lad was calling to drop sails and anchor; they'd continue on the raft the rest of the way... right after the lad made use of the restroom one last time.

Supplies were loaded, and before the group was even halfway to shore, something caught Bowman's eye.

"Looks like there's a boat up in the weeds on the beach there," he said.

Jim stood quickly, squinting to see. "Is it a canoe?"

"I'm not sure yet," replied Bowman. "It's partially covered—have to see when we get to it."

The shore was reached, the raft pulled up on the sand, and the group made their way over to the small vessel.

"This is it!" cried Jim. "It is my father's cave-boat!"

He frantically searched through the canoe, but nothing of note was to be found. Eyes soon turned to the area up ahead, where something new to all of them could be seen. Trees they were, but not the regular woods they were used to. The trees here were different somehow: huge, wide, and vine-covered, with large, vibrant, green leaves of a strange shape. This was no forest; it was a jungle.

Each member of the group slung a heavy pack of supplies over their shoulder, then moved together towards the ominous mouth that was their way inside. Wild, unearthly sounds came from within, for the animals that lived there were unlike any other in Skiddle Earth.

Many brightly colored birds were perched upon massive, twisted, moss-covered branches, and some flew here and there overhead as the group entered. They saw winged specimens of red, purple, yellow, green, blue, and a few other colors they didn't even know existed. Some had long, flowing tails that streamed far behind as they glided under the glowing, green canopy. There were those with thin beaks which poked out straight like a needle; others with thick, curved ones that nearly stabbed the birds in their own chests; and at least a couple with beaks that circled their heads three times, coming to a rear-facing end. Small, furry, bug-eyed creatures zipped around the trees and amongst the leafy plants of the jungle floor as well.

The group looked on in wonder as they followed what looked to be an old path between the giant trees. It was slightly overgrown but offered little resistance to their advancement.

"Look here!" said Sally, stooping over on the path's right side near some gnarled roots.

She was somewhat skilled in tracking, as was Bowman, who quickly joined for a second opinion.

"Someone definitely came through here recently," he said, examining the broken foliage that contained a few pieces of loose thread.

"Let's keep moving this way and see if we can find any more clues," said the lad. A bird pooped on his shirt. He scraped it off with the side of his palm, then used it to pat Jim on the back, giving a few unnoticeable wipes. "We'll find him," he reassured.

***

Two hours later, an empty bag was found at the base of a tree. Jim confirmed it belonged to Papa-San. Several items, including some rotting hams, were seen strewn about the area. Grass was trampled and low-hanging branches were snapped.

"Looks like he may have been attacked," said Bowman. "Stay on guard."

"We don't know which way he went from here," the lad stated. "I say we split up and search each side of the trail."

Bowman gave a look of concern. "Alright, but don't go too far. I'll take this side," he said, motioning to the right of the path behind him.

Sally and Jim followed Bowman, while Bombir joined the lad to look in the opposite direction.

The plants were much thicker off the path, coming up

past the lad and Bombir's waists as they carefully waded deeper into the more untamed regions of the jungle. Their feet tripped frequently on unseen roots below.

"I hope there's nothing deadly lurking beneath all this," Bombir complained. "The sooner we figure out what happened to that old cavester the better. I can't wait to head home."

The lad walked just ahead, brushing vines and branches out of his way. Without turning around, he replied, "C'mon, Bom. We may never get another chance to do anything like this. Would you rather tell your future grandchildren of how you loafed around in your own backyard eating buttercakes your whole young life?"

"I think we've had enough excitement for a few decades by now, the lad. We've already almost died like six times, unless you forgot."

"Ehh, what's a little more? We'll be heading off toward home soon enough. Then you can sit around all you—"

'WHOOSH!'

The lad froze as a man-sized thing flew past him in the air. He kept his voice low and tried not to panic.

"Bom... am I going nuts, or did you see that too?"

"I sure saw something, the lad," whispered Bombir. "I'd *really* like to get out of here now if that's alright with you."

"Right..." the lad replied. "Right, let's turn back and find the others."

The two spun around, now with Bombir in the lead, making their way back to the path double time and cutting through the damp, swishing jungle plants with much haste. The lad stifled a cry as BombirThin was snatched away before his very eyes, swiped up by that flying jungle creature. The lad gripped the handle of his sword, spinning all around and looking for an imminent attack.

Nothing was to be heard aside from the constant chirps and squawks of the surrounding birds. He began to draw out his Saber but was quickly grabbed from behind. He was soaring through the jungle now, up toward the canopy. The lad soon realized they were swinging by a vine. An arm held him tightly across the chest, so he began fighting to free himself. He managed to slide himself down a little, then chomped down on the arm of his abductor.

"OHHhhh!!" cried the unknown thing.

The two of them plummeted through the foliage, crashing through layers of branches until they slammed into the jungle floor. The lad was somehow mostly unhurt and stood to his feet from the depths of the planty floor, eager to lay eyes on the assassin. The broad leaves ahead rustled as the person struggled to get up. The figure rose: a tall, old, bearded man in dark yellow robes with a pointy hat.

"Papa-San, I presume?" asked the lad, looking up at the towering man and still gripping his sword handle just in case.

"Nay," the man replied. "That is one whom I am not."

The lad's eyes widened, his memory jolting into action once more.

"You... you're," he stuttered. "Rudolph? Could it really

be?"

"Rudolph?!" exclaimed the man. "NAY!! Behold! I am Randolf... Randolf the *Bronze*. A Wizard that has come to guide you on your journey to no particular place."

"Would you spell that name for me actually?"

The Wizard rolled his eyes. "R-A-N... D-O-L-F, got it?"

"It *IS* an F like you'd think!" the lad loudly said to himself. "I have so many questions."

"You may quickly ask three," said Randolf, rolling the R when uttering the number.

"Where is my friend? Did you know my unclecousin, Bobill? Is that a skirt you're wearing? No, no, scratch that last one. I meant, what journey are you referring to? Our journey here is almost over."

The Wizard took a breath, took off his hat, ran his fingers through his long, bronze hair, then set the hat back in place.

"I needed to speak with you alone, so I put your friend to sleep and placed him on a branch. I certainly did know Bobill, though I assumed he would have told you enough about *me* for you to not have to ask such a question. Finally, no, your journey does not end here, for that is why I have come. I know of what you discovered: a thing that would've done well to stay where it was forever."

"I don't know what you're talking about! I didn't find a ring of *any* kind!" The lad noticed his mistake even as it left his lips.

"Your unclecousin was unaware I knew of its existence.

I had concerns that this object may be of evil origin, so I looked into history and lore concerning it wherever I could. Bobill had lost the ring, another secret he thought he alone knew. It lay hidden somewhere in that lake, of that I was sure. So, I have spent many a year keeping watch over the area in my spare time for any who might come looking for it. You and your little friends are in serious peril now that it is in your possession. This ring was forged long ago, by a cruel and evil king known as—" Randolf paused, looking back and forth suspiciously. Then, with lips extended toward the lad, he whispered, "*Raauusssooonn....*"

The lad began to ask more questions, but Randolf cut him right off.

"I still don't know the extent of this ring's power, but I do know its maker wants it back, and has sent many a vile creature to seek it out for retrieval. There is a town, out the far side of this jungle, called Debris. Follow the road to the town as quickly as you are able. Someone I sent for will be arriving soon to lead you there and protect you from harm. For now, I must go to the Hall of Wizardness and discuss this matter with my council before making any further decisions. Wait with them in the town, probably at the motel if possible. I will come back to your group and meet you there as soon as I can."

"Wait!" yelled the lad. "This is crazy! How are you so sure this ring used to belong to some evil king? Maybe it isn't the same one. I'm sure there are plenty like it."

Randolf snorted in irritation. "Time is of the essence! But if it must be proven, then hold it out in your hand."

The lad took the ring from his secret pocket, placing it

in his outstretched palm for the Wizard to see. Randolf yanked the bottle from the lad's side, then poured some of the cool water over the ring.

"Look closely," Randolf said.

The lad leaned in, squinting at the shining band. Words appeared on the inner side within moments.

"I see words," said the lad. "It's some strange form of writing that I don't understand."

Randolf circled around behind the lad, peeking over his shoulder to read the inscription.

"The writing is an ancient style called cursive, which few can still read. What it says is this: 'Made in Dormor'. An accursed land which was under the rule of that terrible king thousands of years ago. He was eventually defeated, and this ring was lost to him then, undoubtedly draining him of most of his strength. You see, until very recently, it was believed he had been destroyed entirely, but some bits of him must still remain in his old place of dwelling for such events to occur as they are. If he were to get it back... who knows what may happen. With its great value, he could sell it, and use the cash to buy all sorts of weapons of destruction!"

The lad's brain felt as if it might catch fire trying to process all this information.

"We were looking for our new friend's father," the lad stated. "He got lost or attacked in this jungle. My friends won't understand this whole ring business anyway, but we need to find Papa-San before we do anything else."

Just then, Sally came running up.

"The lad! We found him—come quick!" she shouted.

Randolf had swung up into the treetops before Sally could spot him.

"Go on back," the lad answered. "I'll be right there."

"Alright. Hurry though. It's straight this way." She took off, running back in the direction from where she'd come.

Randolf slid down a vine, BombirThin still fast asleep under his arm. The Wizard set him on the ground. Then, with a staff he pulled from off his back, tapped Bombir lightly on the head, waking him up fully and instantly.

"AHH! What happened?!" Bombir cried, looking all around and flailing his arms.

"You're fine, Bom," said the lad. "This is Randolf the Wizard, he knocked you out so he could talk with me. I'll explain everything, but Papa-San has been found and we need to get over there." He then turned to the Wizard. "Randolf, I don't know why you're trying to keep yourself all mysteriously hidden, but stay here please, just for a little while. We may need your help—otherwise we won't be going on your looney quest."

"Quest?" asked Bombir.

Randolf leaned on his staff, then lowered his eyelids and scrunched his mouth to one side in impatience. "Very well," he said, "but *DO* hurry. I'm going to make a call."

He pulled out a small rectangular piece of glass and began poking at it with a finger. The lad decided not to even ask what it could be, grabbing Bombir by the arm instead and speeding off to the other side of the path to join the others.

When the lad and Bombir arrived, Bowman and Jim were extracting Papa-San from a hollowed-out tree. He *had* been attacked by something and was forced to hide inside it for days.

"Hip... ohh hip. Was a-a hip-p-p," the cave man muttered.

"He's been repeating that since we found him. Hasn't said much else," explained Bowman.

"His left leg is broken in sixty-eight places," said Sally. "I'm guessing that's what he's referring to. We'll have to make a splint and find a way to carefully carry him back without making it worse."

Jim helped Sally with binding the leg while the others gathered sticks and vines to construct a stretcher. About ten minutes passed before a very annoyed Randolf swung down into their midst.

"Do you not know what the word *haste* means?!" he yelled.

"Stranger!!" screamed Sally, as she chambered a rock into her slingshot and fired it at the Wizard.

Randolf smacked it away, more frustrated than ever now.

"Wait!" the lad cried. "This is an old friend of my unclecousin, Randolf the Brass Wizard."

"That's *Bronze*!" snapped Randolf.

"Oh... yeah, I-I meant Bronze. Anyway, he says the item

that I may or may not have found, and/or possibly do or don't still possess, is dangerous. Says we need to bring it to a place where we *and it* can be kept safe from prowling weirdos who want it for some specific reason. It's a little more complicated than that, but we have to hurry along and see that Papa gets home so we can head to a town called Debris."

The lad's friends just looked at him, unsure of how to respond.

"There's no time!" said Randolf. "Servants of darkness roam this area even now. You must leave right away. As for this Papa-San, I will have to change some things around. An apprentice Wizard is coming to bring you to Debris, but now I suppose he'll have to stay here, and I will have to figure out someone else to send ahead." He pulled out his glass rectangle and poked at it some more, then continued. "He'll be here soon, he can take care of those injuries easily enough, though he's only been in practice for several hundred years.... His name is Thoroughbob the Ironic, but he goes by the simpler name, Bob."

"Thank you for the help, sir," said Jim.

"Think nothing of it, good cave man," Randolf replied with a sigh. "I have met your father before. I was there when he helped the lad's unclecousin, Bobill, across the lake on his quest many years ago. I would say that this is payment for his troubles back then, but I remember seeing Bobill give him quite the sum of gold when he departed from us."

"What?!" yelled Jim. "Gold?! Where did that go? I have never seen any gold."

Randolf just shrugged, then gave some final words of departure. "I am going now. As soon as Bob arrives, the lad must take to the road at once and make for Debris—if any of you can accompany him, it would be most helpful. Remember, stay on high alert for assailants. Papa-San himself likely ran into one of them already. Goodbye!"

The old Wizard spun around and jumped high in the air, grasping a vine and swinging away into the distant trees until he vanished from sight.

"Dang it," said the lad. "I meant to ask him why he didn't attend Bobill's funeral. Not that he would've given me an answer.... Kind of irritating that he didn't pay his respects since they were supposedly such good friends."

"Well, none of us has *ever* seen him," said Bombir. "Maybe he grew distant and just didn't know, or he's been busy... for the last couple decades. I dunno."

"Yeah, could be, but hopefully I get to see the geezer again so we can talk about it some more. He probably knows more about Bobill than I do."

The lad fell silent in thought, and the group continued working on the stretcher to carry Papa with while they waited for the next magical fellow to appear.

***

A bunch of minutes after Randolf had left, a shorter, stockier Wizard came shuffling up to them from around a large tree. His robes were of a light gray color, as was his low-hanging hat that obscured his eyes. A rounded nose and an unlengthy beard of bright brown were about all that could be seen outside the mound of baggy clothing.

"Haillo!" said the Wizard. "I was sent by Randolf to tend to an, uhh, injured cave person?"

"A HISPO!!" screamed Papa-San.

"Yeah, it's him, this guy's father," said the lad before pointing at Jim.

"Ah yes, I see," replied Bob. "Looks like he may be feverish. Don't you worry, we'll get him home and patched up good-as-new in no time."

Papa-San was placed on the makeshift stretcher, then Jim lifted the front while Bob used magic from his staff to lift the back. Everyone made their way over to the main path of the jungle, and as Jim turned toward home, he looked back at the rest of the group.

"I cannot thank you all enough. I never would have found my father alone. I just wish that I could help you on the rest of your journey."

"No problem, man," answered the lad. "You just get him home and healed up. You're welcome to use whatever you can find on the Ark-Cheese if you want. I think we've got enough supplies with us. Don't have time to backtrack anyway. We've got this though. We'll get it sorted out and be back by your place to see how Papa's doing before you know it."

Jim nodded. "Alright then. Goodbye, the lad, Bombir, Bowman, and of course my newly found cousin, Sally. I will not forget your kindnesses."

The others waved and said their own goodbyes in return, then both groups headed in opposite directions. Though they had no idea of the distance, many more miles of jungle lay ahead of the lad and his crew. It was still around early afternoon, but they wanted to get out of there before the sun began to get too low, lest they lose their senses in the maddening vines and shrubbery. Along the way, the lad attempted to better explain their situation; he was fairly confused himself, but not even Randolf had *all* the answers.

"What exactly is coming for the ring? Did that fossil say anything else?" asked Bowman.

"No, not really," replied the lad. "Just, evil, dark creatures... or people maybe. Enemies of some kind. *'Servants of darkness'*, I think he called them. You were there. I don't know what they are. I guess we have to assume anyone we cross is likely an enemy."

"How helpful..." mumbled Bombir.

Sally piped in with a hushed voice. "We probably shouldn't even be talking about it, or using the word *ring* out loud."

"You're right," the lad said. "Let's keep our noise to a minimum."

So, they continued without another word for some time, walking as silently as they could manage.

Chapter 13:
An Unpleasant Evening

Plenty of hours had passed. The lad and his friends grew weary, and the sun dropped to the horizon. It was getting hard for them to see, and they were ready to rest and have themselves a meal. Sally started a cooking fire in a clearing not far from the path while Bowman and the lad collected extra wood, hunted for small game, and checked the immediate area for threats. Bombir unpacked the tents and bedrolls, then began preparations for dinner. Within an hour, they were all gathered together around the fire, each of them still able to mostly eat things they preferred. The lad wasn't out of oranges just yet, but he *was* beginning to run low.

As they ate, Bombir held up an odd-looking, bumpy, green and yellow oval with a few slash marks in it.

"Found this while I was cooking," he said. "I remember seeing a drawing of these in a cookbook once. Pretty sure they're wild jungle melons called Züt-Fruits. Supposed to be pretty good... if you can get them open." He frowned down at his poor attempts of getting inside it.

"Lemme see that," said the lad.

The melon was handed over and the lad quickly sliced it to pieces, revealing juicy, tannish-purple fruit-flesh within. The lad passed them around to everyone and they all tried it at the same time. Bombir raised his eyebrows and nodded, fairly satisfied. Sally just shrugged and kept eating. Bowman didn't react, as though he'd consumed something similar enough before. And finally, the lad took a huge, excited bite. He chewed the watery pulp for several seconds before spraying it out on the ground beside him.

"Bleh!!" he yelled. "Züt-Fruits? More like Püp-Fruits! Disgusting!"

The rest of his slice was cast far into the distance, and he went back to the comfort of his oranges.

After their dinner was complete, Bombir started to nod off. He bid the rest goodnight and made his way to his tent. Not long after, Sally did the same. The cooking fire was reduced to a little pile of glowing coals, barely lighting the lad and Bowman's faces as they sat in silence for a time. The lad noticed Bowman pull out a small box from the pouch on his side. From out of the box, Bowman retrieved a thin, white stick, which he promptly placed one end of between his lips.

"When'd you pick up that habit?" asked the lad casually.

Bowman drew in a deep, slow breath, removed the stick, then exhaled a sparkling white cloud into the air. "I dunno," he replied. "My pop used to give 'em to me every once in a while. Guess I got hooked on the flavor at some point."

The lad leaned forward, one eyebrow raised. "You know how much sugar is in those things?"

Bowman stared blankly at the lad, head leaned to one side without the slightest hint of concern on his face.

"How much?" he blandly asked, assuming correctly that the lad had no idea.

"Well, a lot!" responded the lad. "I mean... that's what adults always said at the grocery store when I asked about the candy cigs anyway."

Bowman pulled out another stick and held it up with a half-grin. "Would you like to see?"

The lad let out a long sigh. "Nah, I've already got a serious citrus addiction. Don't need to add another thing."

"Suit yourself," said Bowman with a shrug, sliding his pack of smokes closed and stuffing them back in his pouch. He reached a finger up to the tip of the one still in his mouth, pushing it in. Then he crunched on the candy as a few more sparkly puffs left his lips. "Good stuff," he said with a thumbs-up.

Before he could even put his thumb down, a loud 'CRACK!' was heard nearby. The noise did not come from the direction of their two sleeping companions. It was almost certainly the sound of a fallen branch snapping in half from being stepped upon. Bowman put a finger up for the lad to keep quiet, though it wasn't necessary. The lad was well armed and had been through many dangers and fights on this trip, but something about this place, this situation, was a new level of unsettling he had never felt before. He didn't dare make a movement, neither of them did; anything could be lurking in the shadows beyond the firelight. The two waited for many agonizing minutes with their hands clamped around their still-sheathed weapons, straining to hear another noise of any kind. A sudden grunting, gurgling sound began, nearly making the lad jump out of his skin.

After a moment, he and Bowman realized it was coming from Bombir's tent. Their sleeping friend had apparently grown uncomfortable in his slumber and changed positions, causing him to start snoring. The snore grew louder by the second, making the lad and Bowman quite nervous. Back in the other direction, a little further clockwise around them from the first sound they'd heard, came another light crunch. It was difficult to hear over Bombir's racket, but something was moving around their camp in a circle—a something that seemed to be making an attempt to stay unheard.

Another shuffle of vegetation, this time, much closer to their small clearing. It couldn't be more than a dozen and a half feet away now. Bowman motioned for the lad to move toward the tents, so the two of them carefully slid from their sitting places and dropped to their bellies, slowly crawling away with the utmost silence. As they did this, Bombir was heard clearing his throat a couple of times, his snores finally ceasing.

The lad and Bowman rounded Bombir and Sally's tents, not waking them yet, but positioning themselves at the far openings to yank them away quickly if their stalker turned out to be a serious threat. The coals of the fire were burned very low at this point, and almost nothing could be seen from where they sat peering past the tents. The lad began to shiver, but not just from the sting of fear washing over him. An icy chill filled the air, making his breath begin to visibly steam from his nose and mouth. As he looked down the length of the outer tent wall, he noticed a layer of frost expanding across its surface.

"What in Skiddle Earth is happening?" he thought to himself.

Nighttime it surely was, but they were in a jungle in the middle of summer; a thing like this should not be occurring.

Movement... near the fire. The lad blinked, leaned forward, and squinted to try to make out what was entering the area. A long, dark, formless blob slid out from the deepest inky shadows beyond the farthest campfire seat. It appeared to be something crawling low to the ground like they had just done. A thin, black tendril rose up, feeling around at the top of the log that Bowman had recently been sitting upon.

After staring a moment, the lad realized it was a boney arm. Another arm raised itself next to the first and the dark blob on the ground used the log to pull itself slowly up to what looked to be a crouched position. A featureless head twisted back and forth, scanning the clearing. The lad wanted to go now, to get out of this place as quickly as possible. He glanced to Bowman, who was still studying the unearthly being and trying to figure out exactly what to do. Then the lad looked back to the campfire. The thing raised one arm; a single finger flicked twice, evidently beckoning something else to join.

An enormous beast crept up behind it, swaying side to

side as it walked in impossible quietness. The lad could see a low, wide head, followed by a much larger rounded body, but the details eluded him in the darkness. A slow rhythm of deep, heaving breaths could just barely be heard coming from this second creature, matching the clouds of steam issuing forth from its nostrils. Its eyes seemed to glow a dim red. Whether it was reflected by the coals, or cast by some evil force within itself, none could say with certainty. Either way, it only enhanced the already overwhelmingly menacing sight.

The lad wasn't waiting for Bowman to make up his mind any longer, boat or not, he was still the captain of this excursion, and he was ready to leave immediately. He carefully grasped the bags in between the tents, motioning for Bowman to do the same. Slinging two of them over his shoulder, he gestured again that he planned to grab their sleeping companions and drag them out.

He held the five fingers of his left hand up over his right arm toward Bowman, curling his thumb in to make four. Next was his pinky, the shortest. He dropped it, bringing the count down to three. It was then followed by—

'BWAAAP!!'

Bombir loudly split wind in his sleep. The sound was like a blast from a trumpet filled with lard. So violent was its force that the sides of the tent slightly expanded, and the very ground briefly trembled. The lad cast his hands onto Bombir's shoulders, yanking him with all his strength.

Bowman reached into Sally's tent and grabbed... an empty sleeping bag. He felt around, but there was no one inside. He stood, looking all around in a near panic.

The lad was dragging Bombir toward the main path, slapping him in the face to wake him and get him moving on his own.

Bowman looked back to the center of the clearing, the dark thing was snapped to attention and moving his way, the great beast following closely behind it. Where was Sally? She had to have been out of the tent before he left the fire. Was there more than one pair of these things? Did another one silently take her?

Without thinking it through, he pulled out his bow, quickly nocked an arrow, drew back the string... and fired. The arrow whizzed between two of the tents, making straight for the smaller creature's face, if it had one. A hand came up, snatching it to a stop as quick as lightning. Ice formed thick over the arrow, turning it into an icicle. Then the dark, boney hand squeezed, shattering ice and arrow to tiny chunks that sprinkled the ground.

Bowman threw his bow onto his shoulder along with the supply bags that sat next to him, then turned and sprinted unlike he ever had in his life toward the main path. He stumbled through vines and tripped over roots, coming up to a large tree on his left. It was too dark for him to notice that someone had stepped into his path from behind it.

'WHAM!'

He collided with the person, sending them both crashing to the ground. He went for his daggers, but quickly realized the person was Sally.

"Sally! What are you..." he trailed off, too confused to form a sentence.

She got up and dusted herself off. "Sorry, had to use the ladies' room. I guess I was longer than I thought. Was on my way back right now."

"Oh, thank crud you went this way!" Bowman loudly whispered. "Some kind of evil creature snuck into our camp. Forget about our stuff, we've gotta get as far away from here as possible right now. I did grab this though." He handed her bag to her. "Let's go, the lad and Bombir should be up ahead."

The two ran, eventually making it to the path. After only a minute of running later, they reached the lad and Bombir, both of them collapsed against trees and trying to catch their breath. Bowman spoke up right away.

"No use trying to fight it. I shot an arrow at the thing and it grabbed it right out of the air. Then it... well... froze and shattered the arrow... as absurd as that sounds. I watched it happen."

Loud crashing and rumbling came from behind them, and the lad cried out, "We need to get off the path! I don't think we can outrun it! Let's cross to the other side, quickly!"

Bombir was still half asleep, and had been told very little, but he picked himself up and ran with the rest of them into the dense, devouring blackness of the jungle. They had no light whatsoever and could only guess and hope they were going in the right direction to get out soon—all while falling, tripping and running into trees and spiderwebs every several seconds.

***

After forty or so minutes of constant running through the merciless wet chaos of slapping leaves and snagging vinery, the four companions decided to risk a short stop to regain their strength. It would be some time before the sun rose—several hours at least. The path through the jungle lay around fifty feet to their right, and they watched the direction carefully as they tried to quiet their gasping breaths.

Wiping sweat from his brow, Bombir whispered in the dark, "What *is* that thing?"

"If you remember," answered the lad, "Randolf said it was likely there were already things out here looking for the... item I found. Don't know if they can tell or feel it being nearby and are able to track us like that, or it was just random chance. That creature was the most unnatural thing I've ever seen—though, honestly, I didn't see it real good. Who knows what it's capable of doing? But that's why we're heading to this town, to meet with someone who's supposed to somehow keep us safe from this... *thing*... until Randolf gets back to us."

"The Wizard *did* make it sound like there was probably multiple enemies here, but he never said they'd have supernatural abilities..." said Sally.

"Well, he was in a hurry, I guess," replied the lad.

Bombir began to whine. "I don't wanna be here. I wanna be—"

"Alright," Bowman interrupted. "If we can manage, we need to keep moving."

"You're right," whispered the lad with an unseen nod. "Let's get out of here."

No sign of their pursuer had been detected, but they weren't taking any chances. They remained off the path, still trying to stay quiet, but moving at an easier pace now.

Another twenty minutes passed, and the lad came to a sudden halt.

"Shh," he warned. "I think I heard something."

A soft snorting sound repeated thrice, then all fell silent.

"Are we supposed to be this close to the road?" asked Bombir.

Now that he looked, the lad saw they must've been veering to the right, for now the path was only several feet away, just on the other side of a tree they were all huddled next to. Another sound was heard then, a squishing of moistened dirt underfoot of something large, followed by one more snort. The lad slowly slid himself around the tree, suffering a quick glance. There it was, passing lazily by within twice the reach of a leg: a tremendous round beast ridden by a skeletal man-like figure in tattered, dark brown robes. That chill returned to the air once more.

"Is that a... hippo?" whispered Sally.

The lad reached out to clap a finger over her lips, accidentally stabbing it into her eyeball. She reeled back and stifled a cry while the lad wiped off the eye juice on his pants. He felt terrible when he realized what he'd done but couldn't say anything out loud. Miraculously, Sally's words didn't seem to have been heard. The lad tried to give her an apologetic pat on the shoulder, but somehow ended up catching his fingers in her other eye. He immediately felt the force of four knuckles impact his cheek and twist his head nearly backwards, causing him to sprawl flat on the ground from his seated position.

He laid there a while, unmoving, before finally pushing himself up to take another look at the path. Beast and rider were gone without a trace. Thinking back, it *had* looked like a hippo, though easily double the size of what one would think it should've been. He turned his head to the right from where it had come—there it was again! He got low and slid back around the side of the tree, hoping he hadn't been seen.

'How did it get back there so fast?' he thought. But no, it hadn't gone back, this was a *second* evil hippo.

The tree, the plants, the ground, all turned cold again and began to frost over. The air became difficult to breathe, stinging the throat with its rapidly plummeting temperature. The lad leaned out slightly but saw nothing on the dark path.

'SNORT!'

The sound came from the direct opposite side of the tree from them... the rider had stopped. The lad was so paralyzed with fear that he practically forgot about the pain in his recently punched face.

A shuffling noise... it was coming around the tree now,

only a couple feet from him at most. Without properly thinking it through or saying anything to the others, he jumped up and unsheathed the Super-Deluxo-Saber, holding it high over his head.

"Wait!" hissed Bowman, but it was too late.

Just as the boney brown rider leaned into view, the lad dropped his sword down with all the fury he could muster.

"TAKE THIS!!" he shouted almost involuntarily.

The blade struck it in the shoulder, sinking in ever so slightly and bringing the rider to the ground on its side. With frightening speed, the rider reached out and grabbed the lad's wrist as he was raising the sword for another blow. Thick ice spread across the lad's hand and up his arm until he yanked away from the nightmarish fiend, causing him to drop the Saber in the process. The others were already on their feet and sprinting, with Bombir grabbing the lad's non-frozen arm to pull him along. He was dazed, but began to run as well, right arm still icy and hanging limp at his side.

The tree they'd been using for cover suddenly exploded into splinters at the base, sending everything above crashing through the jungle. The monster hippo had burst into the foliage, its rider climbing back atop. Bloodcurdling shrieks and deafening roars echoed past the lad and his crew, but they dared not look back; they just kept running, zigzagging, winding, and twisting through the plants trying to throw the wicked heckspawn off their trail.

Chapter 14:
The Rhyming Weird

"I can't step another step!" cried Bombir, collapsing to the dirt.

Dawn had still not come, and the lack of visibility was wearing down the sanity of all.

"We've gotta get out of the jungle, Bom!" said the lad.

"I don't care! Let that demon's fat hippo come and swallow me whole! I ain't movin' an inch until I've had a rest!"

"Fine... take five," said Bowman. "Just keep quiet, I'm gonna check behind us." He then quickly disappeared into the darkness.

"I'm really sorry for the... eyeballs thing," the lad said to Sally.

"Well, I'm sorry for punching you... so hard. But—you know—twice and all."

"Right. I guess I deserved it. Anyway, I'm gonna have a look ahead real quick through these bushes. Maybe we're finally getting close. I'll be right back."

Sally nodded and sat on the ground with, but not terribly *near*, Bombir, who was non-stop grumbling under his breath.

"Be careful!" the lad heard her loudly whisper to him as he strode away.

Though the ice had melted away from the lad's arm, it was still cold and quite numb, aside from a sharp burning sensation. He rubbed at the spot furiously in an attempt to warm it up as he approached a seemingly impenetrable wall of branches and leaves that stood before him. There'd been a few tight places throughout their trek in this jungle, so he figured he'd just feel his way down until he found an opening somewhere, hoping they wouldn't be forced all the way back to the now-distant road.

Eventually, he came to a soft spot and started pushing his way through leaves that were still fairly dense. He imagined seeing an open field on the other side, free of trees and bushes of any kind. How he would rejoice at such a sight, even if it wasn't yet light out. His eyes strained in the pitch dark, trying to make out the shapes of the branches so he could keep them from stabbing him in the face.

Something strange appeared, somewhat elliptical in shape and lighter in hue than the surrounding flora. The lad pushed his face closer for a better view, but instantly regretted doing so. The shape in front of him, not more than six inches from his nose, was a wide-eyed, grinning face. As if that wasn't enough to incite the lad's heart to pop, the hovering face spoke aloud in a gleeful tone.

"Hey there, fella. How can I help ya?" said the face, shining white teeth settling back together into an excessively large smile.

The lad ejected himself backwards out of the bushes, rolling and flipping across the ground. He scrambled to get up, then sprinted like a madman back to his friends. Sally leapt to her feet upon seeing his hysteria.

"What happened!?" she asked.

"A friggin face! A man, i-in the bushes up there!"

Bombir was standing up now too. "Okay, slow down a bit the lad. What was this man doing?"

The lad gulped hard, looking behind him repeatedly.

"Just... staring. I only saw his face—it was so close I almost ran right into it! Then, he spoke to me... asking 'how's it going' or something like that."

"How bizarre..." muttered Sally.

About that time, Bowman came walking back toward them. The lad explained to him what happened, and Bowman suggested they all go together for another look.

"Doesn't sound like one of those brown riders, but I say we all stick close and stay alert. We have to keep pressing forward, weird bush-face or not. Take us to the spot, the lad."

So, the lad led them to the place where he'd seen the bush person. Bowman told them to wait and stay silent for a moment so they could listen before pushing into the shrubberies. A voice was heard, not close, but also not very far. It sounded like... singing. The lad hesitantly leaned into the bushes a little and could barely make out the shape of a short round fellow dancing on a stump. The song grew a bit louder, and they began to make out the words:

'Stick, stones, and water too,
he invented the color blue!
Thick bones and knobby knees,
he is older than the trees!
Brick thrones and ancient kings,
he can fly cuz he's got wings!

Sing loud, Ron-a-thants!
Dance along and clap your pants!
Backflip, kick a neck!
Send that hippo back to heck!
Yes, R.B. is here!
There is nothing left to fear!

Quick loans and golden spoon,
he has visited the moon!
Sick groans and ginger tea,
he slayed eight dragons easily!
Trick zones and secret lever,
he can hold his breath forever!

Sing now, Ron-a-thoes!
Skip along and snap your toes!
Spin 'round, punch a mouth!
Send the riders runnin' south!
Now, he'll sit and pour a cup!

Cuz he never makes things up!
Find the knife and grab a fork!
For his name is Bomblethork!!'

The song was quite unusual to say the least. The four listeners couldn't believe how ridiculously nonsensical it was, all except the lad of course, who'd heard similar things, albeit in his dreams. This fellow also seemed to sing a few lines about running off the hippo riders, which meant he couldn't be all bad. But what kind of person stands on an old tree stump in the jungle at night, clapping, doing high kicks, and singing about how some person has done a whole bunch of random fantastical deeds?

"I'm going to try talking to him," said the lad.

Bowman grabbed his arm. "You don't know if that lunatic is dangerous! I say we all go and confront him together, weapons at the ready."

The lad brushed the hand off, deciding that this was somehow a great moment for a pinch of confrontation.

"Listen here, Bowman, *I'm* still pretty much the leader of this little expedition, and I say you guys can cover me from here. You've got your bow, Sally has her slingshot, and Bom... well, he can be an extra set of eyes. I'm going alone."

The lad really didn't know if the idea was very wise; he guessed that he simply wanted to regain a bit of the confidence he'd lost earlier, and maybe seem like a tough guy in the process. He'd recently known a level of fear previously thought to be impossible, making him look like a coward and a weakling to his friends. Perhaps he could take more control, keep his cool, and earn himself a widthy slice of sweet reputation.

He began to rise up and move through the hedge, but two of Bowman's hands clamped the lad's shoulders, forcing him back down.

"No, *you* listen!" said Bowman in irritation. "You can call yourself the leader all you want, but you have very little experience being out in the wilderness and dealing with threatening situations. You've been living in town your whole life, spending most of your time eating oranges and throwing rocks at things. I know you like adventure, and you're still upset at the loss of your sword, but rushing into the unknown like this is nothing short of foolishness. Now, I say we all calmly walk in and introduce ourselves at the same time. Is that cool with you?"

The lad sighed, then he yelled, "You don't tell me what to do! No one does! And you better keep your dang hands off me before I pop you in the mouth, Smokey-Joe!"

"Think you're a bad dude, huh? *HUH*?! You little orange-sucking melon-dome! Go ahead! Try and take a swing!"

The lad's bottled insecurities erupted forth, manifesting into raging fury. He lunged at Bowman, throwing punches left and right.

"The lad! Stop this!" cried Sally.

Bowman leaned, ducked, and blocked most of the blows, still catching one in his eastern eyebrow and another in his favorite kidney.

"Quiet down, someone will hear this racket!" said Bombir.

Bowman tried repeatedly shoving the lad back, not wanting to return fists, but his patience had worn thin. He tackled the lad to the ground, pinning him.

"Cut it out, you dumb little punk!" yelled Bowman.

The lad got one hand free, immediately firing off a knuckle sandwich toward Bowman's face, but its length was depleted within an inch of his chin, bringing the lad's arm to a straight-snapping halt. Bowman snickered at the failed attempt, just before the lad wrapped his fingers around Bowman's goatee and yanked.

"Take that, arrow-boy!" the lad mocked.

Bowman slapped away the lad's arm, then drew back a fist to plant it into the lad's face. As the blow fell, Bowman felt his arm jerk to a stop, a hand grasping his wrist.

"Well bless my shoes and call me 'Dear', what the heck's a goin' on here?" said a mysterious voice.

Bowman leapt to his feet and quickly shuffled back to where Sally and Bombir stood behind, dragging the lad along with him.

"Who are you? What do you want with us?" asked Bowman.

"Want? Nay, nothing at all. Just wonderin' what's the point of this brawl. But whomever am I, you've a need to know? Ron Bomblethorpe's by the name that I go."

The man came closer, revealing himself, so the group

took in a good look at him. He was bright-eyed and circular-faced, and wore a tall, rounded, fiery-orange hat with a few small holes poked through it. The hat perched upon what looked to be an unruly swoop of electric neon-blue hair, connecting through wide sideburns to meet with a thick beard of matching color. Below that was a square-shaped formal jacket, the same eye-melting orange as the hat. It looked to be clean and pressed, which did not reflect the appearance of his legwear: dirty, ripped, dark green corded denim pants that had been cut off into shorts of nigh inappropriate length. All that remained beneath their jagged and frayed edges were stubby, surprisingly sparsely haired legs that came to an end in long, brown shoes which kicked up high at the toe, making them look like reclining L's.

"We were, uh, just fooling around," said the lad, standing to his feet. "That song... *you* were singing it, right? It sounded like you mentioned driving away those beast-riding creeps. Did you really?"

Ron gave a quick nod and a laugh. "Aye, ol' Ron did just that, sent 'em runnin' like a rain-soaked cat."

"How is that possible?" asked Bowman. "They have... quite unnatural powers. Are you a Wizard or something?"

"The King of Wizards, Ron was long ago. He taught the rest all the magic they know. But alas, nearby, the riders still roam. Safety and answers can be found in my home."

"You're offering to let us stay at your place?" Sally asked. "How do you know we're not bad guys?"

Ron chuckled. "So many questions... wait until day! If

it's shelter you seek, Ron's home is this way!"

He somehow did a backflip from a standstill while jumping forward over the ten-foot bushes, then ran into the dark. The lad and his friends took off after Ron, almost losing him. They eventually caught up after a few minutes when he stopped suddenly next to an exceptionally huge tree.

"Ron's house is up there, at the top of this tree. His wife, Stickaletta, is waiting on he," said Ron with a grin.

He did a quick, complicated knock on the tree's trunk, a few raps with the backs of three left knuckles, then three kicks with his right shoe. He followed this with alternating slaps with each palm several times, spun around and banged it with the bottom of his left shoe at least twice, then finally, he smashed his forehead into it. A squeaking sound was heard as a square platform lowered with ropes from the high branches, coming to rest silently on the jungle floor.

Ron waved them on. "Now, up and away ol' Ron's tree we'll go. Leave worries and fears in the darkness below."

They huddled close as Ron stomped the platform once, and it began to rise. "This tree was planted by Ron himself, in millennia past, before Dork, Man, or Elf."

At least half of Ron's guests didn't believe that, along with several other claims they'd heard him make so far. Assuming he wasn't trying to kill and eat them up there though, they'd just nod and smile for the time being. The platform reached the lofty boughs of the enormous tree, the branches almost seeming to move out of the way before anything came in contact with them. Lights could be seen now, glowing in the windows of a small house above them. It looked to be near the tree's top, held fast between huge beams that diverged from the trunk. The vast majority of the leaves grew only on the very ends of the branches, leaving the ascending travelers suspended in a wide-open space within a tremendous green orb.

"This is incredible," mumbled the lad. "You'd never even know this was up here."

The rest of the way up, Ron bounced up and down, humming a tune that sounded much like the song he'd sung earlier, a wide grin still filling his face. The platform slowly came to a stop next to the door of the house, which was illuminated by a small hanging lantern.

Ron turned to his guests and proclaimed, "That, good friends, is the end of the ride. Let's open the door now and go on inside."

With that, he twisted the knob and flung the door open, leading the others into a short entryway.

He called out, "Stickaletta, my darling, your Ron has come back. Four guests are with him, would you grab them a snack?"

Ron hung his orange jacket up near the door, then continued into an open area between a kitchen and living room. He stepped aside and allowed the group to have a look at the place and meet his wife. She was standing by a kitchen island, platter full of snacks in her outstretched hands. None of them knew what to say, they just stared at the sight before them. She was very obviously not a living person, but many bundles of sticks tied together to create a lady-like statue. It even had facial features carved or placed on the front of the head, giving it a slight, welcoming smile.

"Well now, there's no need to be shy. Go on, grab a bite, meet my wife and say hi."

The lad gulped, then cautiously stepped forward. He reached Stickaletta and bowed, though it was not the custom of his region.

"Hello there, I'm the lad, and these are my friends. Thanks so much for your hospitality."

He took one of the food items from the platter, looking to be a little cracker-and-cheese sandwich of sorts. Then he turned to Ron who motioned to the dining room table. The lad sat in a chair as the rest greeted Ron's fake wife and got snacks of their own.

"Eat up, relax, unwind and sit tight. Ol' Ron's gonna make sleep arrangements for the night," Ron said as he vanished down a hall into a back room.

"Pleased to meet you, ma'am, we appreciate your kindness," Sally was the last to say, taking her cracker sandwich and joining the others.

The four sat at the table, munching the small morsels and keeping their heads down without a word. Soon, Ron was heard coming back down the hall. The lad looked up as he rounded the corner, arms overloaded with pillows and blankets. What the lad did *not* see, was the stick woman.

"Where's Stickaletta?" asked the lad.

"Poor gal was tired, had to lay down her head. I told her to go back and get into bed."

The lad glanced at the kitchen island and saw the snack tray sitting there.

"How did that pile of sticks get moved away and that metal tray set down without making any noise or us noticing?" the lad thought to himself.

The others shared a look of concern. Ron laid out the sleeping materials across couches and floor, then bid them goodnight.

"Sleep well, my friends, Ron's off to count sheep. Tuck yourselves in and have a good sleep."

Ron snapped his fingers, which extinguished all the lights in the house, save one that burned on the living room coffee table. Then, the group heard his footsteps fade down the hall and his bedroom door shut.

After that, they figured they might as well try to get some sleep, eerie as the place seemed. Sally and Bombir took the couches, while the lad and Bowman slept on the floor. This gave the lad a chance at a much-needed apology.

"I'm... sorry for earlier, Bowman. I was a gigantic jerk. You were right, I just wanted to look cool and ended up looking like a turd."

"It's no big deal," replied Bowman. "We were all getting tense from being in this jungle so long. I suppose I could've been less rude myself."

The lad breathed a sigh of relief, thankful to know he'd apparently escaped permanent friendship damage along with any serious consequences to his moronic actions as well.

"Goodnight," said the lad.

"Night," said Bowman.

"Nighty-night," said Sally.

"Goodnight, guys," said Bombir.

The lad stretched up and blew out the candle on the table, sending the room into pitch darkness.

A moment later, he heard a whispery, "Goodnight." It was a female voice, but not Sally's... so faint that he wasn't sure if he'd really heard it.

His heart sped up, but he decided not to say anything when none of the others seemed to stir. He told himself that he was hearing things from a lack of sleep, so he forced his breathing to slow. His heart returned to normal, and he slipped off into dreamland.

Chapter 15:
Breakfast at Bomblethorpe's

The lad awoke to the sound of talk, laughter, and a sizzly noise. He rubbed at his blurry eyes and blinked a few times, only for them to be met with stinging white smoke. He took one last hard blink and wiped away the streams of tears, then began searching for the source. Golden beams of sunlight poured through the windows, piercing and brightening the ivory fog that rolled across the room.

"Is the house on fire?" thought the lad.

It was then that his nose kicked into action. The smell of frying bacon permeated his sniff-holes, undoubtedly the thing creating the smoke and sizzling. Sally Kim was just sitting up as well, stretching her arms and yawning wide.

"What time is it... and why's it all smoky?"

The lad said nothing, but noticed that Bowman and Bombir's blankets were empty, so he stood to his feet and made his way through the grease clouds toward the dining area.

"I think the others are in here," the lad called back to Sally.

When he got a few feet closer, he saw his other two

friends sitting at the table, plates and cutlery at the ready. To his left, in the kitchen, Stickaletta stood in front of a stove, multiple fires roaring under pans and griddles.

"Don't stare," said Bombir. "She'll never get anything done that way."

The lad looked to Bowman, hoping he had something to say that made more sense.

Bowman put his hand to the side of his mouth, shielding it from the direction of the stick woman and silently mouthed the words, 'She's real'.

The lad's confusion only grew, so Bowman gestured for him to sit down.

Bowman leaned in close and explained in a whisper. "We don't quite understand it, but she... does things... when you aren't looking at her. She never moves if she's in your field of view... but glance away for a moment, and when you look back, you'll find that she's made progress on whatever she was doing. We even heard her humming and moving things earlier."

"You *do* know that's far more creepy than interesting, right?" said the lad.

"Yeah, but I won't question anything that gets me free bacon," piped in Bombir.

"Where's Ron?" the lad asked.

"He left about half an hour ago—said he was going to fetch a few things for breakfast," answered Bowman.

"Even though it's probably lunch time or after," added

Bombir.

Sally came in to join them, slumping down into a chair with her eyes nearly closed, looking as if she'd fall right back to sleep at any moment.

"You guys catch her up," said the lad. "I'm going to go check something out."

He rose from his seat, making his way into the kitchen. Bowman began to protest, but figured he'd just let the lad do as he pleased and went back to talking. The lad slowly approached the stick woman, eventually coming up to stand right next to her. Four disgusting eggs were frying on a skillet, appearing to be newly cracked due to the see-through liquid surrounding the shiny yellow yolks.

"Smellin' good, Mrs. B!" said the lad, leaning over her stickly shoulder. "What kind of bird-rear did these pop out of? A rooster? A pelican? Turkodactyl?"

He lingered there, eyes fixed on the ever-crispening eggs and the nearby spatula in the grasp of a twiggy hand.

"Don't blink, don't blink!" the lad thought to himself.

But the smoke overcame his watering eyes, and he involuntarily snapped his lids down. 'CLANK!', he heard, in the billisecond his peepers were closed. In no time at all, they were fully open again, and beheld the eggs sitting neatly on a previously empty plate with five new ones having taken to the skillet. The lad got a sudden urge to shove the stick woman to see what she'd do, but after brief consideration, he realized he feared to know the answer. Just then, the lad's attention turned to a noise from behind;

the front door was open, and Ron was stepping inside.

"Ol' Ron's come back, and brought more to eat. With fruit and bread, the meal's now complete!" he cried, stomping over to the kitchen island and dumping out the contents of a burlap sack.

Lengthy rolls of bread tumbled onto the counter, followed by two dozen or more rounded fruits. There were some apples and peaches for sure, but the lad had eyes for another item of edibility: glossy spheres of pure perfection which shined like the morning sun. Their color lay somewhere in the space between red and yellow, and they happened to be the lad's utmost preferred consumable. He swiped up every last one, scanning the room suspiciously and growling at anyone who dared meet his gaze. It had been nearly twelve hours since he'd tasted an orange, and he'd lost his own supply when the brown riders came upon them.

"Now, don't be greedy, there's plenty to spare. Let's split those up for all to share," said Ron as he reached for an orange.

The lad's face struck at Ron's hand like a springing cobra, attempting to sink teeth into his thieving digits. But Ron had an otherworldly swiftness in his bones, for most of the oranges were taken and spinning aloft on his fingers before the lad could even chomp down. The lad's teeth rattled as he clamped them into thin air. Ron winked, still smiling as he juggled the oranges.

"I see you like 'em, but they have more than one use. R.B.'s gonna press some over there and make juice."

He walked to some kind of mechanical device on the counter and tossed a few of the citric orbs inside it. Then, he began to push buttons, turn cranks, and pull levers. The machine made a rhythmic sound, almost like music, as pipes tooted out steam. Ron danced and sang a song, somehow coming up with at least four words that rhymed with 'orange'.

At the song's end, the steam hissed to a stop and Ron slid glass cups under one end of the machine. He flipped some switches, pressed a large button, and from out of a small faucet poured golden juices of orangeness. The lad and his group were so intrigued by the spectacle that they hadn't noticed Stickaletta come by and serve the food. The large platter was in the center, and all their plates were heaped with breakfastic splendidries. Strangest of all, the lad's plate was the only one which contained no eggs. How could she have known?

"She couldn't know..." thought the lad. *"Maybe she was annoyed with my behavior, so she didn't give me any."*

The lad shook his head at the notions and decided to just sit down and eat. Ron came over to the table with six full glasses of juice and even some buttered toast from the bread rolls. All began to eat. Even Stickaletta had taken a place at the table, though, no one had actually seen her sit down.

The four guests made sure to simultaneously glance away at times, giving her a chance to partake.

"Where'd you get this amazing bread?" asked Sally after swallowing a bite.

"The fruits, I found in trees far and near, but the bread comes from my baguette plants right here."

"You... grow wheat, you mean?" Bombir asked.

"For these rolls, ol' Ron's made a better technique. They sprout from the ground whole, like a carrot or leek."

The room became quiet then, as if something had been said that sounded a bit odd. Aside from a lot of loud chewing and crunching, everyone ate for a while in silence.

Eventually, Ron spoke up once again. "You're welcome to stay as long as need be. I could always use help with work 'round the tree."

The lad knew they couldn't stay much longer, but after hearing mention of work, he wanted to leave even sooner.

"We can't thank you enough for taking us into your home for the night," said the lad. "But we have some terribly important business we gotta tend to in the nearby town of Debris."

Ron nodded. "Well, eat your fill now, and bring some for the hike, but before you head out, you can wash up if you like. Fifth door on your right, just down the hall. Hot water and towels, size large down to small. Before I forget, if clothes you need clean, just near the tub is a washing machine."

Bombir was the first to finish eating, so he went on back to the bathroom while the others continued talking to Ron. He told them of how he was best friends with the greatest scientist who ever lived, and that's where all the amazing inventions and ideas came from for the machines and technology he possessed. Though later, he clarified, saying *HE* actually invented those things and taught them to others, and that's the only reason his friend was able to become a scientist.

Ron also spoke of the brief time he spent as a king in the icy north, but had to give it up to pursue his dreams of working as either a paleobotanist or a barber. He had decided on both before retiring several decades later, only to come back out of retirement to join the army of a far eastern kingdom as a medical specialist. When the wars of that time had ended, he was discharged with the highest honors ever given, and was sought out by folks all over the world for his expertise in medicine and healing.

A time came, however, when he could not be located, since the next twenty-six years saw him deep beneath the surface of the earth showing the Dorks how to improve on their mining and smithcraft. The following few decades took him on the high seas, to uncharted lands in distant continents across oceans of unimaginable vastness. When he came back, he set up shop on the beach as a tailor, specializing in beachwear made of tinted glass from the surrounding sand. That job only lasted him a year or so before he headed back east once more.

He studied at Bookingham University, and within three months, he'd earned a master's degree in maritime law. Unfortunately, he never got any use out of it since he had moved very far from water and wasn't planning to go back. He felt that he was a bit overqualified for such an occupation as well, so he signed up for a job in forestry, working at a lumber mill right outside the south end of

Grabthorb Forest. It was there he encountered an ancient, secret race of tree-folk, and eventually, the half-tree daughter of the Forest King. He ran off with her one night without the leave of the King or giving two weeks' notice to his boss at the mill. Stickaletta, of course, was her name, and they were soon wed.

They continued to move further away from her home, seeing Ron come back again to more western parts. They found this very spot one day and decided to settle down. Ron then began working to build the house of their dreams in a tree he just happened to plant there in the long distant past. The story came to an end just as Sally, the last of the four to get cleaned up, was rejoining everyone at the table.

"That's some amazing stuff," said the lad, quite unsure of how much was factual.

He began to tell Ron about a few of their own adventures that he thought the fellow might find interesting, but Ron raised an eyebrow more than once, saying with a chuckle he believed the lad may have been stretching the truth a bit.

"Well, I think it's time for us to be on our way, Ron," said the lad, trying his best not to be offended by the man's accusations, lighthearted though they seemed.

"Pack up your things, then we'll head down. Ol' Ron's gonna take you mostway to town."

The lad and his friends said their goodbyes and many more thanks to Stickaletta, as weird as it still was, then Ron joined them on the lift and rode it down to the jungle floor. He led them around the back of the tree, where a very large, square bush stood. Ron pulled a hidden lever off to the side and a secret door swung wide open, revealing the bush to be some kind of garage covered in thick vines. Ron whistled, and a horse slowly trotted out from the dark opening.

However, upon quick inspection, it appeared to be no ordinary horse. It was shiny and smooth, with a forked tongue that often flicked out from its mouth. No fur or hair was seen anywhere on the animal, for instead, its hide was of slick scales like a reptile. Ron pulled out a cart and began to hitch it to the strange beast.

"Took in this girl a-many years back, her leg had been injured by a monkey attack. Slitherhoof, she's named, and she doesn't bite, hop up in the cart and you'll see it's alright."

Slowly and reluctantly, the group circled wide around the animal, threw the few supplies they possessed in the cart, then climbed aboard. Ron took his seat up front, and soon they were off, crossing his yard and passing through a thick hedge of bushes that moved itself out of their way.

To their great surprise, only about five minutes had gone by when they finally reached the end of the jungle at last. Open sky and vast green fields greeted them like an old friend. The relief that came to them was nearly overwhelming.

The lad saw Bombir fidgeting with his sword, Spit, which made him think of his own weapon—lost to him in the deep jungle or taken by some wretched demon. His chest ached at the thought, and he longed for its safe return.

"Hey, Ron," said the lad.

The man lifted the brim of his orange hat and half-turned toward the lad with eyebrows raised in expectation.

"If you happen to do any traveling a bit to the west of where we met you... I lost my sword somewhere in that area. It's killing me now that I think about it—possibly just lying around in the dirt, ready to be picked up by who or what ever passes by. It was close to the path next to an exploded tree. I would've liked to go there first and search myself, but I'm not sure the riders are gone, and I really don't have the time now. If you don't see anything, I'll look when I get back from Debris. Shouldn't be more than a few days."

"Of course, my boy, Ron will keep out an eye. Stop and check in as you're passin' back by."

They all talked a bit more on the way down the long, dusty, featureless road, until at one point, Ron stopped the cart.

"This right here is as far as Ron goes. From now on, you'll have to use your own toes."

So, the group got out and said plenty more goodbyes and thank-yous to Ron.

"Thanks for the food, safe place to sleep for the night, and the use of your facilities, good sir. I don't know how we could ever repay you," the lad said, finding himself bowing again.

Ron bowed as well, along with tipping his hat to them.

"Ron's happy to help, any time, any way. You're all

quite welcome, goodbye and good day."

With that, Ron turned his cart around and rode back to his home.

The lad took one last look, and the thought came to mind. *"Snake... horse? Why does that feel so familiar? Still really weird though... oh well."*

It was back down to the four of them now, out on the open road in a strange land completely unknown to them. As they began to walk, something sharp hit the lad in the back of his neck. Bombir saw the object fall to the ground, so he bent down and picked it up.

"Looks like it's for you," he said to the lad.

Then, he handed it over for the lad to examine. It was a single sheet of paper, folded many times to form a shape that could glide through the air. The name 'the lad' was written upon its top side.

The lad straightened the page, revealing a note within that read, "This place is unsafe, so pray do not tarry. Make haste for Debris with the item you carry. - R.B."

The lad did not read it aloud, but showed it to the others, who were just about as shocked as he was. None of them had a clue how Ron could have found out. The lad even checked his secret pocket to make sure it was still there. He fought off a passing urge to pointlessly don the allegedly evil fingerbelt and quickly rezipped his pocket. He looked to his friends, carelessly shrugged, then motioned to the road that lay ahead.

"Shall we?" he said.

Chapter 16:
Debris

The group of companions had been walking for three hours since their departure from Ron Bomblethorpe. There was no sign of anyone else on the road, and aside from a few small clusters of trees, the occasional boulder, and possibly one or two distant farmhouses, the scenery continued to stay about the same. Light snacks were consumed on the fly, for they desired to reach the town before nightfall, an occurrence which would be upon them within the next couple hundred minutes.

"Up ahead," said Bowman. "Something's coming down the road."

"Over here!" the lad raspily whispered.

The four of them huddled in behind a sizeable rock just off the road's side.

Soon, the squeaks of bouncing wagon wheels and the thuds of a large animal's feet came into hearing range. Sally was the only one that could get a view without being immediately spotted. She was lying to the stone's left side, peering around it through a patch of dry weeds.

"Can you see what it is?" asked Bombir.

Sally nodded her head. "Kinda. A freaky, tall animal I've never seen before, but it's not a hippo at least. It's pulling a really big cart—almost looks like a small house. I think I see a guy driving too.... No one else around, unless they're inside."

The lad was about as satisfied as need be that his group could deal with this wagon driver, so he peeked a look over the boulder's top edge.

"I know that animal," he said to the wonder of his companions. "It's a giraffe. Bobill told me about them. He saw some on one of his journeys. Though I remember him describing the color a bit differently—tan with brown spots, I think? This one is pure white without any spots at all."

"Albinism, perhaps?" said Bombir.

"Nah, Bobill didn't drink, so I doubt he was seeing things."

Bombir frowned. "That's not what that—"

"Evening friends!" shouted a voice. A voice that came from the driver's seat of the approaching wagon.

It was the wagon driver. The lad's group was busted, so they went ahead and stood up from their concealment.

"Hope you're not planning on doing me any harm or trying to rob me!" the wagon man called out as he slowed to a stop.

"Nope," replied the lad with hands in the air, "we're just travelers on our way to Debris. We had a few run-ins with some nasty folk further back, so we figured it was best to be careful."

"Oh, I hear ya," said the man, setting down a loaded crossbow he'd been hiding. "Smart thinking. You sound like you could use some of my merchandise. Why don't you come have a look?"

The group high-stepped over the weeds and back onto the dirt road to get a closer view, varying levels of suspicion still present amongst them.

"I'm called the lad, and these are my friends," he said, pointing to each in turn, "Sally Kim, BombirThin, and Bowman Slim. Who might *you* be?"

The man jumped down, revealing the superior stature those from outside Vim Valley usually possessed, which was more than a foot taller on average. He circled around to the side of his large wagon, then pulled a lever which folded out the wagon's side like a store front, displaying all kinds of items from necessities to luxuries. There were shelves of breads, dried meats, vegetables, and fruits; racks of jewelry, weapons, armor, and clothing; and display cases of books, maps, tools, and cookware. The man stood proudly and pointed to the sign at the top of the wagon, reading it aloud.

"Clenjamin Thriskwhistle's Moveable Marketplace. You can just call me Clen, o'course. I'm a traveler just like yourselves. Take a look around and see if anything catches your eye."

The group browsed for a while, each finding a few small things they thought could be of use. Bowman bought all the arrows Clen had, which was around twenty or so, along with a carton of candy cigarettes and some jerky. Sally purchased a few upgrades for her slingshot as well as a bag of precision steel ammo and a few jumbo peppermint sticks. Bombir already had a choice weapon that needed no attention and didn't quite have the amount of cash the others did, so he chose to only buy several food items: chocolate-covered salt cubes for now and various edibles and spiceries for their inevitable trip back home. While everyone else stuffed their new snacks in their mouths and admired Clen's giraffe, the lad grabbed a convenient brown paper bag and stuffed nine oranges inside—the wagon's entire stock. Then, he eyed the weapon racks.

"What's the cheapest sword ya got?" he asked the salesman.

Clen flipped through a few, scratched his chin, then raised a finger like he'd just remembered something. He opened a small cabinet door on the side of the displays near the bottom and pulled out a slightly rusted, somewhat bent sword. After screwing the handle on and wrapping it tight with twine, he held it forth for the lad to analyze. It felt like a total piece of crap, but the lad desired to have something he could swing at no-gooders until he could get his old weapon back, or otherwise the money for a begrudged replacement.

The lad let out a long sigh. "I guess it'll have to do for now," he said.

"Excellent," Clen replied. "That will be $3 for the oranges, and $5 for the sword."

The lad set the items on the counter and patted himself

down as if looking for something. "I don't really carry cash on me.... Do you take high-fives here?"

Clen looked at him in thought, then pulled out a notepad and pen. "Let me see... high-fives... currency exchange rates this year... inflation adjustments.... How many high-fives do you have?"

The lad blinked, shrugged, and shook his head, then threw out his best guess. "Maybe thirty-five before my hand gets too sore."

"Ahh," Clen said with a nod.

He took to the notepad once more, furiously scribbling and mumbling to himself until he began to sweat.

"Here we are. Thirty-five high-fives will exchange into a dollar amount of"—he paused and re-read the amount—"zero dollars, point zero, zero cents. I'm sorry, but you'll have to come up with a little more than that, son."

The lad shamefully began to put his items back when he noticed each of his three friends holding out a dollar.

"That's enough for the oranges at least," said Sally. "You don't need that junky sword."

"Good friends you've got there, the lad," said Clen. "How 'bout we make a deal. You tell everyone you can about my shop, and I'll throw in the sword free of charge. You can even keep your thirty-five high-fives."

The lad's face lit up. "You're too kind, sir. Thank-you, really."

"It's my pleasure!" cried Clen. "If that'll be all, I'll be on my way."

"Is there even anyone to sell to down there?" asked Bombir. "We really haven't seen a trace of anyone besides a few far away houses, and those were only within the last couple miles."

"Oh yeah, there's a few places," Clen replied. "Just gotta know where to look. I've been this way more than once, and I usually find a sale or two lurkin' around." With that, he closed up his wagon and climbed back aboard.

"Stay alert," said Bowman. "Like we said, we were attacked in the jungle and barely got away with our lives. They eventually left us alone, but we don't know if they're still in there or not."

"I appreciate the concern, but don't you worry, old Clen here can take care of himself." He gave them a nod as he patted his crossbow a few times. "Remember, spread the word about Clenjamin Thriskwhistle and his Moveable Marketplace! You folks have a good evening now!"

The salesman gave the reigns a flick and the white giraffe lazily trotted off, pulling the clattering wagon along behind.

***

The sky was beginning to dim, the sun settling down into a puffy bed of dark purple clouds low on the reddened western horizon. The four friends continued on with haste, passing increasingly more farmhouses. Some were even fairly close to the main road, and a few of the occupants began to light the lanterns at their front doors. Several wagons and people on horseback passed by, no doubt on the way back to their homes in the country from inside the town limits.

Full darkness had arrived at the same time the group did to the western gates of Debris. A good bit of the town was fenced in, and a deep water-filled ditch lay just beyond, perhaps as a mild deterrent for sneak-ins. A man sat in a guard tower near the open gate, but he said nothing as the group crossed into the town's interior. The rustic look of the place differed greatly from the more modern appearance most of Hometown maintained. Most of the houses looked to have been made from rough timbers or mortared uncut stone; some had roofs of wooden shingles and others were covered in tightly packed straw.

A few shopkeepers on the main stretch of the cobblestone road that cut through the center of town were beginning to close up their stores and go home, giving the lad and his friends odd glances as they passed by in the orange light of the burning streetlamps. The group ignored them, pressing on in the search for the aforementioned motel. The town was larger than they expected, and many of the buildings blended together, not giving much of a clue as to what they were.

Alleys and other lanes split off from the main road on occasion, disappearing around turns or halting into dark dead ends.

"It would've been much easier to find in the daytime," mumbled Bombir.

"Well, we don't have much choice now," stated

Bowman. "Let's just follow the road to its end. It's likely a motel will be out here and not in some obscure corner of town."

And he was right, for after the next curve was rounded, they easily spotted the place. It was a stone three-story building with a stable attached to one side, its entirety much larger than any surrounding structure. A sign was lit brightly over the front entrance displaying the establishment's name:

'The Motel of the Glancing Goaty'.

The lad opened the door and strode inside, his companions close behind. Most of the ground floor was a wide-open sitting area with tables and chairs scattered about. On the far end of the huge room were a selection of couches and other things to sit upon comfortably, all facing a massive stone fireplace that was currently roaring and crackling away. As the four stood near the doorway staring, a soft voice spoke to them from the nearby counter.

"Evening! How may we serve you?" asked a young smiling girl.

She looked to be no older or taller than any of them. The lad stepped forth and spoke up.

"We're supposed to be meeting someone here. My name's the lad."

The girl reached for a book and flipped it open. She searched through the pages with her sparkly green eyeballs, her thick red curls swaying as she scanned each line.

"I see a Thlad Porchnel, and a Ladethor Smirkin. Either of those you?"

The lad shook his head.

"What was the name of the person you were meeting?" she asked.

The lad shrugged. "We never heard it. A Wizard named Randolf said someone would be here for us, and that he would get here himself when he could."

The girl nodded and went back to the book. After a moment, she looked to the lad once more.

"There's an Olfrand Zebron listed here—but that's not even close. Actually, it sounds like a really made-up name. Says he hasn't checked in here in years."

The lad sighed. "Alright, I guess for now we'll just order dinner for four and a room for the night."

"You got it!" said the girl, beginning to scribble on a notepad. "That'll be $52.50."

The lad patted his pockets, then turned them inside-out.

"Would you happen to accept high-fi—"

Bowman stepped up and nudged the lad out of the way. "Here you are, ma'am," he said, handing her the full amount.

"Thank-you!" she replied. "Here's your key—room number fourteen upstairs. Take a right and it's the third door on your left, just before the corner. You can have a look or wait in the sitting area by the fire if you'd like, then pick up your dinners back here in about twenty minutes. My name is Pencilla by the way—Pencilla Picklepants. Give me a holler if you need anything else."

Sally and Bombir tried to give Bowman some of their remaining cash, knowing he had to be quite low by now. But he waved them away.

"It's fine, I'm not totally broke yet," he said.

"How about we sit by the fire while we wait?" suggested Sally.

So, the group walked single file across the room between tables filled with cross-eyed, slack-jawed weirdos until they reached those blessed couches. They each sunk their aching bodies into the velvet-covered cushions of splendor, and simply stared into the fire wordlessly for a time. Bowman casually slid out his pack of smokes and drew one out. The very moment it touched his lips, however, he heard a cry that came from his right side.

"Hey, you little delinquent! No smoking in here!"

Before Bowman could react, an old man reached out, snatching the candy cigarette straight out of his mouth.

"Dude, what the heck!?" cried Bowman.

The old man threw the sugary stick over the rug in front of them where it landed in the fire with a hiss. Bowman looked over at the man with fury painted across his usually patient face, but the man was slouched down on the next couch over, eyes closed and starting to snore.

"Sorry about that," said Pencilla, coming up from behind. "That's my grandfather, Percy. He's supposed to be retired, but sometimes he hangs around in here harassing people." She circled his couch and tapped the old man on his forehead. "Time to wake up, Gramps, you're bothering folks again. Let's get you back to your room."

She pulled him to his feet and led him stumbling away.

"Six years!" yelled Percy as he was hobbling in behind the counter to a back room. "For six darned years everything tasted like cowpies... the wrong end of 'em too!"

"Sure, Gramps," said Pencilla while shutting his door. She then slid four plates of food onto the counter and rang the bell. "The lad! Party of four!" she cried.

Chapter 17:
The Stranger

The lad and his friends sat eating in the main dining area of the inn. There were few others still present, as it was beginning to get late. The group couldn't help but notice a ragged, greasy-haired man occasionally glancing at them from the far end of the room. He was eating from a heaping plate of spicy chicken wings and seemed to be downing each one whole, bones and all. His dark clothes were tattered, faded, and dirty, due likely to long travels or years of hygienic negligence. The lad was almost sure he saw a rat peek out of one of his pants pockets. Flies were circling the man's head, landing at times upon his nose, cheeks, and eyeballs, but they received no reaction from the man as he continued to slurp and crunch away at the glistening red poultry appendages. The pungent scent of the meal was apparently inferior to that of the man to the insects, making the lad thankful he wasn't any closer.

The thankfulness was short-lived however, for the man let out a long, floor rumbling burp, dabbed his mouth with an old sock, pushed back his plate, stood from the table, and made his way straight for them.

He stopped uncomfortably close to the group's table,

leaned down slightly without looking at any of them, and spoke in a growlish whisper. "You're the ones I was sent to protect. Is that correct?"

The lad nodded and replied, his voice cracking. "Ye-EAH—" He stopped to cough and clear his throat, then continued. "Well, I think so. Randolf didn't say what your name was or what you'd even look like."

"You may call me Stranger, for that is the name I am known by in these parts of the world and all others. Now, have you rented a room here? A place where we can discuss things more privately?"

"Hold on just a second!" said Bombir. "How do we know you're not pulling a fast one? What makes you think we'll simply trust you?" The others nodded in agreement.

The man sighed, then drew forth a wallet from within his cloak. He flipped it open, revealing an identification card for them to examine. There was a well-drawn portrait on one side that looked just like him, and next to that were the words, 'The Stranger: Professional Bodyguard, Bounty Hunter, Weapons Expert, Pest Exterminator, Horse Trainer, Tuba Player ~~and Tax Analyst~~'. The last profession in the list was crossed out for some reason.

"That's all the proof I've got to offer," said Stranger. "But you are in serious danger right now. We need to get to a secluded area so that we may speak of things more openly."

The lad scraped the last few bits of food from his plate into his mouth, and while still chewing, replied, "Alright then, follow us."

The four companions made their way up the steps to the second floor with Stranger trailing behind.

Bowman leaned over to the lad's ear and whispered, "We should've questioned him further before doing this. He seems a bit... *off*."

"Right, Bowman, just like the bad feeling you had about Ron and everyone else..." the lad replied.

"What do you mean, '*everyone* else'? Who else did I say that about?"

"I don't know... just everyone."

"*No*, name someone."

"I don't remember! But I'm pretty sure there was others."

"I'm not going to keep arguing with you, the lad, you can think what you want. I'm just trying to be cautious to keep us from getting stabbed. Looks like we're committed now though, so stay on high alert and keep a hand near a weapon at all times."

Sally was holding the key, so she unlocked the door for all to enter. The room was clean, though smaller than they imagined it would be, and a single window overlooking the street out front could be seen on the far wall. Aside from that, the first thing to enter their minds was how the cramped space and the presence of only two little beds may have made for a somewhat awkward situation later. But that could be worried about when the time came—at the moment, they needed to keep cool and not let their guard down around the mysterious fellow who was now amidst them in the dim, candle-lit room.

Stranger began to search around, knocking on walls, sniffing pillows, and peeking under furniture.

"I think this place is secure," he eventually said. He pulled up a chair from the corner to the foot of the two beds that the lad and his friends sat upon. "May I see the object?" asked Stranger.

The lad was hesitant. "Why? Don't believe I have it?"

"I know you do. I just want to see what I'm dealing with here."

"That's probably not a good idea..." mumbled Bombir.

The lad looked across to the other bed where Sally and Bowman sat, pleas for another opinion written on his face.

"It's your call," said Bowman.

"We trust your judgement," added Sally, a possible hint of doubt in her eyes.

"Okay," said the lad, reaching into his secret pocket and retrieving the grief-strickening chunk of cold metal from within. "Here it is."

There it sat in the lad's outstretched palm. Stranger's face shifted to a look of something other than stone-hard seriousness for the first time as he leaned in for a closer look. After a minute, he relaxed, slouched back in his chair, and chuckled.

"What?" asked the lad. "What's wrong?"

Still smiling, Stranger replied, "It's fake. A replica. I can tell that right away."

"You're kidding me!" yelled the lad.

"Nope, it's worthless junk. Ol' Randolf must be losing it. If you give it to me, I know the perfect garbage can to toss it into."

The room became heavy with fear and suspicion upon the words 'give it to me'. The lad gripped his discount sword and chose his next statement carefully.

"Randolf saw the ring himself. He showed me how to tell that it was real and proved it to me. Give us a reason not to strike you down, and quickly."

Stranger looked back and forth between them, then burst into laughter. "I was kidding!" he cried. "I was sure you could tell I was joking. I'm truly sorry, perhaps my humor isn't as clever as I'd like to think."

The lad's group didn't ease up quite yet. They sat still, staring him down and very much unsatisfied by his cheap explanation and apology.

Stranger continued. "Listen, in all seriousness, I am more than capable of bringing it to a place where it can be kept from evil. You can go on home and let me take care of it. *OR*, if you're unwilling to part from it, you can go right ahead and carry it yourself while I guard you with my life. It's completely up to you."

The lad thought for a moment. His tension had receded a little, but not much. All he knew, was that no one but *him* would be carrying the ring anywhere. So, he put it back in his inner pocket, zipping it tightly.

"I'll be carrying it," he said to Stranger.

"Excellent. We'll head out to meet with Randolf at first light then. Get some rest."

With that, he walked over and slid down on the floor against the room's door.

"We'd actually prefer if you wouldn't stay in here," said Bowman. "We still don't really know you and you made a fairly poor first impression."

Stranger replied, "I know it's kind of odd, and I sincerely apologize again for my bad joke, but the holder of the ring is under my care now. It's my full responsibility that no harm shall come to him. You're welcome to stay up with me if you're uncomfortable, but there are potentially two entrances to this room I must guard, and enemies could very well be lurking just outside as we speak. I will stay put here."

Bowman grumbled, then moved the chair back to the corner. He sank into it with a dagger in one hand and his bow across his lap. Sally kicked off her shoes and rolled into the bed farthest from the door. The lad let Bombir take the other one while he himself pulled the window curtain shut, extinguished the candle, and lay upon a blanket on the floor between the two beds. The circumstances were not ideal, but eventually they each drifted off to sleep—Sally after only five minutes, Bombir, fifteen. The lad took all of forty-five minutes at least, and Bowman lasted two full hours before finally passing out, despite his plan to stay up all night.

***

It was about two in the morning when something stirred. Somehow the window had been expertly breached without a sound. A chill entered the room as a shadowy figure emerged from the dark curtains. It crept slowly and silently over to the spot where the lad slept, keeping low to the floor. All were still fast asleep... aside from Stranger. He quickly became aware of the presence and leapt into a furious attack with his sword.

The dark figure dodged back and forth, then drew its own weapon. It struck back with a vengeance, causing the sound of clashing metal to ring out and sparks to fly. Everyone else in the room woke up in shock, unsure of what was happening.

"They're here! The servants of evil have come!" cried Stranger.

In the nearly total darkness, they could only see two even darker blobs flailing about, crashing into walls and kicking over what little furniture there was in the room. Sally fumbled to relight the candle, but once she did, the flickering flame cast enough light on the scuffle to see that Stranger had dropped his sword and gone stiff. A look of horror was on his face... as the weapon of the intruder plunged ever deeper through his belly. The sinister blade was twisted, then yanked forcefully back out. Blood spilled from the wound, and Stranger's eyes rolled back as he collapsed to the floor. Bowman had an arrow ready to let fly but stopped short when he saw the lad rush at the assailant, cheap sword swinging chaotically.

"Die, fiend!" cried the lad.

"Wait a moment! Please!" said the dark figure in a surprisingly unthreatening tone of voice. The lad's continued blows were all deflected by an unusual weapon. What at first looked to be some kind of spear, was in reality, a pitchfork. The lad's attacks slowed as he began to grow weary, and they eventually came to a stop. He stumbled back, hoping he wouldn't be run through before one of his companions could take over.

"Take him down!" yelled the lad, raising his sword once more to point it at the intruder.

"Stop! I beg you!" called out the unknown thing, dropping its bloody farm tool to the floor and raising its hands high in surrender. "This man was not the one you were meant to meet with. *I* am!"

Bowman pulled his string tighter. "Why should we believe that?" he growled.

"I am the one called Stranger. I had been traveling for days to get here when an old beggar on the side of the road asked if I had something to eat. I foolishly dropped my guard for only a moment to look through my pack when he cut a rope and dropped a net over me from the trees above. He then clocked me over the head with a rock, revealing himself to be not quite so old as I thought. He was long gone when I awoke, and for some reason, the only thing of mine he had taken was my wallet and... another thing."

The lad eyed the man for a minute, his comprehension barely functioning due to being dead asleep only moments earlier. He lowered his sword and rubbed at his face.

"Well... how did he know to come here then?" he asked. "Why would he know about meeting us?"

The man answered, "It hadn't been long since I was discussing the plan with Randolf on my uhh... message device."

"You mean like that square, glass-looking thing Randolf was poking at?" asked Sally.

"Oh, you've seen one!" he answered.

"Yes, that was the other belonging that was taken from me. It was given to me many years ago by the Wizards, since I have long been a friend to them."

"I know people who have long been Wizard friends and *they* never got a fancy messaging glass," said the lad.

The allegedly actual Stranger gave an uneasy shrug. "I'm sure there's a reason, it's a complicated business, the affairs of Wizards. Anyway, I'd like you to know that I arrived just in time. Your fake pal here was standing over your unconscious body about to cut your throat, undoubtedly so that he could relieve you of the item you possess. Look there." He pointed to the floor, where next to the lad's pillow lay a jagged knife.

"Well thanks, if that's true and you didn't just plant it there," said the lad. "He *did* make it seem like he was trying to get me to give him the ring. Said it was fake and worthless, then tried to save himself by passing it off as a joke."

"I would never ask you for it," replied the man. "Rather, I would say do not let anyone else see or touch it, for it could easily be misused or turn a good-natured soul into a mindless, greed-filled monster in a frighteningly short time."

The lad sighed, sliding his sword back in its sheath. "I see... well your odds of not getting killed are slightly improving, but how about you throw back that hood so we can get a better look at your face at least."

The man did so, showing his appearance to be a bit more like the ID card portrait than the other fellow.

"If you don't mind, I'm going to kneel down and retrieve my belongings," said the man.

The lad glared at him through narrowed eyes, then gestured for him to go ahead.

"Don't reach for that weapon just yet," said Bowman, somewhat less tense, but still holding his bow at half-draw.

The man nodded and began to go through the clothing of the slain imposter. He found the wallet, which he stuffed into his pack, then he turned the body over and continued searching.

"Have a look at this," he said to no one in particular.

The lad took a few steps forward to see. Bombir, who had remained totally silent since waking, leaned over the foot of the bed for a view as well. The back of the dead man's shirt was lifted, displaying a large tattoo that read:

'RAUSON RULES!'.

"Only a servant of darkness would bear such a marking," said the most likely real Stranger.

The lad and his friends were in various levels of shock, now realizing how close they had come to having their lives ended by this wretched deceiver.

"Alright," said the lad. "I think I believe you now. You really are the true Stranger."

Stranger pressed his hands together and bowed in thanks, then he went back to his searching. In one of the corpse's back pockets, he located his messaging device.

"Ah, here it is," he said. "Surprised it didn't get broken being kept in—" He froze as his eyes scanned the glowing screen.

"What's wrong?" asked the lad.

Stranger held the device up for him to see. When looked at straight-on, the thin glass rectangle gave off a blue light. Within that light, words could be seen floating, as if they were white foam drifting in an illuminated pool of water.

The lad read the words line by line:

'-He's incapacitated, heading to the motel now.

-They finally came in. I'll make a move soon.

-I've got them. Just waiting for them to fall asleep.

-Doing it now.

-Compromised! Broadcasting location.'

"We need to get out of here immediately," asserted Stranger. "Grab your things, quickly!" He gave the piece of glass in his hand a thoughtful look-over. "I really hate to do this to such a priceless artifact, but there's no choice." He then dropped it to the floor and stomped it to pieces.

After picking up his pitchfork, he turned to find the lad and the others suited up and ready to leave.

"Out the window! Go!" he cried.

Bowman went out first, stepping onto a narrow, angled roof. Next came Sally, then Bombir, followed by the lad. Stranger checked the room door one last time before climbing through himself. They all sat motionless as their worst nightmares appeared through the fog: four hulking beasts trotting two by two down the lane below, ridden by skeletal creatures in brown robes. Stranger motioned to some close rooftops nearby.

"Follow these around if you can," he whispered. "Stay as high as possible until you reach the gate on the far end of the main road. That's the east entrance. We need to go north though, so follow the town fences counter-clockwise until you reach the North Road."

"Why can't we just cross here if we need to go north?" asked the lad, pointing to a thick cable just above them that stretched to a building on the other side of the central street.

"That's risky—but if you think you can do it, go now. I'm going to drop down and try leading them away."

Stranger then slid himself down the side of the motel. He let go and landed silently behind a barrel near the stable entrance. The lad reached up and tested the cable, yanking it a few times. It felt pretty strong, so he seized it with both hands, then threw both legs over, wrapping them securely around. The slow shimmy across commenced.

"I don't know if I can do it," whimpered Bombir.

"You've got this, Bom," said Sally. "Don't even think about it. I'll go first and Bowman will be right behind you."

She jumped up, grabbed the cable with hands and legs, and inched her way over, glancing down briefly to see that the unholy hippos were almost directly underneath them. Bowman helped Bombir get his feet hooked on and soon he was on his way as well, though quite unhappy about it. The lad was having trouble gripping, for ice began to form over the cable due to the presence of the evil riders. Bowman had barely started climbing when he heard the loud voice of Stranger below.

"Eat dookie, you ugly fossilized bonebags!"

He had scraped up a mound of horse excrement in his hand and proceeded to high-speed pitch the dung straight into the face of one of the riders, sending it sprawling to the ground. It let out an ear-piercing shriek as it climbed back aboard its rounded steed and drew forth a large sickle. Stranger turned and bolted down the street to the east, and the screaming demons furiously pursued him upon their great beasts.

The lad continued across, ice quickly melting away now that the hippo riders had moved on. He eventually made it to the other side and let his legs swing down to touch the roof. The others reached the destination as well, and soon they were hopping from roof to roof, following another main road to the northern gate. When the last building was reached, it was low enough to easily jump to the ground from. The group carefully and silently did so, then made their way past the fence and finally out of Debris.

Chapter 18:
On the Run

The lad and his friends stopped about a quarter mile outside of the north gate of Debris, finding some bushes to take cover behind on the side of the road. They waited and watched through the darkness and mist for signs of Stranger or the hippo riders.

"What if they got him?" asked Bombir. "We've seen what those things can do. He could be dead, and we're next!"

"Cool it, Bom," said the lad. "I think he's probably more clever than that. We'll wait here until he comes."

The lad was right, for not five minutes had passed, and Stranger quietly crept up to them out of the weeds nearby.

"Good, you made it," he said. "They're a little confused as to where I went for now, but hopefully I led them far enough away from the town that they won't try going back just yet. Let's continue down the road at as quick a pace as we can manage."

So, Stranger took the lead, speeding up to nearly a jog. The others were hard pressed to keep up, being shorter in stature than he, and eventually they were forced to slow down. A few questions were asked along the way, but Stranger refused to answer any of them.

His only reply for some time was: "Answers can wait until daylight."

Even when the first light of dawn came, they kept moving, beginning the long, subtle incline that led to the foothills on the southern side of the Mimson Mountains in the far distance. The lad's attention darted to and fro, at small patches of trees, large boulders, and grassy hills. His mind wandered, showing him images of lunging, foamy-mouthed hippos, and evil, sneaking, brown-robed skeleton men. Bowman and Sally seemed quite on edge too, though none so much as Bombir. He was sweating, gulping, trembling, and wishing he could just go home. He finally couldn't take it anymore and began to protest.

"Okay, I've tried to keep my mouth shut and keep moving, but I've got to have a sit-down and a snack at least, or you'll have to leave me here to die alone."

Stranger came to a halt. "We'll take a quick stop then. It *is* about breakfast time."

A fire could not be risked, so they ate what provisions they had that did not require one. There was enough still to last them a few days if they were careful, and that was likely how long it would take to get to their next destination.

"May I ask where you are even taking us?" mumbled Bombir.

"To Drivenrail, Mr. Thin," answered Stranger. "A land

which wherein lies the home of BellJohn the Elf—a secret place that is well-guarded and safe. It is my hope that Randolf will be there so we can speak with him *and* Master BellJohn on what our course of action should be."

Bombir's face lit up at that, for he had always wanted to feel how pointy an Elf's ear really was, and this could be his big chance.

After twenty minutes passed, Stranger stood to his feet, urging the others to do the same. They reluctantly gathered their things and joined him back on the lengthy road. They walked all that day, encountering only a few travelers and briefly stopping twice more for lunch and dinner.

Later, the miserable day of near-constant walking was coming to an end, the sky darkening once more. The chirps of crickets and croaks of bullfrogs were heard all around, and the lights from the butts of fireflies danced throughout the surrounding trees. Not much had been said in the last couple of hours until the lad broke the silence.

"Do you expect us to walk through the night too? Or can we find a place to sleep? We're all running on empty here."

"Of course," said Stranger, as he scratched at his bristly beard. "I believe there is a place just ahead where we might find a bit of shelter."

Several more minutes after, they turned off the right side of the path a little ways, where a fifty-foot cliff jutted up from the ground behind a row of thick evergreens. Halfway up the cliff was a wide ledge with enough room for all of them to sleep with reasonable comfort. Stranger found a way to climb up to it in the dark, and the others were able to follow once he threw down a rope. Bowman, Bombir and Sally wasted no time unrolling their blankets and attempting to sleep, but the lad stayed up a while longer with Stranger.

At first, the lad said nothing. He simply watched the man as he gathered up sticks and rocks in the immediate area. When he was satisfied with his haul, he began to craft an intricate mechanism of sorts. Ten minutes later and the lad could tell that he was crafting a tuba. Another five and Stranger was softly playing the instrument.

"Are you trained in Wizardry?" asked the lad.

Stranger released his lips from the mouthpiece and replied, "As a matter of fact I am, though I learned only a little. I was able to reach the rank of Grassen—that's the second level of Wizdom if you didn't know—but I gave it up shortly after. However, I did not gain the skill of making musical instruments out of various items in nature from the Wizards, truth be told. I learned it from an acquaintance of mine, a short man named—"

Stranger was abruptly cut off when a loud roar suddenly echoed through the night. The riders were close by.

"Get down!" whispered Stranger, and the two of them dropped to their bellies.

They both slowly crawled to the edge and watched for movement beyond the cluster of trees in front of them.

"There," said Stranger, pointing at the road to their

right.

All four of the riders were traveling together, moving off in the direction the group would be heading in the morning. They could only hope the devils would be long gone by then—if they didn't circle around and find them on the ledge first anyway.

"Horrible things," said the lad. "I wonder what in the heck they are."

"They are the personal butlers of the ancient and evil King Rauson," replied Stranger. "They're known as the Wazgalls, or sometimes Ringwafers, due to their pursuit of the ring and wafer-thin bodies. They're neither sleeping nor awake, and their only desire is to take that thing you've got in your pocket and bring it back to their master, possibly giving him a chance to rise to power once more. They can feel the great worth of it, and their hunt will be unending unless we can find a way for you to get rid of that little round problem."

The lad said nothing, but had plenty to dwell on now. In time his eyelids began to grow heavy, and soon he was off to sleep.

***

The lad woke to dark gray skies. It was early in the morning and a light rain was beginning to fall. He sat up, looking around to find everyone but Sally gone. She was still passed out in a very twisted, uncomfortable-looking position and making a lot of unconscious mouth noises. The lad left her be and shuffled to the cliff's edge to look down. He heard the sounds of talking and banging just below. When he moved a bit to one side and squinted through the fog, he could see that Bombir and Bowman were speaking with Stranger and looked to be building something. The lad grabbed a rock and used it to etch the words 'just below' on the ground near Sally.

He then packed up his things and climbed down the rope to the base of the cliff so he could find out what the others were up to. When he reached them, his eyes were drawn to a large box made of widthy sticks which were lashed together in rows by a mixture of makeshift ropes.

Upon seeing the lad approaching, Stranger spoke. "I wish I had thought of this beforehand. It would've saved us time and certainly been built with better quality."

"What is it?" asked the lad.

"Don't know a wagon when you see one?" replied Stranger.

"Just looks like a box to me," answered the lad.

"How about now?" said Bombir, as he and Bowman retrieved two great wooden circles from behind them.

Stranger helped securely fasten one to each side of the box, then the three of them, quickly joined by the lad, lifted the whole thing off the ground and flipped it over. A crudely made, two-wheeled cart it surely was.

"That's pretty cool," said the lad, "but what's going to pull it? You?"

Stranger smirked, letting out a puff of air that resembled a momentary sound of almost-laughter. "My friend will pull it. He's always nearby."

With that said, Stranger pulled a brown paper bag from one of the many pockets on his outfit. He proceeded to smooth it out then squeeze the opening down tight by wrapping his fingers around, leaving only a small hole through which air could pass into the bag. It was lifted to his mouth, and he blew a long breath inside, filling it to near bursting with a single exhalation.

Next, the end was twisted and tied off, causing an even higher level of pressure to build within. Stranger drew a knife from his side, and with one swift movement, pierced the bulbous paper with the very tip of the well-honed blade.

'PEEEEEEE!!'

An incredibly high-pitched whistle suddenly burst forth from the tiny pinhole, so shrill that it could barely be heard, but enough to cause irritation and discomfort. The lad, Bombir, and Bowman covered their ears after twenty seconds of it, still without a clue as to what it was supposed to accomplish.

After a couple of minutes went by, the bag was running low on air and some members of the group were starting to get bored. Right around the time the last toot of air escaped, another sound was heard: the rhythmic thudding of four fast-moving hooves. Bowman kept his cool, but the lad and Bombir almost panicked, believing it to be a charging hippo that had been drawn to the whistling bag. Their fears were soon washed away when a sleek and shining, gunmetal gray horse appeared, sliding to a stop at Stranger's feet. He patted the animal's head and gave it a carrot sandwich with extra salt.

"*This* is my friend," said Stranger with a smile. "His name is Hoofhaver, The Steed of Steel. He is descended from The Great Thunderclop of elden days, and I promise he could beat up any horse you've ever laid eyes on."

Stranger then began hitching his horse to the small cart.

"What was the deal with the bag?" asked the lad.

"Oh, that," replied Stranger. "I'm not the best whistler, and this fellow only responds to a very specific pitch for some reason. A pitch I accidentally discovered could be made through a small hole in a paper bag once. I make sure to keep a stack of twenty on me every time I head out just to be safe. It's fairly tedious, but I wouldn't trade this beast for any other."

"Should've seen the horse we were taken to Debris by the other day," said Bowman in keeping with the equine-related conversation. "Half horse and half snake if you can believe that. Wouldn't have myself if I hadn't seen it. We all did." Bombir and the lad nodded.

"Ah, so the line of legendary snake-horses lives on then," said Stranger. "I've heard tales of them—may have even seen one long ago. They were said to have inhabited the jungle to the east and were originally created by some kind of Wizard magic. You say you were pulled along by one. What kind of person could tame such an unearthly creature?"

"His name is Ron Bomblethorpe," said the lad. "He took us in and kept us from being killed by the Ringwafers. Sorta like you're doing now, I guess. He's a pretty weird guy. Speaks in rhymes and whatnot."

Stranger had a look of surprise on his face. "Amazing," he said. "Very few have seen the abode of Ronathan Bomblethorpe. I've met him once or twice myself, but I've never been to his house. They say that he's an excessive truth-stretcher... and only one out of every three statements he makes is true."

"Well, every single thing he claimed was incredible," said Bombir.

"Correct," replied Stranger. "So even if two thirds of what he says is false, he's still quite the impressive fellow."

All of the sudden, a howling shriek cut through the air, echoing off the nearby cliffs. The Wazgalls had come once again.

"The lad!" cried Stranger. "Run and get Sally! We must stay and protect Hoofhaver and the cart, they may be our only way of evading them."

The lad nodded and sprinted back to the cliff. He grabbed the rope and clambered up as fast as he could. When he pulled himself to the top, he was met with a scene of dread. Sally was backed into an inner corner of the ledge, her path blocked by a brown-robed demon. It was raising its black sickle, ready to bring it down on Sally's head. She had her knife out but was in a terrible position for a countering strike, even if she could match the Wazgall's supernatural strength and icy grasp.

"Hey, dirtbag!" screamed the lad. "Over here, you walking carcass!"

The Ringwafer spun around, hollow eye sockets in a

charred skull fixed on the lad from under a brown hood. It stooped low, placing a boney hand to the ground. Then, it raised the hand up, palm still flat, creating a long, icy shaft underneath. It took hold and snapped the ice free. The ice shard flipped in its hand so the sharp end was facing the lad, then, the spike was hurled with great force straight at his heart. The lad swung his cheap sword with all his might, expecting it to break against the magic ice. But no, the ice was shattered on the blade, exploding in all directions around him.

He spotted an opening and went for it, running at the Ringwafer and diving to the ground. He slid between the boney legs under the tattered robe, his feet nearly getting hacked off by a quick swing of the sickle.

"Slingshot! Climb on!" was all the lad managed to blurt out.

He turned quickly, allowing Sally to jump onto his back, then grabbed her legs tightly and walked at the Ringwafer once more. Sally chambered one of the new steel rounds into her slingshot and fired it over the lad's head, cracking the skeletal nightmare square in the forehead. The Wazgall stumbled back, shaking its head as Sally pulled back and fired another. It struck it in the cheekbone this time, causing its head to twist around. The lad began running, screaming, and waving his sword like a maniac, still trying to hold on to Sally with his free hand. He would collide with the Wazgall within the next few seconds if he didn't veer off.

Sally let one more metal ball loose and it went directly into the Ringwafer's eyehole. Instead of bouncing off, it seemed to stick inside, causing the creature a significant amount of discomfort. It clapped a skele-hand over the hole and began thrashing about.

The lad body-slammed the creature, being careful to use his shoulder and not Sally's face, which sent the Ringwafer tripping and flailing backwards. It came to a stop on the very edge of the thirty-foot cliff, and Sally fired a final projectile. It miraculously smashed directly into the other eye socket, sending the Ringwafer tumbling over.

The lad and Sally heard a 'CRASH!' at the bottom, and without even letting her down, the lad dropped off, grabbed the rope, and repelled back to the ground below. As soon as his feet landed, the lad let go of Sally and told her to follow him. The two sprinted the short distance through the trees to see that Stranger had pulled out onto the road with Bowman and Bombir in the cart.

"Hurry!" they cried to Sally and the lad.

They booked it for all they were worth and dove into the cart with their friends. Stranger's horse immediately squealed hooves out of there, reaching speeds that were somewhat terrifying in the rickety stick-cart. The coast looked clear for a few minutes—until a hippo burst through the foliage from their left, its tremendous feet thundering against the dirt. Its rider swung a sickle, but Stranger swerved away before it could bite into anything.

Moments later, another hippo came out of the trees on the other side, followed by a third just behind it. The group fought with all they had to push them back, but the Wazgalls kept coming. Sally's steel rounds and Bowman's arrows were frozen and smashed to dust in midair. Evidently, the fourth Ringwafer that still trailed behind was either clumsier than these or just confused by the lad and Sally's double-stacked running attack. They stopped wasting ammo and drew only blades, desperately attempting to deflect incoming blows.

Up ahead, a waterfall cascaded down the cliff to their right, spilling into a deep river that cut across their path. A narrow rope bridge spanned the fifty-foot width of the river, and none knew for sure if it could hold the weight of the loaded horse and cart. The fourth rider caught up then, and all closed in on the lad's group in a final assault; for they too were uncertain of their ability to cross the bridge and needed to make sure the cart was stopped at all costs before reaching it.

By this point, Bombir had only taken a few swings with his sword, mostly wanting to stay further back and do some cowering. But his terror reached its peak when two of the Ringwafers grabbed the cart by its sides, and ice began to form across the tightly bound sticks. The other two were straight behind, straddled upon the heads of their monstrous hippos for better reach. They were swinging their black sickles wildly and missing by mere inches. Something snapped in BombirThin at that moment, and the sword in his hands seemed to respond to it.

Spit, The Sword of Doom, glowed a burning, pulsing, red. Bombir stood from his previous fetal position, pushing between his friends to stand upon the open back edge of the cart. Just like the sword, Bombir's eyes were alight with a crimson fire. He muttered an unintelligible phrase, sharp and commanding, that sounded as if it came from the mouth of some deranged, ancient king. When he finished, he raised his fiery sword and called out one more word.

"BURN!!" he bellowed as he swung the sword downward through the air.

A huge wave of fire leapt from the blade, followed by the loud crackling sound of superheated air exploding all around it. Dark clouds quickly formed overhead, twisting into a whirlwind and sucking in the flames. The spinning, blazing fury swept back and forth behind the cart, following the moving tip of Bombir's outstretched sword and the burning gaze of his eyes. Fire consumed each of the Ringwafers one by one as Bombir's companions looked on from behind him in utter disbelief. The demons screamed and their steeds roared, one after another smashing face-first into the dirt and writhing in agony.

Just then, the cart dropped onto the wooden rope bridge, causing it to dip down far enough to touch the water's surface. They were still moving quickly and made it halfway before the last burning hippo did a nosedive, flipping, rolling, and coming to a final splintering crash straight through the bridge and into the water. The ropes snapped, causing the back end of the bridge to fall and begin drifting downstream with the current.

Stranger cracked the reigns of Hoofhaver furiously as the water level reached the floor of the cart. It started to float and slide to the left, but the mighty horse prevailed, galloping swiftly off the last bit of bridge, yanking the cart safely to dry ground on the other side. Stranger brought the horse to a halt, giving himself and the others a minute to calm their nerves. Those in the back were still white-knuckle clutching to the sides of the cart with hearts racing. All except for Bombir, who was peacefully passed out and snoring on the floor.

Chapter 19:
Of Meetings & Mountains

"What in Skiddle Earth just happened back there?!" yelled Stranger as he pushed dark, sweat-soaked hair from his face.

"We're just as shocked as you," said Bowman. "He doesn't usually do that."

"Well, he's out cold for now," added Sally after smacking Bombir's cheeks a few times and receiving no reaction.

Stranger began to speak again, but a concerned and focused look filled his face, his eyes drawn to something behind the cart. The others turned to see a steaming, mud-caked Ringwafer crawling up the bank of the river toward them, robe torn and partially burned. It slowly stood to its feet, blobs of slush raining from its cloak. It raised its sickle and ran at the cart, shrieking with liver-curdling terror. Stranger pulled forth his gleaming, silver pitchfork and rolled backwards off his horse. His feet met the front of the cart and he vaulted into a backflip over its occupants. He twisted in the air and landed in a full sprint at the incoming Wazgall, feet crunching into the ever-thickening frost that covered the grass.

The sickle and pitchfork met with a sharp 'CLING!'. The lad and his conscious friends watched as Stranger's skills in weaponry were put on glorious display. The Wazgall was unnaturally strong, seemingly unfazed, and free from all the weariness that should have been inflicted by Bombir's inexplicable onslaught and subsequent swim against the crushing current of the river. It dodged, rolled, and swung like a churning puff of brown smoke.

But, despite its speed and fury, Stranger matched every step and his pitchfork turned away the Wazgall's blows with flawless precision. Like a spring chicken with a sugar rush, he began to drive the monster back with faster and faster strikes, moving it ever closer to the river's edge. The disoriented Ringwafer attempted to keep up the pace, swinging chaotically and beginning to make mistakes. Stranger made a quick thrust after a deflection of the sickle, the silvery spikes of the shining pitchfork plunging deep into the Wazgall's wretched and filthy cloak. The fork was twirled, and like a lump of pasta, the garment was ripped away from the vile creature, openly revealing its true form in the full light of day.

A charcoal-black skeleton, bones covered in an oozing tar-like substance perhaps due to its recent aquatic excursion, stood hunched and swaying, gripping its wicked blade and staring at Stranger with hollow, black eyesockets. It hissed and called out in a language unknown to all who heard, causing the patch of frost that blanketed the ground around it to rise up into short spikes of ice. It began to form on Stranger's shoes as well, followed by his legs. By the time he realized this, he was unable to move.

The Wazgall suddenly leapt backward, the rapidly freezing water of the river now up to its boney knees. It then threw the sickle with all its might, straight at Stranger's unshaven chin.

The unexpected move was too quick for Stranger to lift his pitchfork and whack it away, so he was forced to quickly lean back. His shiny black mustache was nearly grazed as the spinning blade passed over his face, then it continued until it reached the others. The sickle stabbed into Sally's pant leg, pinning it to the side of the cart.

Stranger cut away the ice that held him, his weapon making quick work of it. Now disarmed, it was all over for the dirty Wazgall.

"To the grave with you," said Stranger as he stepped forth and made a wide, sweeping swing with his pitchfork that struck the Ringwafer in its neck.

The powerful blow tore right through, sending the ashen skull sailing into the air and flipping repeatedly before coming down to land at Stranger's feet. The decapitated skeleton body wobbled and collapsed, turning to dust as it fell into the water. It became nothing more than a dark cloud of silt that spread out and washed downstream.

Stranger looked down at the skull and drew back his foot to kick it, but it crumbled apart and was taken away with the wind. The chill in the air and frost on the ground receded as he sheathed his pitchfork and turned back to his protectees. He found the lad reaching down to pull out the black sickle that held Sally to the cart.

"Wait! Don't touch it!" cried Stranger.

'BZZZT!'

The lad was tossed off the cart onto his face, hand smoking.

Stranger sighed and helped him up. "The sickle mustn't be handled by mortals—it is a tool of evil."

The lad looked at his palm. It was bright red and tingly, but thankfully intact.

"How the heck do we foist it out then?" asked the lad in frustration.

Stranger drew his pitchfork once more, using it to twist against the sickle's handle. With a swift yank, the foul weapon was flung to the ground.

"Whew, thanks," said Sally in relief. "That was a close one. I don't even want to think of what that thing would've done to my leg. Sorry you got zapped, the lad. I was about to try getting it out myself, but afraid to look down in case it had gotten me."

The lad half-closed his eyes and bobbled his head around in acknowledgment, while Stranger dug a hole and buried the Wazgall's blade, already having enough cursed artifacts to deal with.

"We keep moving," Stranger said. "I'd like to get well away from this place before making any more stops."

He climbed upon his horse and set off on the road yet again. For the next few hours, the passengers said nothing as they were bounced around in the cart. Bombir continued to sleep up until about midday when the word 'lunch' was mentioned. While they ate, he was asked all sorts of questions, but really didn't recall much about what had happened earlier.

"I guess I kinda remember swinging the sword around," he said. "I thought that was in a dream though. Everything's pretty hazy still."

So, the rest of them, aside from Stranger who wasn't looking when it had taken place, told him the tale of his amazing attack on the Wazgalls.

"It was like you suddenly transformed into an absolute fire-wielding storm god!" cried the lad.

Bombir just shook his head, unable to believe it.

"We'll have to keep an eye on that weapon," said Stranger. "It could be dangerous. Perhaps Lord BellJohn can have a look at it when we arrive."

"No!" screamed Bombir.

Stranger looked up at him. "What's that?"

"I said, um... 'ohh', as in 'oh-kay'."

Stranger narrowed his eyes at Bombir, then went back to whittling a stick. He looked back up when the lad called out to him.

"Hey, Stranger, those were some pretty kick-butt moves back there. You think you could show me a few of those techniques? I'm decent with a blade, but that was some seriously next-level stuff."

"Certainly," replied Stranger. "I suppose we could do a

quick training session before we head out again. Couldn't hurt for you to gain some skill in weaponry. Anyone else care to join?" Bowman, Sally, and Bombir all looked at the ground and kept eating. "Suit yourselves."

So, the two made their way to a spot away from the others to practice. Stranger went over some brief posturing tips before taking several steps away and turning to face the lad.

"Above all, remember this," said Stranger. "Overconfidence is key, but too much overconfidence leads one to a swift downfall. Of course, if you come across a situation where too much is necessary, then by all means utilize it, just never go beyond that. Do you understand?"

The lad nodded like it made sense.

"Alright then," Stranger continued. "Let us begin."

The two came at each other, swinging quickly and carefully. It went on like that for several minutes so that Stranger could examine the lad's skill level and fighting style.

After he was satisfied, Stranger suggested various adjustments for improving his timing and footwork, then began to show him a handful of techniques best suited to his abilities. In a surprisingly short amount of time, the lad managed to learn 'The Curving Slash-Crack', 'Seventeen Poke-Stabs', and 'The Almighty Heaving Gouge'. He had almost nailed a relatively complicated move called 'Air-Surfing Spiral Slice' before an unexpected rustling disturbance was detected nearby.

The lad and Stranger snapped their attention to the spot simultaneously.

"You heard that?" asked the lad.

Stranger gave a nod. In the shadows of the tree line, a pile of bushes moved about. The others were up now as well with weapons in hand.

Suddenly, the bushes parted, and a figure in charred brown robes slowly emerged.

"Good grief, not another one..." said the lad.

The others came in closer to the lad, and Stranger took the lead. The Wazgall approached, but something was odd about this one.

Bowman noticed it first and told the rest of the group. "It looks... wider than the other ones. Like it's got something stuffed under its robe. It walks different too."

Stranger decided to call out to the thing. "Who are you, and what are you planning to do? Answer quickly or there will be trouble!"

It stopped walking and fumbled around for its hood, making a few muffled sounds. Everyone leaned in and tensely awaited what lay underneath. The long sleeves fell back to reveal human hands that reached up to the sides of the hood and grabbed hold. The covering was cast back, and the face it once concealed belonged to none other than their previous and brief companion: Cave-Man Jim.

"Hey there, guys, I did not mean to frighten you," he said.

"Jim!" cried all but Stranger.

They ran to him, shook his hand, patted his back, and embraced his oversized person.

"How'd you find us?" asked Sally.

"Well, I sat with my father until his condition improved some. I also got to know that Wizard, Bob, a bit and trusted him enough to leave my father in his care while I went to make sure you guys were alright. I spoke with a traveling salesman who had seen you, then some folks in Debris told me you had gone north, so I followed the road up this way."

Some of the group's faces became filled with concern when hearing their route was being freely shared by folk from the town, but they let the cave man finish his story.

"I had to swim across a river since the bridge was out," Jim continued." I got very cold, but I ended up finding this discarded cloak on the other side and decided to put it on."

The lad sucked in through his teeth and winced. "I would *probably* not wear that if I were you," he said. "I know where it's been and trust me, it's not pleasant."

Jim gave a careless shrug and dropped the robes to the ground. It was then that the mystery of his peculiar width was solved. He'd been carrying a crap-ton of gear that was strapped down all over him. He began to untie and lay out the objects for observation.

"I picked this stuff up on my way through the jungle," he said. "I figured it likely that you did not mean to leave it behind."

Just about everything was there: the tents, the blankets, the cookware, the extra food and supplies. Of course, it was all soaking wet, but it would dry out.

"Wow! This is incredible," said the lad. "If only you—"

Before the lad could utter another syllable, Jim reached to his back and pulled forth the Super-Deluxo-Saber, then handed it to the lad with a grin. The lad took the sword and held it across the palms of his hands.

After a moment, he leaned his head down and wiped his face on his sleeve. "Friggin dust just kicked up in my eyes," he mumbled. "Thanks, man, really. We definitely owe you for this."

"No. You guys rescued my father. This is the least I could do. But, if you will have me, I intend to travel with you until the end of your journey and continue to help in any way that I can."

The group agreed and introduced Jim to Stranger. Soon after, they realized their cart would not support another passenger.

"Hoofhaver and the cart wouldn't have been of use to us for much longer anyway," said Stranger. "Our path into the mountains is rocky and treacherous, so we must bid him farewell for now and continue on foot."

Stranger cut away the cart and pushed it down a hill for his own enjoyment, then, he slapped his horse's buns and sent him neighing off into the wilderness. The others gathered their things into bags and packs, and in no time, they were on their way again, heading into the first slopes of the Mimson Mountains.

***

The group struggled along, up the narrowing path over boulders and loose rocks. Stranger led the way of course, followed closely by the lad. Behind him were Sally, Jim, and Bowman, still full of energy and ready to tackle the perilous road ahead. Bombir lagged behind, complaining constantly and scratching at the seat of his pants. He'd dropped a few logs earlier and mistakenly wiped with a pile of scorchweed leaves, one of the more poisonous plant varieties in this part of the world. Stranger had given him an ointment along with a dose of very unpleasant liquid medicine to drink. They dulled the burning pain a bit, but the itching was relentlessly and incessantly persistent. The lad was annoyed with him for a while, but after considering how miserable his friend must've felt, decided to go back and walk with him.

"Sorry about that, Bom," he said. "You came with me on a short trip that turned into a crazy, dangerous quest, then saved all our lives. You'll get the rest you deserve soon, and we'll be heading back home before you know it."

Bombir let out a long puff of air. "I don't mean to whine so much. I'm just not used to all this. I've actually had a pretty good time, aside from a few sucky things. We'll all have some amazing stories when we get back, that's for sure. Though, I may leave a few parts out around my parents."

The lad smirked. "Well, I appreciate you sticking with me. The worst of it's most likely over... now that those robe-demons are wiped out."

The lad went to give Bombir a free high-five until he saw how swollen and red his friend's hands were. So, he patted him on the shoulder and moved back up the line to speak with the others.

After some mindless chitchat, he fell back into his previous spot behind Stranger and kept moving in silent thought for a time. His mind began to wander, and without realizing it, he took the ring out from its secret hiding place. He rolled it from hand to hand, flipped it in the air a few careless times, then looked down at it. Quite surprised to see it there, he brought it closer to his face, examining it. It was like he was looking at it for the first time, and he found it to be far more interesting now than ever before.

For no particular reason, he slipped it over his left pinky. Aside from a sudden bad taste in his mouth, nothing seemed to happen. He was also fairly certain he wasn't unseeable. He switched the ring to his other pinky, and to his shock, he could see much farther than normal. However, the field of view in his sight was narrowed, like it would be when looking through a peepingtube. This change in vision nearly made him fall on his face, so, he quickly removed it but made sure to keep a mental note of such a useful feature.

Ironically, the left and right ring fingers didn't appear to have any discernable effect. The left middle was much the same, yet the lad did feel... slightly lighter... somehow, *and* gained a strange urge to punch someone. He shook his head and tried the right middle finger next. Nothing with that one either. At least, not until he heard gasps and a string of interjections coming from behind. He turned to see his friends wide-eyed and open-mouthed.

"What?" he asked with impatience.

"Dude, your hair is like... on fire or something," said Bowman.

The lad started slapping at his head but felt no heat or pain. He then moved some longer strands of hair into view and saw that it was all alight with a white-gold brilliance. Now that he thought of it, the ground beneath him was ever so slightly lit up by his radiant cranium.

"It's not fire," he said, still eyeing a handful of hair. "It's just... glowing."

A moment later, he glanced back down at the ring on his finger, then took it off. Instantly, the light was extinguished. The lad felt the sharp slap of a hand on his shoulder. It gripped tight and spun him around. It was Stranger.

"NEVER, NEVER DO THAT, YOU DUMBUS!!!" he shouted in the lad's face. "What are you thinking?! Putting that accursed band on can and *will* attract very unwanted attention. I thought you already knew this. Use your brain and quit playing with the darned thing."

"Alright, alright!" said the lad while putting it back in his pocket. "My mind was somewhere else at the moment—I'll be more careful. Sheesh."

Stranger leaned in close and studied the lad's expression, then loosened his grip from his shoulder. "Very well," replied Stranger. "The path levels out after the next mile or so and becomes a bit easier. As long as we don't run into anything nasty, we'll make good time and reach Drivenrail by noon tomorrow. And yes, that includes a few hours' sleep tonight and a couple of quick meals."

Stranger's words were not incorrect, for the path did flatten, and their pace was quickened. The mountains loomed high above on either side of them now—towering gray spires jutting upward like the world's own set of teeth. Night would be coming in less than three hours, and Stranger wanted to make as much progress as possible before then.

The lad and his friends were staying in tight formation, talking and letting out the occasional laugh, when things took an unexpected turn. Stranger motioned for them to be quiet and get down behind a boulder on the side of the path. He peered over another large rock just ahead of them, then snuck back without a sound.

"Not good," he whispered.

"What is it?" asked Sally.

"Something I thought had been wiped out long ago," answered Stranger. "It's a Giant. But not just *any* Giant. His name is Mimson Moe, and he has slain men by the dozensworth. I'd heard a group of warriors killed him many years back—even brought his head in for a handsome reward. Guessing it must've been a convincing fake, 'cause that's him alright. I can tell by that long, crooked nose and the scar across one pale eye. Best to try and sneak around him rather than attempt any sort of conflict."

The rest agreed right away. The lad listened as Stranger whispered out a plan to get around the Giant, but he became distracted by the sound of crunching coming up the path behind. The lad turned to see what it was, followed by Sally and Bombir. Stranger shut his mouth and looked as well.

"Get your weapons ready," he said.

The source of the noise came into view. It was a Troll, stumbling along with an angry scowl like it had just been through the worst day of its life. One of its two upturned horns was half broken off, and it carried a sack in its right hand while reaching in and grabbing fistfuls of roast buttons with the other, undoubtedly cold and chewy. It stuffed a pile of them in its huge, drooling mouth as it came ever closer to the group.

"Stay still and he may not spot us," said Stranger.

The Troll immediately spotted them and threw down the worn and stained sack.

The creature bellowed out a croaking holler and proclaimed, "Ol' Tubben's eatin' good tonight!"

The Troll then broke out into a sprint toward the group as they fumbled to draw their weapons so tightly packed together. Tubben reached out as he ran, big tongue flapping out the side of his mouth and eyes glazed over with the insanity that only an unexpected free meal can bring. Bowman loosed an arrow, and it struck the Troll square in the chest. There was a flinch, but it did not stop him. So, Bowman fired three more, hitting him shoulder, the neck, and finally, the right eyeball. The Troll slid to a stop less than thirty feet away, shook his head violently, yanked the arrow out, and clapped a large, stubby-fingered hand over the devastating injury. Eye jelly poured through the fingers and the Troll erupted in a furious rage.

"YOU'LL PAY DEAR FOR THAT!!" he roared.

The ground rumbled, as if an earthquake had begun.

At first, the group thought the Troll was causing it, but he hadn't even moved yet. They saw his remaining eye grow huge with intense fear, and his jaw and shoulders dropped. The lad looked up in time to see an absolutely massive form leaping over them with something huge in its hands. It was Mimson Moe, and he was clenching a gigantic metal hammer above his head, winding it back as he sailed through the air.

A moment before the Giant landed, he swung down the great hammer with an indescribably powerful force. It connected with the Troll's head and kept traveling downward without the faintest hint of resistance.

It looked like an oversized anvil that had fallen from the clouds and landed on a ripe watermelon. The group was rocked by the almighty boom of the ensuing shockwave, as mist and pulp sprayed the surrounding ground and cliffs with a thick coat of redness. The Giant stood to his feet, pulling the hammer free from the freshly made crater, then, wiped the splatter off his face and beard.

"Now!" whispered Stranger.

He threw himself over the boulder and waved the others on. They quickly scrambled over as well and began running hard when they saw Stranger do so. None looked back, but after several seconds had passed, they heard thunderous cries and earth-shaking footsteps closing in behind them. They'd been seen by the Giant.

"Keep running!" Stranger called out.

The narrow path they followed began to gradually open up wider, then slope down. There was a large area ahead like a shallow, grassy bowl sparsely dotted with trees, and the jagged peaks of the mountains continued their sharp, upward stabbings around either side.

Everyone sprinted down the loose gravel of the hill with all they had, then kept on going once their feet reached the grass. Bombir, however, was getting tired. His legs slowed and his heart was pounding. He tried to suck in more air and push through, but it was no use. With arms flailing, he took a few short and unstable last strides before coming to a halt. He bent down, gripping his kneecaps and gasping for breath. The tremendous rumbling of the Giant's feet grew louder, but Bombir's doughy, numb legs would take him no further. The world was spinning, and he thought he heard muffled shouts in the distance.

"Just go..." he managed to respond.

'SLAM!'

Something hit Bombir in his side, swiping him off his feet. It was Stranger. He'd come back and grabbed him up, then ran back toward the others. The group kept moving, approaching several large, ice-covered conifers that lay on each side of the shiny, seldom-used path ahead. Alas, their troubles increased exponentially at that point; for from out behind some of those trees... stepped three Ringwafers. All were on foot, unrobed and without a hippo in sight, but they were now blocking the group's only escape from Moe. Each of them held out their black sickles, ready for combat.

Chapter 20:
A Pickle on the Peaks

"Three each way, back-to-back!" cried Stranger.

Bowman, Sally, and Jim faced the unmoving Wazgalls while the lad, Stranger, and the still-recovering Bombir turned to meet the gaze of Mimson Moe. The Giant slowed to a casual walk, showing a hint of satisfaction on his face at the predicament the group was in.

He stopped about thirty feet away, eyes fixed on Stranger, then he spoke in a thunderously deep and guttural tone. "So, we meet again, Stranger."

Stranger gripped the center of his pitchfork with both hands, setting the end of the handle into the grass at his feet so he could stare at the Giant between the fork spikes.

"I guess so," he replied. "Thought I heard you were dead."

The sixteen-foot monstrosity let out a booming grunt of amusement, then put a thumb to one nostril and blew a massive snot rocket into the dirt that actually shook the ground. He rubbed a hand across his twisted nose and wiped strings of green mucus on his great loincloth—a garment which looked to be made of multiple large brown bear pelts.

"Nay," said he. "The Folks Flattener is alive and well."

"That's still a terribly corny name," said Stranger. "And alive *perhaps*, but you don't look too well from where I'm standing. I see that eye of yours was a total loss, thanks to Silvorkiel." He twirled the pitchfork in his hands as he uttered the name.

Moe frowned, and anger flowed across his hard, gray, rock-like face. "If you'd only tried rolling a half-second later... The Dimension Subtractor would've put you through the earth."

He spun the black twelve-foot hammer with a single hand, then let the colossal square head drop to the ground with a shocking thud.

"You're just too slow, I guess," Stranger replied.

Moe's frown turned to a bitter scowl; murderous rage shone through his narrowed good eye.

"Bom," croaked the lad. "Think you can do some of that firestorm sword stuff you did before?"

Bombir gulped. "I don't know. I don't even remember how it happened. But... I'll try."

He took a step in front of the lad and Stranger, then drew forth Spit from its sheath. The metal rang out with a shrill hum as Bombir pointed the tip of the blade at Moe. All was still and awkward for several seconds while he tried to trigger the sword's powers. He pulled in a deep breath and began grunting and growling, attempting to somehow will his own life energy into the weapon.

Nothing happened, and Mimson Moe laughed loudly at the display.

The lad leaned up and whispered in Bombir's ear. "I think you said some words. They weren't anything I understood, but I know you yelled '*burn*' right before the fire came."

"Gotcha," replied Bombir.

So, he planted his feet firmly, swung some kind of crisscross pattern through the air with Spit, then pulled the weapon close to himself. He took another deep breath, then plunged the sword into full outstretch, screaming at the top of his lungs.

"BURN!!!"

Sparks flew from around the hilt, then a wave of fire passed up the length of the blade to its point. The ball of flame sat there smoldering for a moment, then plopped to the ground, extinguishing in a quick and quiet 'psss'. Bombir fell back between Stranger and the lad.

"I suppose that means you're done with that little embarrassment then," scoffed Moe. "So, let's get to it."

The Giant issued out an explosive roar, then charged the group with hammer held high.

"Scatter!" yelled Stranger, and all six of them dove outward from the incoming blow.

The Dimension Subtractor impacted the ground where they'd all been standing a brief second earlier. Moe wrenched the hammer from the dirt and followed up with a horizontal sweep. The lad pressed himself tightly to the ground as it passed over, but Bombir was right in its path. Stranger shoved him down and only had time to raise Silvorkiel and try blocking the hammer's mighty force.

'CLING!'

The fork held up, but Stranger was thrown about fifty feet away. He flipped over several times and came to rest flat on his back. His hands were buzzing, but still holding his weapon.

By this point, the Wazgalls had decided to attack. In order keep them at a distance, Sally fired the steel rounds from her slingshot while Bowman shot his arrows. Jim was also throwing what rocks he could find, but none of the projectiles were doing any damage. Eventually, the ammo ran low, and the black skeletons advanced in even closer on the trio.

The lad and Bombir continued to dodge and roll from under repeated hammer strikes, and in the process, led the Giant away from the backs of their other three friends. Bowman and Sally switched to blades, and Jim drew the spear from his back. The shrieking Wazgalls came in swinging, and the trio could only do their best to keep from getting hit, for none of them had hand-to-hand experience enough to defeat the skeletal demons. Even if they did, their weapons lacked the effectiveness that Stranger's silver pitchfork had shown against the vanquished Ringwafer from before. Or so they thought.

One of Sally's strikes made it through her opponent's defenses, hitting the nightmarish fiend in left arm and sinking into the dark bones. She leaned back and twisted the blade free, severing the arm at the elbow. The appendage dropped to the ground and instantly turned to ashes. The Wazgall screeched in fury and brought its sickle down fast. Sally tried side-stepping, but it caught her in the left side, opening a small, yet agonizing, gash. She felt as if she'd had boiling water thrown across her entire torso and fought to keep standing.

Jim took a graze on his arm as well, but when he saw the condition Sally was in, he attempted to assist by swinging his spear wide and hitting her Wazgall in the leg, knocking it off balance. He was quickly punished by a slash across the chest. Sally pushed through the pain when she saw the opportunity she'd been given.

She hurled her knife at the Wazgall's face point blank, and it passed right on through the black skull. It came to a stop with half the blade sticking out the back of the head. The creature wobbled, then stumbled back. Sally was unarmed now, and had no idea what to do next, so she simply watched as the Wazgall collapsed to its knees. Bones began to separate, crumble, and turn to dust. She'd actually done it. She had defeated a Ringwafer.

'SLISH!'

In a flash, the partial remaining arm of her dying opponent swung in a quick arc, bringing the cursed sickle's blade deep into Sally's thigh. Her eyes went wild at the sight, but then came the pain. Electric fire erupted throughout her leg, stinging and tearing like a river of swords through every blood vessel. She crumpled to the ground and screamed while rolling and pulling at the lodged weapon. Just a few feet away, the Wazgall she'd fought fell on its face and turned completely to ashes. Meanwhile, Bowman and Jim continued to fight off the remaining two, unable to lend her any sort of aid.

Back on the other side of the grassy bowl, Stranger was trying to get himself up and back into the fight, but his heavily rattled body would have none of it. He grabbed fistfuls of grass and dragged himself toward the place where Bombir and the lad were still fighting Moe. The Giant took a few swings at the lad who was directly in front of him while Bombir tried to get in an occasional thrust of his sword from behind. After a successful stab into Moe's calf, Stranger saw the Giant give a backward glance at Bombir while seemingly pretending to keep trying to hit the lad.

"Bombir, look out!" cried Stranger as the Giant's mighty, sandaled foot flew back and collided with Bombir's chest.

The boy let out an 'OOF!' and he sailed through the air with the wind knocked totally out of him. He flew tumbling right over Stranger and faceplanted in the dirt, his sword clattering far away.

The lad now stood alone against the towering Folks Flattener. The Dimension Subtractor came down, and the lad rolled to the side just in time. He shielded his face as dirt and chunks of rock showered across him from the destructive slam. The hammer was pulled up, then swept close to the ground once again. The lad sprung to his feet and jumped over it, feeling the smooth metal graze the soles of his shoes.

All of the three fighters still on their feet were getting quite worn out and would soon be overtaken by their opponents if they didn't think of something. Bowman had been trying to do just that while deflecting sickle swings, and a plan began to form in his mind.

He had it—at least, as good of one as there could be. He took a couple of long strides back from the Wazgall, then switched to his bow. There were but three arrows left in his quiver, and he'd have to make them count. He spun 'round and fired the first one, planting it into the Giant's forehead. It had little effect. In half a moment, the Ringwafer behind him would either strike him or go after Sally to finish her off, so he had to be quick. He loosed another, and it sunk into the Giant's bad, pale eye. That got his attention. Moe raised his hammer and ran at Bowman, stepping over the lad. Bowman went back to his daggers and turned around in a flash to face the Wazgall once more. He crossed the blades and used them to block an incoming blow from the sickle.

In the reflection of one of the blades, Bowman could see the Giant just starting to swing the hammer down. He let himself fall backward, then pushed off with all his strength, launching himself between Moe's legs. The anger-fueled attack was the Giant's hardest yet, and the Wazgall Bowman had been fighting was right in its path. The charcoal demon looked up, let its sickle fall, then raised its boney hands upward in a pathetic attempt to stop the devastating impact.

The hammer flattened the Ringwafer, punching four feet into the ground beneath and causing a puff of dark powder to blast out from around the head of the unstoppable weapon. It was all that was left of the Wazgall. Bowman wasted no time while Moe began to pull the hammer back out of the earth. He circled the Giant's left leg, scooped up the now-unconscious Sally while calling for Jim to get out of there, then ran toward Stranger and Bombir.

Now, at least, the group had all their enemies on one side of them. It was soon apparent that the two were not in league however, for the Wazgall grabbed hold of Moe's hammer and tried to freeze it to the ground in retaliation of its vaporized companion. This was the perfect time for the lad to lay down a heavy assault on the distracted Giant's rear end, if only his own attention hadn't been elsewhere. For he looked on at Bowman as he ran by toward the others with Sally's pale and seemingly lifeless body. He could see the dark sickle protruding from her leg as Bowman tried to hold it still and keep the blade from causing further damage. The lad wondered if she would ever be able to walk again... or worse: if she would even make it through the injury alive. He'd never be able to forgive himself for bringing her along.

A shriek was heard, and the lad's focus snapped back to his enemies. Moe's hammer was completely encased in solid ice, and the Giant could not budge it from the ground no matter how hard he pulled. What happened next was quite unexpected. The Wazgall knelt and placed its boney hands to the spots where the other two had fallen.

Ash and dust kicked up in the air as if from a sudden gust of wind. It formed together in a swirling double-vortex that split and ran up each arm of the wretched creature. Its boney frame thickened and grew, and its features became more hideous than ever. The jaw extended down, teeth within lengthening into dagger-like points, and from the sides of its skull grew twisted black horns. Next, two extra arms sprouted out from beneath its original pair, bringing the total number to four. A second sickle was picked up from the ground by the Wazgall, then it cried out in a long, shrill screech once more. As it did, whirling, icy wind surrounded the creature, covering it in a layer of what looked to be jagged armor made of solid ice. The sickle blades were coated in the magically evil substance as well, adding to their length.

It was then that Moe abandoned his hammer and attacked the Wazgall with his monstrous bare hands. Fists flew rapidly into the Wazgall's ribcage and skull, knocking the creature all around before it could react. This went on for a few minutes until the devilish Ringwafer was cast down and repeatedly stomped into the dirt with the utmost violence. Finally, the Giant grabbed the limp creature and threw it with all his might at a tree. So powerful was the throw, that the tree was shattered apart in the center and the Wazgall traveled another sixty feet before landing and flipping to a stop. Regardless of this punishment, the Ringwafer rolled over and slowly stood to its feet. Moe did not hesitate; he charged with fists clenched together overhead, ready to bring them down in a crushing slam.

Just as he did so, the Ringwafer jumped high, past the falling fists and even Moe's head. It spun in midair and landed on The Giant's back, sinking all of its newly formed claws in tightly. Moe shook, twisted, and tried in vain to reach his arms around and get a hold of the Wazgall. Ice began forming across Moe's back, then down his arms and legs. It eventually covered the Giant's entire body until he was entombed in a huge block of ice. With Moe out of the way, the Wazgall turned now toward the lad and his group.

Stranger had tended to Sally during all this, carefully removing the sickle and bandaging her wound. "She's stable enough for now," he said to the others. "But we need to get her to Drivenrail quickly or she'll lose this leg."

Still fairly injured themselves, Bombir and Jim stayed with her while Bowman and Stranger joined the lad, who was certainly glad to see he wouldn't be facing this Super Wazgall alone. The three stood side by side with weapons gripped in hand, watching as the boney terror ahead of them closed in.

Out of nowhere, it broke into a run, bent low at the waist and dragging the icy sickles across the grass. The first swing came up at Bowman, and only by using all his strength was he able to deflect it away from splitting his face in half. After that, he figured he'd better keep his distance and lend support when necessary.

"Let me handle this, the lad," said Stranger. "Only a blade imbued with fancy Elf magic can put an end to a Ringwafer, and Silvorkiel is just such a weapon."

The lad took a few steps back but stayed ready for anything. Stranger went at the Wazgall with a fury unlike anything the others had seen from the man thus far. The glistening fork spun and twirled through the air, whistling with intense speed, and meeting the Wazgall's iced blades with ringing excellence. The two of them were locked in combat for a good deal of time, neither able to overcome the other apart from a few nicks and grazes. One of these came in the form of a slash from the Ringwafer to Stranger's left facecheek.

The stinging pain caused him to falter for only a moment, but it was enough for the Super Wazgall to quickly gain the upper hand. Its lower set of hands, which had done little aside from making obscene gestures up to this point, took hold of Silvorkiel with a fiercely strong grip. Though Stranger tried, he could not get his weapon back. Nevertheless, he would not let go of it, leaving him open for the Wazgall's upper arms to do their worst.

The lad and Bowman saw what was coming. The two sickles were raised high, ready to plunge into Stranger's shoulders and make him dead. Reluctantly, Stranger released his pitchfork and tried to jump back, but the Wazgall let go as well... and seized the man by the flesh of his waist-sides. Silvorkiel clattered on the ground, and in a flash, Bowman found himself sliding between the two, grabbing it up. He spun quick, then thrust the fork into the Ringwafer's back. The weapon lodged into the bones, sticking in deeply and causing the Wazgall to arch its back in response.

Now it was the lad's turn. This was his adventure—his quest. It was time for him to be the hero and save them all from this terrible mess. He came in fast from the right side, Saber trailing loosely behind. While running, he launched himself as high as he possibly could, bringing his sword up over his shoulder where his left hand came in to meet the right on the handle. Immediately, he twisted his entire body into a slow sideways roll and went into the Air-Surfing Spiral Slice.

It was the most complex move Stranger had taught him, and he'd never quite gotten it right. In addition to the barrel roll, the lad also began tumbling forward in a series of front flips, giving the appearance of a total loss of control. Out of this spinning ball of chaos, the Saber was being spun the same direction independently, rapidly switching from hand to hand in order to stay perpendicular from the ground as it passed around the lad's body. The precise and interwoven motions granted the sword a hypercharged increase in striking speed that would not be possible otherwise. The Wazgall glanced over just in time to see the lad coming in hot. Like a crank-powered circular sawblade geared for triple-maximum velocity, the Super-Deluxo-Saber sheared through all four arms as easily as through air itself.

As the limbs fell to the ground, the lad landed, slid to a stop, and came right back for another strike. This time he took a simpler route and used the Curving Slash-Crack. The sword hit the Wazgall in the spine just above the pelvis, tearing straight through. More than enough damage had been done already, but the lad did one last quick-spin and followed up by taking off the cursed demon's head before its upper half could even hit the ground.

"Take it! Take all of it, you stinking heap of rotten filth!!" the lad screamed.

The black bones of the Super Wazgall separated, crumbled, and turned to dust. The last of the known Ringwafers was defeated... probably. The lad dropped to his backside to take a breather while Bowman retrieved Silvorkiel and handed it back to Stranger.

"Thank you... both of you," muttered Stranger. "I would've been finished if not for that display. Looks like quick thinking and some of my training paid off... along with some other things...." He looked to the lad's sword and raised an eyebrow but kept it low so no one would notice.

A rumbling sound was heard in the distance then. Most assumed it was merely an impending thunderstorm, but that was not the case in the slightest. Mimson Moe's icy tomb had melted away, and the Giant was beginning to stir.

Moe roared, pounded the ground in fury, and ripped trees from the earth. To say he was angry would have been a statement of less than adequate representation.

After his half-frozen good eye had thawed enough to see clearly again, he spotted three of the little pests who'd trespassed on his territory and nearly cost him his gigantic life. He gritted his big teeth and ran at them, taking his hammer back in hand along the way. The lad happened to be the closest to him, so that's who the Giant chose to flatten first. Stranger ran to the lad's side and threw his pitchfork at Moe. Silvorkiel stabbed into the Giant's left pectoral square, slowing the brute but not stopping him. The lad was still on the ground and shuffled himself back, trying to get up. Moe's hammer came down fast, and all the lad had time to do was try deflecting it.

The massive head of The Dimension Subtractor met with the business end of the Super-Deluxo-Saber, shoving the sword's handle to the ground next to the lad. However, it came to a quick, ear-splitting halt due to a large rock the lad happened to be sitting over, which in turn caused his face to be pelted with shards of shattered stone. The force of the hammer was cataclysmic, but the Saber was completely undamaged. The lad was flat on his back now, nose nearly touching the front of The Dimension Subtractor. The hammer was lifted, and confusion flooded Moe's face when he saw the lad still in three dimensions. The Giant also seemed to not notice the sword stuck into the head of his hammer. He raised it for another blow and the lad stabbed his discount sword into the top of Moe's right foot, which proved difficult due to the skin being as tough as a six-month-old biscuit. The Giant hollered in reaction to the sudden discomfort.

That was the moment when Bowman loosed his final arrow. It whizzed through the air and sank far into Moe's mighty tongue. Without thinking or looking, the Giant brought down the Dimension Subtractor one last time. The handle of the protruding Saber punched into the stone once more, pushing the blade straight up through the other side of the hammer, splitting it in half. The two tremendous fragments thudded to the ground on either side of the lad. Moe yanked the arrow from his mouth and the fork from his chest just as the lad pulled his cheap blade from the Giant's foot.

When Moe looked down at the wreckage of his beloved weapon, all believed he would reach a new plateau of rage, so they braced for the worst. But it was not so. The Giant simply stooped down, picked up the fragmented pieces of his hammer, studied them with a pathetic frown for a bit, then slowly limped past the trio of fighters. Without looking at any of them, he continued up the path they had all come down earlier and disappeared over the hill.

Stranger sighed. "Next time then, perhaps."

Less than one minute later, loud booms shook the ground. Everyone was sure Moe was about to come rushing back down, but the sound was coming from the other direction. Bright yellow bolts of electricity were striking all over the area and moving their way.

"Just ahead now! We'll get them!" yelled a raspy, echoing voice.

"What now?" said the lad.

The lightning strikes ceased, and through the smoke could be seen a large gathering of persons. As they came closer, it became clear who they were. Elves, a small army of them, all being led by one single old guy in the very front and center: Randolf the Bronze.

"The lad! You're alive!" cried the Wizard. "Some bugs told me your group was nearby and having an epic battle with Wazgalls and Giants, so we came with all haste to rescue you."

The lad gave a sarcastic nod while he rubbed at a sore spot on his right arm. "Yeah, well there was only one Giant, and he just foisted off. You guys got here just in time to miss him. Thanks for trying though... I guess."

Stranger then spoke up. "The Wazgalls have been defeated, but some here have sustained serious injuries. We must get them to BellJohn's house, and fast."

Randolf gestured behind him, and a few Elves came running up with stretchers. The wounded were loaded on for carrying, and those who could walk proceeded onward in the midst of the Elf warriors.

Chapter 21:
The Secret Elven City

The lad was tired, as were the others who'd partaken in the battle that were still on their feet. They'd been marching by torchlight for hours, descending down the mountains and encircled completely by dozens of pointy-eared folks carrying shields and spears. The lad would have liked to talk with Randolf but decided in his weariness to let Stranger give the Wizard the details of their journey. A few snacks were eaten along the way since they hadn't the time to stop for any kind of meals or rest.

It was of the greatest importance to reach their destination as quickly as they could, for Jim and Sally both had received grave wounds from cursed weapons, with Sally's being by far the more serious. Bombir was on a stretcher as well, having smacked the ground with his face at high speed. He desperately wanted to take a nap, but some random Elf kept jolting him awake by yelling 'NOPE!' every time he started to drift off.

Eventually, the path narrowed, and the Elves' formation tightened down to three across. As the large group progressed, twisted trees with enormous trunks were set ever closer to one another on either side, dense bushes filling the gaps between. The path began to turn sharply back and forth, and the taller members of the party were forced to duck and pull their arms in, even after they'd switched to a single file line.

"If this road gets any smaller, most of these guys are gonna end up crawling," the lad thought.

No sooner had such a thing crossed his mind than the entire host of Elves came suddenly to a halt. The lad tried leaning around the protruding bottom of the Elf in front of him to see what was going on.

"What's happening up there?" asked Bowman from behind him, trying to look as well.

"They're tryna foist open some kind of... gate, or a secret passage maybe," the lad replied without certainty. "Sounds kinda like something Elf people would do anyway."

A muscular Elf at the head of the pack was stooped in front of a tangled mess of vines and branches so thick that it was impossible to see through. He flicked a branch or two as if they were levers, twisted another, and gave a single vine a few pulls. Then, he mumbled some words that sounded very much unlike normal language. The wall of foliage began to unravel, then it all retracted to the sides at once, leaving a small opening for the group to pass through.

They set off again into an open space, immediately coming to an arched bridge spanning a bubbling stream in the darkness beneath. The lad and Bowman couldn't see much, aside from the lights of tall lamps burning over small roads and candles in the windows of buildings clustered together ahead. There were plenty of sounds to hear, mostly soft things like the rustlings of leaves in the breeze, a few waterfalls of varying distance, the melodic tooting of Elvenflutes, and some kind of odd, tinkly noise that never seemed to stop.

At first, the lad assumed that it must be the guy running toward them covered in bells, but the sound didn't seem to come from him. It was more like it was coming from the lad's own ears... or perhaps his very mind. Whatever it was, he ignored it so he could listen to the bell-robed Elf.

"Bring them into the medical room at once," the lad heard him say.

Jim, Sally, and Bombir were rushed off to the left side of a large, central building, then the Elf spoke up so the rest could hear.

"I am BellJohn, Lord of this humble city we call Drivenrail. For those who are weary, follow Elfelfius to the second floor of the main house where he will show you to the Hall of Sleeperies." He motioned to the muscular Elf that opened the secret door earlier, then continued.

"If any are in need of a warm meal, I've had my cooks prepare some various things to eat. Accompany Melleniel, and she will guide you to the Hall of Eatleries on the first floor." BellJohn extended his hand toward a female Elf nearby to point her out.

"As for myself, I am urgently needed in the Hall of Healeries"—he paused in heavy thought, as if just realizing it might be a foolish-sounding name—"to... tend to your friends' wounds." He then gave a quick bow and scurried off toward the left wing of the main house with abundant gracefulness.

The lad was quite hungry, despite feeling he would collapse from exhaustion at any moment, so he followed the Elf called Melleniel with Randolf. Bowman and Stranger chose to go with Elfelfius, wanting nothing more than to close their eyes in a comfortable bed.

The two groups walked in parallel until they came to the front doors of the main house. Fancy-looking Elves stood guard on either side and quickly threw the huge doors open upon the groups' approach. The guards bowed and rolled forth a flattened palm to the guests as they passed inside. Elfelfius turned to ascend one of the stairways in the foyer with Stranger and Bowman close behind, while Melleniel headed straight, where more guards opened yet another door.

They came into a grand hall which was mostly filled with a long table. It sat in the center of the room under a spectacular chandelier, and was flanked by two tremendous fireplaces, one on each side.

"You may sit wherever you please—your server will be with you shortly," said Melleniel just before vanishing out of the room.

The lad and Randolf made their way to the far end of the table and seated themselves across from each other.

"I assume that you have more questions to ask of me," said Randolf with eyes aglow. "You may do so. And if you're lucky, I might just even answer a few."

The lad's head was spinning. He was excited for this moment, but for some reason he felt a bit concerned about what could come out from between this Wizard's wrinkly lips. Were there things he didn't necessarily *want* to know? He forced himself to wave the notion away and proceeded carefully.

"First off, if you were such good friends with my unclecousin, why have I never met you, and why didn't you come to his funeral?"

Randolf scrunched his forehead in thought while straightening out his beard with one hand.

"There are many doings and happenings in the world to which a Wizard is more or less obliged to oversee, attend, and/or take part in. I tried to visit once a year or so to keep in touch, but increased activity in the dark lands of the east took much of my attention for some time. I saw you twice when you were naught but a babe, and though still young, twice more after the tragic disappearance of your parents."

The lad felt his chest tighten at those last words. He was normally fine to discuss it when the topic arose, since he'd only been three years old and barely remembered them, but it felt strangely different coming from this old codger who knew more about his family than he did himself. Regardless, he kept his cool, nodded, and Randolf continued.

"Upon my last visits to Bobill, he seemed more irritable than ever before, and sometimes was not even at home. I never spoke much with anyone else in the town, but I can assure you, had I known of his passing, I would have been there. Would you care to tell me of what happened?"

The lad cleared his throat and took in a deep breath, staring down at the table. "Like you said, he left home a lot. I didn't know what *for* until recently. A little over a year ago he told me he was gonna be gone for a few weeks or more. I was already staying in my parents' old house by myself anyway, but he was just letting me know he wouldn't be around for a while if I were to need anything—"

Just then, a fancy Elf swished in through a side doorway and up to the table. He placed glasses and cutlery down in front of the lad and Randolf, then began filling the glasses with a dark liquid from a large pitcher. Through ever-closed eyes, the Elf somehow seemed to notice the lad's raised eyebrow.

"This is our finest chilled purpaberry tea," he said. "I will be right back with some much more solid ingestibles."

The lad watched him speed away, then looked back to Randolf.

"No menus?" he asked, half-joking and two-thirds serious.

Randolf just shrugged. "Perhaps its due to the time of day... or night rather."

"Well, anyway," the lad continued, "when he stayed gone for much longer than he'd said, I mentioned it to a few of my friends' parents. People began asking around and searching, but no trace was found for many months. Aside from that crazy trip with *you*, I heard he'd never been away anywhere near that long in his life. Eventually, his ripped-up clothes were found... along with his bones... up in the mountains near the lake. That was early this year. We buried them in his backyard, boarded up his house, and a lot of people showed up to pay respects there in the freezing cold that day."

The Serving-Elf came back to the table just then, laying out plates of food before them. It was mostly bread and vegetables with a few morsels of some sort of thinly sliced meat. It was not things the lad would normally eat, but he was famished, so he began to shovel it in regardless.

"You got any oranges here?" he rudely asked the server with a full mouth before he could get away.

The Elf held up a finger and headed back into what the lad figured to be a kitchen. A moment later, the server was back with two orange-colored spheres. The lad could hardly contain his excitement.

"No way! I can't believe it!" he said.

"Well..." replied the server, "they are not exactly oranges. They are tangerines. Unfortunately, that is all we have at here at this time, but they are very similar to an orange."

The lad's smile faintly dropped, then he sliced one open and took a bite. "It tastes a little... off... but it'll do for now."

The server nodded and exited once more.

"I'm very sorry to hear that," said Randolf.

The lad looked up and wiped his mouth. "Don't be," he

responded, "they're seriously fine. I mean, at least he didn't bring me like grapes or something." He shuddered at the thought.

"I mean about your unclecousin," Randolf clarified. "It's a shame that such a decent fellow should come to such an end. All for the desire of that wretched fingerbelt. I feel a fool for not confronting him about it when I had the chance."

The lad said nothing. A minute of silence passed between them until they went back to their plates. Randolf was eventually the first to finish eating, and after dabbing his mouth with a napkin, he slowly rose from his seat and gave his back a few twists.

"I believe we may be here a while," he said. "So, we will have plenty of time for more conversation later if you wish. For now, I must rest my eyes, as I'm sure you'll want to do as well. Just follow the stairs in the foyer to the right—all the rooms on that side are usually available to guests. I bid you a good night!"

"Alright, goodnight then," replied the lad.

Randolf nodded and walked to the entryway they had used earlier. He opened it up, stepped through, and the door shut behind him. The lad scooped in a few more bites, then rested his chin on his hands for a while, staring down at the elegantly patterned, silky golden runner that partially hid the glossy finish on the dark, knotty wood of the tabletop beneath.

"All finished, are we?" a voice suddenly said.

The lad nearly jumped out of his skin, then he began stretching, yawning and trying to crack his neck in an effort to conceal his fright when he realized it was only the server.

"Ohh, uh... yeah sure. Thanks."

The Elf produced an enormous, perfect-toothed grin upon the lower half of his impeccable face, then quickly swiped the plates up with one hand while wiping down the table with the other.

"It has been my pleasure. My name is Brin-Gamiel by the way," he continued while pointing to the nametag on his white and gold jacket. "I hope everything has been to your liking. If you need anything further... then I don't know what to tell you because I'm going to bed! Have a good night, sir!"

With that, he took his final leave of the room, passing into the kitchen and making a few sounds before the lad saw the light go out. The candles in the chandelier above were already quite dim to begin with; now the room was even darker. The lad was only slightly creeped out by the sudden loneliness of the place. He knew he needed some sleep, but also wondered about his injured friends. Perhaps he'd be able to peek in or ask someone about them so he could rest more easily. He got up from the table and moved toward a door on the front left side of the room. When he opened it, he found a dark hall with no one in it. Thinking it may lead to the medical section, he went ahead and followed the hall to its end. Paintings of Elvenfolk and majestic landscapes hung between the low-burning wall sconces, alternating with small, carven statues and potted greeneries.

After a bit of sneakish walking, the lad came to a door at the end. A sign that read 'Hall of Healing' was hanging upon it. The last three letters of the final word had been struck through and written over with 'eries', so that it now appeared as 'Healeries'. The lad knocked softly a few times but received no answer. So, he grasped the knob and gave it a turn. The door was unlocked and swung freely open. He passed through and into an open area filled with chairs. Likely, it was some kind of room for waiting in. To his left, the lad spotted a reception window, but the room behind it was dark and no one seemed to be there. To the right of the window was another door; this one had a sign secured to it displaying the words 'Please Wait To Be Called'.

"Ehh, what the heck..." the lad thought as he reached for the knob.

The door suddenly flew open, missing his outstretched hand and his face by mere inches. A shadowy figure stood in the darkness on the other side.

"Holy friggin heck!!" yelled the lad.

"Sshhh!" the figure responded. "What do you need?"

The lad's eyes adjusted, and he saw that it was BellJohn.

He breathed a sigh of relief and answered, "I didn't think I'd be able to sleep if I didn't try checking in on my friends."

"I see," said BellJohn. "I can assure you—they are doing well. The girl, Sally, will take some time to heal, but further damage has been prevented. For now, they are all stable and asleep. I am going now to my quarters for the night, as should you. Don't worry, nurses will be keeping an eye on them until morning."

"Oh, alright then," said the lad. "Thanks for all this."

"Certainly."

BellJohn escorted the lad back to the foyer and wished him a good night. Then the lad finally climbed the stairs and headed down the hall to the right like he'd been told to. Eventually, after a few tries, he found a room to be unoccupied. He locked the door behind him, cast his belongings to the floor, and threw his filthy, greasy, grime-encrusted self on the immaculately clean bed. Within minutes, he was out cold.

***

The sun was shining brightly through the white draperies of the lad's bedroom window. Birds were screeching out ear-piercing songs, and some were even pecking away at the outside of the house. The lad attempted to drown it out by wrapping his pillow around his head, but after growing quite tired of trying to ignore the sounds, he went ahead and sat up on the edge of his bed. While rubbing his eyes and preparing to stand, he could've sworn he heard someone in the room trying to get his attention.

"Psst. Pssst!"

The lad spun around, but no one was there. He shook his head and smacked the side of his face a couple of times before finally getting up. He stretched a bit and took note that there were three doors in his room. One was the exit, but he was unsure of the others. The first of the remaining two was checked and found to be a closet with stacks of various cloths inside, so he shut the door and moved on to the next. This one led him to a washroom with a toilet, sink, and even a shower the lad suspected might feature hot running water. After turning a knob, the lad breathed a delighted sigh as the warm droplets struck his outstretched palm. His soiled clothing was quickly thrown to the floor as he dove inside and pulled shut the curtain.

When he had finished, he whipped a bright white towel around his waist, combed his coconut-shaped hair, and reached for his clothes. Upon seeing them, he stopped his hand. They were caked in dirt and smelled like deceased manure. He stood for a moment, frowning down at them and trying to figure out what he could use aside from a towel to cover his ladly physique.

"The closet..." he thought.

Going back to the closet, he found a set of clothes in his size that were exceedingly comfortable and not even terribly goofy looking. The grayish brown shortpants were for his legs and the silvergreen three-button shirt covered the area just above them. The garments were light, breathable, and smooth as water. Apart from one fairly important artifact, the lad didn't bother to grab his gear, knowing he certainly wouldn't be leaving any time soon. He stuffed the item into an unfortunately zipperless pocket, then simply walked out the bedroom door into the hall, where he was met with a knuckle-punch to the nostrils of breakfast-time aromas.

He hurried down the stairs past some guards that

heeded him not, and into the Hall of Eatleries. Stranger, Randolf, and Bowman were seated at the table and finishing up towers of butter-soaked waffles. As they looked up from their plates at his arrival, the lad noticed a fourth person was with them. It was BombirThin.

"Bom!" yelled the lad as he ran over to greet his still-face-stuffing friend.

They exchanged a free high-five, and the two began talking as the Server-Elf, Brin-Gamiel, laid out a plate of waffles with a single tangerine on the side for the lad. Bombir had been cleared to leave the medical area upon waking a few hours earlier.

"I'm feeling great actually," he said. "A little soreness in the ol' ribs maybe, but other than that, I think I'm fine."

"It's fortunate any of you made it here alive after the things *you've* been through," piped in Randolf. "When you have finish eating, we'll be heading to the Hall of Healing — err... Healeries... to check up on Sally and Jim. While we're all together, I'll catch everyone up on the happenings that have — well... happened. I've not yet gotten the chance to explain why I did not meet up with you earlier as I'd planned. Not that it's any of *your* business, but some of it does have relevance to further matters of discussion."

The lad nodded furiously while inhaling his food, and just about the time he was washing down the last bite with a splash of watermelon juice, BellJohn entered the room.

"It is time," he said.

The group rose and followed the Elf through halls not

unknown to the lad until they reached an area he'd yet to see. The hallway behind the 'Please Wait' door led them past several rooms, but the last one on the right was their destination. BellJohn opened the door and went inside, motioning for the rest to follow.

An Elf lady pushed back a few curtains that separated the room into sections, and that was the moment the lad spotted Sally and Jim. They were both sitting up in beds somewhat near each other against the far wall and eating soup out of bowls. Chairs were slid up to the beds so the visitors could sit and converse with them.

Knowing well that he wanted to talk to Sally the most, the lad decided to address Jim first and get that out of the way. He circled around to the left and greeted the young cave man.

"Hey, Jim. How ya feeling?"

Jim seemed surprised that the lad would come straight to him.

"Oh, hello, the lad. I suppose I am doing well. BellJohn and his nurses have done a great job and say that I may be back to normal within a few days. I took some bad cuts by those evil weapons, but I was not hurt as much as Sally was." He looked over to her with concern.

"Glad you're still with us," the lad replied. He patted the cave man's shoulder, gave a nod and a half grin of approval, then moved to Sally's bed.

"Any pain?" asked the lad as he took a seat.

"Not as much as the last time I remember being awake,"

Sally weakly replied with a raspy throat. "It's dull now, but deep and persistent. Can't really move my leg at all yet. I'd show you the wound, but it's tightly bandaged at the moment. Guess now I know how Aramel felt. I hit her in nearly the same spot—except it wasn't with a cursed blade obviously.... Of course, she probably didn't get medical attention from Elves afterward either. They're really something here. I mean, somehow, they got this wide-open cut to completely close already, and it's only been like ten hours. It looked like a rough burn mark surrounded by dark purple bruising when I saw it earlier."

Without thinking, the lad started to place his hand on her arm as a gesture of comfort—but he stopped himself short, worried at what her reaction might be. He then diverted trajectory downward, pretending to scratch his knee.

"Sorry you have to go through this," he said. "You were almost hit in the same place once before. It should've been me."

"Nah, don't be like that. I'm glad I came. There have been scary times for sure, and the nearly *dying* part kind of sucked, but it's also been really amazing. The scenery, the new people, the adventure—against insane odds, every one of us managed to survive to tell about it too. Give it a few months and I'll probably have forgotten all about this little scratch. It definitely could've been much worse. Besides, from what I heard, we may not have made it off those mountains at all if *you'd* been taken out of action early."

The lad opened his mouth to attempt a reply but was

cut off by Randolf, who loudly cleared his throat and stood to his feet.

"Now that we are all reunited, I have a few things I must reveal," said the Wizard as everyone in the room turned their attention toward him with looks of puzzlement.

Randolf silently eyed each of them suspiciously, and when he was at least *mostly* sure his onlookers were actually paying attention, he began to speak once more.

"I was meant to meet with you as you were leaving Debris a few days back, but due to possibly unforeseeable circumstances, I was unable. You see, I was meeting with some of my fellow Wizards at the Hall of Wizardness within the Tower of Icingshard to discuss the confirmation of a certain item's finding. We conversed of it thoroughly, then after we'd concluded and the rest of the Wizards were leaving, I was called back inside by the leader of our circle.

"His name is Marazûn, and on top of being my superior, he has been my advisor on staff maintenance and beardcare products for centuries. The words he spoke seemed friendly enough at first, but I soon realized he was trying to get me to tell him the exact whereabouts of the item. Normally, I would trust him, but something in his voice gave me cause for hesitation. I made excuses, and he saw right through them, quickly becoming angry, shouting, and calling me a liar that was in league with the enemy."

Randolf briefly paused and began searching within his yellow robes for something as his audience waited patiently. The sought-after object ended up being a case that contained his bubble-pipe. He fiddled with a tiny jar of liquid and a small stick that was either a fancy match or a miniature Wizard staff, then continued his tale.

"Where was I? Ah, yes... Marazûn ended up smashing me over the dome with his pointy staff, then shocked nine-twelfths of the life out of me until I was unable to attempt an escape. I was tossed in a prison cell which I was unaware existed beneath the Hall, then told I could not leave until I"—he tapped the liquid in the pipe with the mini-staff, causing a faint glow to form—"disclosed the item's location. Several days passed before I was able to convince a rat to seek out and bring me the key to the cell. I retrieved my staff and snuck out the front door without detection. Doubtlessly, he's furious now...

"From what he said and things I saw, I am also quite certain it is *he* who is in league with the enemy. Many ages ago, his father and my own were bitter rivals that fought endlessly for power. My father wanted to go about things the right way and keep the innocent folk of the world in mind—but Marazûn's father saw them simply as lesser beings who were in the way of his designs and wanted no part in working with them or helping anyone. Well... aside from impolite Wizards and sometimes exceedingly ill-mannered Elves. Marazûn and I, however, were good friends, and believed we were meant to break the cycle. But in more recent years, I believe the darkness and evils of Rauson have twisted his thoughts, and he's becoming ever more like his father all the time."

The lad raised his hand, but the Wizard ignored it.

Instead, he blew on his magic pipe a few times, sending transparent spheres of orange and blue dancing up to the ceiling. When he realized no one except Jim looked quite as impressed as he thought they would, he got back to the story.

"After my escape, I came straight here, not knowing of your whereabouts due to the destruction of Flare—uhh... *Stranger's* far-talker. I wasn't here long before I ran across a beetle and a centipede having a discussion on the edge of a bridge. I was about to stomp them into oblivion until I overheard part of their conversation. The beetle was saying that a butterfly had mentioned seeing an incredible fight up on the mountains between Wazgalls, Giants, and several small peoplefolk accompanied by a single, taller one. I haven't a clue how a butterfly knows what a Wazgall is, but of course I set out at once with the Elf army of Drivenrail to aid you.

"Well, that is the story, and it's all I have to say at this time." His brows suddenly lowered, and he cast out a pointed finger at the lad. "And just so *you* know, I saw you whispering and giggling to BombirThin when I mentioned the conversation between the insects. It did happen, and I *can* understand them. Though I don't have to prove anything of the sort to the likes of you. Hmph!"

The lad slid down in his chair and looked away with a frown, then Randolf addressed the room one last time.

"I do not give out information on this level of mysteriousness lightly—so I bid you mark these words well. Lord BellJohn is to call for a meeting on what to do about various situations and objects in later days. One further thing I almost forgot to mention—is that messengers have been sent to Hometown to alert any friends or family of as much about the current circumstances as can be told, and to expect your return whenever possible. For now, get some rest and relax, you're quite safe here."

With all of that said, the Wizard turned and made his way out of the medical halls with a trail of bubbles floating overhead. All sat in silence for a few moments... until the lad broke it.

"Anyone know where I can wash my clothes? They stink like you wouldn't believe."

"Is that what you tried to interrupt Randolf for when you raised your hand?" asked Bowman.

"Well, yeah. I was thinking about it and was afraid I'd forget."

Bowman shook his head. "Geez, man. Didn't you have a basket for soiled laundry in your room? *I* did. I put my clothes in it, sat it outside the door, and someone took it this morning."

"Ah, I'll have to look into that," the lad replied.

Stranger said a quick farewell, taking his leave at that point while the ones that remained continued to talk for a time. Sally began to feel drowsy and sore after a while, so the visitors said their goodbye-for-nows and left the Hall of Healeries.

Bowman and Bombir got conversing on the way back to the main hall and decided they wanted to go take a look around outside. The lad told them he would catch up right after he found a dirty-clothes basket. They parted ways, and the lad climbed the stairs once more, going back to his room in search. Nothing was found, so he simply tossed his pile of clothing on the floor in the hall.

"Not my fault they didn't give me a friggin basket," he thought.

He went to walk to the stairs but noticed a small door at the end of the hall. It didn't look like a whole room could be there, so he assumed it to be some kind of utility closet.

"Aha! Maybe the baskets are in there."

He looked around, making sure nobody was present lest they think him to be up to something. He approached the door and gave the knob a good turn. What he didn't expect, was the door to suddenly fly open from the weight of a thing leaning against the inside of it. A sack fell at his feet with a thud, full of clothespins or fresh dust mop covers most likely. When the lad looked down, he found that the lump of stuff was not in a sack or bag at all, but covered by a sheet, or maybe a cape.

Either way, he could see the edges, so he reached down and flipped it back. His eyes grew several sizes, and he threw himself tumbling backwards down the hall, crying out in horror.

"UGGHHH! DEAD GUY!! DEAD GUYYY!!! GET IT AWAY!!!"

As surely as buttocks blow bad air, there was a corpse on the hallway floor.

Chapter 22:
The Amazing Return

Randolf and Stranger ran up the right stairway to the second-floor hall while BellJohn cleared the entire left flight with a double backflip. There they regrouped to find the lad on his back, shuffling himself away from something with his heels and elbows. He looked up at them and pointed to the lifeless body at the end of the hall.

Stranger made his way over to it at once for inspection, and before he could say anything, the lad's wits had returned to him enough to process the image in his mind. He knew who it was. Stranger bit his bottom lip and let out a long sigh through his nose holes, then knelt down and placed his hand upon the dead fellow's brow. The lad saw Stranger's facial expression change quickly to one of surprise.

He looked to the others and said, "He's warm."

Just then, the body on the floor let out a terrible, heart-ceasing cry.

"AAAAHHHH!!!"

Stranger leapt backwards onto his feet, lost his balance, and crashed through a glass window next to the closet. The others heard his grunts and yells as he thudded down an angled roof and plummeted to a deck below.

"Melleniel!" shouted BellJohn.

She appeared behind him at once.

"Yes, Lord?"

"Go and retrieve the man who just fell out of the window, he may need medical attention."

"Right away, Lord," she responded before rushing back downstairs.

The closet dweller sat up with his back facing the stunned observers and rubbed at his head. The lad stood to his feet and slowly advanced towards him. He stopped short a few feet away and stared, trembling with disbelief.

"Can it be?" asked the lad softly. "Is it really you... Bobill?"

The man on the floor looked back and forth at the surrounding walls before loudly replying, "Who said that? Someone talking to me?"

He shakily rose to a standing position, steadying himself with a hand placed on the closet door trim. After a moment, he turned to face those who stood behind him. He reached out and felt the open air with his fingers, then called out once more.

"Is anyone there? I can't seem to see anything."

The lad answered him with a question. "Have you tried opening your eyes?"

The man's hands dropped to his sides, then his eyes popped wide open in an instant.

"My little the lad!" he cried. "You're here, and Randolf too! Were you following me?"

The lad was confused but knew now for certain that this was truly his unclecousin.

"I don't know what you mean," he replied. "You've been gone for almost a year, and everyone thinks you're dead. Your torn clothes and even your bones were found in the mountains months ago."

Bobill gave a grave look of concern. "I-I just came here to rest for the night—how could that much time have passed?"

"I can give you an explanation," said BellJohn, who came to stand beside the lad along with Randolf. "In the early days of building these halls, that room was filled with a powerful magic that causes whatever is inside to be preserved in a state of dormancy. It was used for various things, such as storing food and drink, and later it was found to be useful for medical purposes. On a few occasions—and against my council—it was abused by those impatient for their birthday or some other special event. After we built a larger, more practical version in the Hall of Healeries, it was simply used as a broom closet. The only trouble we've had from it for the past few centuries was from our dear Mister Gabbin here, and if my memory serves me well, this would be the *fourth* time you've tried sleeping in there." BellJohn glared at Bobill with sternity in his eyes.

"Well, sorry," said Bobill. "All the rooms were taken during those times."

BellJohn sighed heavily. "I *told* you, Mister Gabbin, that some of the knobs will often stick, giving the impression they are locked when they are indeed not. Do not worry yourself over it. I will have someone come and build a brick wall in front of this door soon so that the mistake is not repeated. I see there is much here to discuss however, so I must recommend that it be continued downstairs in the Hall of Sitleries—" BellJohn squeezed his eyes shut, pushing his thumb and forefinger into each of them respectively with frustration as he let out a long exhale. "I really must change those names back," he said.

***

While BellJohn was instructing his building crew Elves to brick up the upstairs closet and repaint the labels of the house rooms, Randolf, the lad, and Bobill sat in the soon-to-be-renamed Hall of Sitleries. Randolf puffed on his magic bubble pipe, and the rest sipped from glasses of purpaberry tea and ate various small snacks while firstly discussing the most pressing matter at hand: what in Skiddle Earth had Bobill been up to?

"You see, the lad, the Dorks had come to visit me on my birthday the Spring before last," Bobill began with a mouthful of fried radish skins. "With their great craftsmanship they had made for me a wondrous yet strange gift. It was a life-sized replica of my own skeleton to display. I was quite unsettled by it—but didn't want to be rude after all the work they'd gone through. So, instead of merely stuffing it in the trash bin, I pushed it into a corner and used it to hang coats and hats on.

"The Dorks stayed for a week, and upon leaving they invited me to an upcoming grand feast they were putting on in celebration of... well... something. I don't really remember. Anyway, I accepted the offer, but just before that time came, there was a gusty day when I went to go check my mail and the front door slipped from my grasp. It flew all the way back, smashing my skeleton coat-hanger into the wall and breaking several of its pieces.

"Rather than lug the entire thing across half the world, I took only the snapped bits with me to see if the Dorks could repair them. They wouldn't fit in my fanny pack, so I wrapped them in a shirt and tied it closed with a pair of pants, leaving one leg loose to sling over my shoulder. I said my goodbyes to you, then headed out of town."

Bobill paused to gulp down the rest of his tea, then loudly slurped at the remaining residue in hopes to attract attention for a refill. He smacked his lips a few times, then proceeded along with his story.

"That's good stuff," he said with a half-concealed burp. "But as I was saying, I had left town. On my way through the mountains, a fog rolled in, and at one point I thought I saw a tiny ghost zip past my feet. I panicked and began to run up the hill, only to be met with a low-hanging branch to the forehead. I ended up rolling backwards down the hill and came crashing to a halt in a pile of thornbushes. When I finally forced myself to get up, I couldn't find any sign of the bone bag, even having searched for a couple hours. The only thing I *did* discover was that the 'ghost' was nothing more than a white rabbit."

He stopped briefly and stared at the table in slight embarrassment. A server Elf came then, replacing his empty cup with a freshly filled one. Bobill took a swig and cleared his throat, preparing himself for more speaking.

"So, fearing I'd end up late to the party if I fooled around too long, I made the decision to forsake the fake bones and perhaps look for them on the way home. BellJohn's house lay along the path I was taking, and I had already planned to spend a night in his halls. Of course, no one *here* knew that, and I somehow slipped past everyone in the late-hour darkness and made my way to a room. Like you've already heard, I assumed they were all occupied, so I ended up trying to get some shut-eye in the broom closet like I did way back on my first journey with Randolf... and a couple times after.... It truly only feels like it's been a single night since I went inside. Such a strange thing, Elf magic is. But that's the tale in full, if I'm not completely mistaken."

The lad was astonished and relieved by the explanations. But he was also excited since Bobill was finished talking now and he'd be able to tell his unclecousin of his own adventures.

"I'm glad you're still with us," he said.

"As am I," added Randolf. "I for one knew quite well you had not yet exited the land of the living."

"What!?" yelled the lad. "You didn't say that yesterday when we were talking about him!"

Randolf cleared his throat and quickly glanced around the room as if planning an escape. "Excuse me, good fellows, there are matters I have to address... outside." He then got up and left the room.

The lad shook his head with annoyance, then went back to talking with Bobill.

"Oh yeah, you will *NOT* believe what I found on the way here!" he exclaimed.

"And what's that?" asked Bobill with a smirk.

The lad suddenly realized he'd goofed. Why the heck did he say that?

"Uhh, nothing. I didn't find anything."

Bobill's grin dropped slightly, and the lad could have almost sworn his eyes narrowed with nigh-undetectable conjecture, had he known what the word conjecture even meant.

Then, Bobill raised an eyebrow. "Nothing, huh? Well, I'm sorry to say I don't find that too terribly interesting."

His seriousness broke, and he burst into a laugh. The lad fake-laughed along with him while trying to think of something else to talk about.

"I did find a few things actually," the lad continued. "Friends, adventures... a junky new sword that I'll probably throw away.... I guess since you're too late to go to that party and I'm waiting for a couple of people to heal up before I leave here, I can tell you the story from the beginning if you'd like."

Bobill's smile grew once more.

"Why of course, the lad, tell me all about it!" he said

with enthusiasm while secretly believing it would be boring.

"Yeah, I'll tell you all of it," thought the lad. *"All but a few things anyway."*

The lad took a long gulp of tea, then began his amazing tale. It took him nearly till lunch just to get to the part where he met Cave-Man Jim, which worried the lad considering what Bobill knew of that location. In time, they were called to the newly renamed Eating Hall, where they met up with a very surprised Bowman and Bombir. Shortly after, they were joined by Randolf and a somewhat grumpy Stranger, whose head now featured a prominent bandage. Despite the injury, Stranger greeted Bobill warmly and acted as if it were not the first time they'd met one another. All were caught up on the happenings of Bobill, and once they'd finished eating, the whole lot of them moved to a grassy area outside by a stream to continue the lad's own story.

A few times, Bombir piped in to add some details, and more than once did the lad have to give him a hard glance or loudly cough to keep him from mentioning the ring or anything that may hint at its finding. Bobill happily listened, and though parts of the account seemed odd or nearly impossible, he knew his own story could be thought of in much the same fashion. With the collaboration of multiple points of view, he had to admit to himself that it must all have been factual, and despite his initial assumptions, he found the tale to be absolutely fascinating. At times, he added in his own experiences for comparison, and the lad made sure to remind his unclecousin often that he knew very little of those tales.

Shortly after dinner that evening, the lad finished the telling of everything he could safely bring up, prompting Bobill to go on and on about how grown and courageous his nephewcousin had become.

"I know I was never terribly straightforward with my own story," said Bobill. "Many years ago, I sat down and wrote it out in full. I planned to never show anyone, considering some of the more private matters within—but to be honest, those things are long in the past and nothing more than a distant memory for me. So, I want to give you this."

He unzipped his fanny pack and drew out from it a green rectangle. The item was placed in the lad's hands, where it was studied by him thoroughly. It was a hardcover book, and on the front, beneath a crudely drawn picture of a single, pointy mountain behind a pile of trees inside a circular frame, was written, 'The Gabbin', in a pleasantly contrasting dark-bluish hue.

"Oh, wow," said the lad as he thumbed through the papery sheets within. "This thing has gotta be almost two hundred pages long! I know what I'm going to be doing for a while. I appreciate this, really."

"You are welcome, the lad. It feels good to know someone else will finally know the whole story. Hopefully it can even aid you in some way with any further adventures you may find yourself on. My own days of adventuring are coming to an end, I think. I'm not the spry young fellow I once was in my youth."

The lad waved his hand dismissively. "Nah, you're not

even, what, your forties yet? You've got plenty of time."

"I'm fifty-eight," replied Bobill.

"Exactly! That's not *that* old. Heck, you were making your way across half the world before coming here. And who knows how much aging you've prevented by sleeping in that closet."

Bobill could only purse his lips and nod in agreement. "Perhaps you're right. With all the crazy things going on in the world these days, we may have no choice but to have another adventure together on the way home from here."

It was a comforting thought to the lad.

After his friends were better and BellJohn decided where to toss that accursed hunk of jewelry, they'd all be heading back to Hometown with Bobill beside them. The group talked for a short while longer until the time for sleeping arrived. One by one, they each said their goodnights and climbed the stairways to the sleeping quarters area. The lad smelled the scent of fresh mortar as he approached his room, which came from newly laid bricks around the old broom closet.

"Goodnight, the lad," Bobill said as he entered the room across the hall.

"Night, Bobill."

The lad closed his door, locked it tight, extinguished the candles, and flopped into bed. That night, he dreamt that his door splintered into a million pieces. Amidst the smoke and debris, Bobill entered the room and grabbed him by his throat, holding him high and shaking him like a ragdoll.

"Where is my ring, you puke-sniffing liar?!" roared his unclecousin just before unsheathing the legendary sword, Stink, and planting it firmly through the lad's fleshy gut cover.

The lad awoke suddenly, flipping out of the bed to the floor, tangled in blankets and soaked with sweat. He got himself up, re-lit his bedside candle, and checked his room and under the bed for any insane relatives. No sign of intrusion was found; it was just a stupid dream. He went to his window and opened it, resting his elbows on the sill and gazing out at the moonlit mountains behind the shimmering mist of cascading waterfalls.

When he'd had enough of that, he went to the bathroom, dropped a massive deuce, splashed his face with cool water, and went back to bed for the remainder of the night without issue.

Chapter 23: Judgement of Steel

A full three weeks had passed since the lad and his friends' arrival in the Elf city of Drivenrail. Jim had been out of the medical area for eight days, and Sally was scheduled for full release at noon. Stranger had left early to 'run some errands', as he put it, and was gone for many hours. Randolf set himself down in the library to study a few history books but ended up staring and poking at his glass far-talker for the majority of his visit to the room. Bowman, Bombir, and Jim went outside to see if they could find a stream to take a dip in, settling instead on a wide and calm pool in the backyard of the main house at the foot of the mountains. The lad was at the Dining Hall table with his unclecousin, eating a late breakfast of hash brown, bacon, and strawberry porridge along with a small stack of Bobill's own homemade buttercakes.

"How are you liking the book so far?" asked Bobill.

The lad stopped his spoon at a crooked angle just before it reached his lips, allowing time for a large portion of oat-slop to slap back into his bowl.

"Uhhh," he droned in dumbfounded thought. "Well, I didn't actually... exactly... quite start yet. I almost read some a couple times, and it seemed pretty cool."

Bobill frowned a bit. "You thought parts you *almost* read were cool?"

"I mean, uh... I skimmed over it a little and saw some of the words. Looked to be written good."

"Written *well*," corrected Bobill. "And by 'skimmed over it', do you mean the description on the back when I first handed it to you?"

The lad looked down at his lap, unable to form a reply.

"It's fine," said Bobill. "Perhaps it would be best if you didn't read it anyway. I'll go ahead and have it back if you don't mind."

"No! It's not like that!" the lad said, louder than he meant to. "I just kept forgetting is all. I've never really been a huge book reader. I'll crack it open tonight. I promise."

Bobill shrugged. "Alright then, I just don't want it to be forgotten and discarded if you're not interested is all. It's the only copy, and I put a great deal of time into it. I know you kids these days will nod right off without an excess of entertainment."

The lad gave his unclecousin his most assuring gaze. "I mean it. I'll have half that sucker read by this time tomorrow. And it definitely won't be discarded, I'd never do something *that* stupid. The story is really important to me."

"Okay, okay, I believe you," answered Bobill. "And though I'm *giving* you the book—would you do me a favor and not eat any of those powdered cheese snacks while you read? You used to make a habit of that when you were too young to understand how *'boring'* books were, and the pages would always turn orange."

The lad quickly nodded, but all he could think about now was cheese... and oranges.

"All right then," said Bobill with a groan as he stood from the table and wiped his mouth. "Speaking of books, I'm heading over to the library to see what Randolf is up to. And—if I'm not mistaken—it's nearing time for your girlfriend to be leaving the Hall of Healing. I'm sure she'd be delighted if you walked her out."

Thoughts of oranges drained from the lad's mind like a flushed toilet, and his face turned as red as one of the strawberries he'd just eaten.

"Wh-wha?" he stuttered. "Sh-she's just my friend! Not *girlfriend*. She doesn't even like me like that at all. I'm pretty sure there's one or a dozen others that'd be on her list before me if she's even considering anyone."

Bobill did that lip-pursing thing again and fluttered his eyelashes before simply replying, "Okay."

He gave the lad a third of a wink, brushed the crumbs from his shirt, and strolled out of the room with exaggerated, dance-like movements.

The lad shook his head and argued with himself about why his own statements were true until he felt the burn leave his cheeks.

A few moments later, he found himself walking down the halls to the medical area. He arrived just in time to head right back out with Sally, who shockingly, was able to walk without any aid.

"That Lord BellJohn really knows his stuff," she said. "Take a look at this."

She stopped and rolled up her pant leg to just above her knee, where a very faint, pinkish line was on display. "Aside from a slight tingling there sometimes, I'm pretty much back to normal."

"That's awesome," said the lad. "Have you been outside at all?"

"No, just saw it through the open windows," she replied.

"The guys are out back right now. You wanna go?"

"Sure."

The two proceeded out of a back door and watched the others while they swam. The lad knew Sally wouldn't be diving in, so he simply sat with her on the edge of a rock with his feet dangling in the water. The group talked, laughed it up, and goofed around like children until dinner time.

As they ate that evening, Brin-Gamiel peeked out of the kitchen and called for Bobill. "Hey, Bobe, would you mind helping me with these buttercakes? I thought I had it down, but the mix seems wrong."

Bobill excused himself, then made his way over to the Elf. Moments later, Lord BellJohn entered the room with a message. He spoke closely to the lad, since it concerned him the most.

"In three days, I will be holding a meeting in a secret room downstairs. I would like you all to gather in the library at one o'clock so that we may all descend down together. Some trusted visitors from other areas of the world are on their way even as we speak. The matter we will be discussing is of great importance to their people, though most know not of it. The ones who are sent may be able to aid in ridding Skiddle Earth of... that certain item.

"I want you to be aware of this beforehand, for I do not want you to think anyone that has been summoned will be a danger to you. It is best Bobill knows nothing of this, and I will make sure he is distracted throughout our time down there. At present, I will be in the Hall of Sitting for a while. If any of you would be so kind after finishing here, I'd like to have a look at any weapons that you have. I've heard there were some exceptional pieces amongst you. Weaponscraft and the lore therein has been a major hobby of mine for many ages. I may even be able to tell you some interesting facts you'd otherwise never have known!"

The Elf turned away and walked into the next room just as Bobill was coming back in.

After plates were cleaned and stomachs filled, each member of the group went to retrieve their respective weapons from where they were stored. Stranger was still away with Silvorkiel, which BellJohn was quite familiar with. He also knew plenty of Wham-Thing and Stink as well, so their owners left them to rest and simply came to hear of other artifacts. The first presented were Bowman's twin daggers and his well-worn bow. Though they looked to be quite ordinary, BellJohn held each with care.

"The daggers I bought at a blacksmith in my town a couple years back," said Bowman. "But the bow was a gift from my dirtbag father. He gave it to me as a Quispness present when I was like seven or eight and I couldn't even begin to pull the string back. I think he said some old hunter gave him a deal on it. I've never been able to figure out what the symbols mean that are carved into the side there."

BellJohn was already looking at the very spot.

"This bow is well made," he said. "It is also fairly old—at least by the standards of men. Maybe fifty... sixty years perhaps. The symbols are ones used long ago by the Lakers of Vim Valley. Strange anyone would still know that language enough to use it, even if it was several decades ago. The Lakers have been gone for nearly twelve hundred years. The name carved here is 'Greywind', but nothing else is indicated. It is a rare piece indeed. May you keep it well."

"Cool, thanks," replied Bowman as he gathered his things and sat down.

Next up was Jim. His spear was crudely made by his father and bore no markings, a thing that BellJohn suggested Jim remedy. At last, after a minute of staring, the Elf lord said it was 'pretty neat' and moved on to the next person.

Bombir slowly shuffled up and laid Spit on the table, wondering suddenly why he didn't just lie or show his toilet plunger instead—the Elf would surely not approve of this sword. BellJohn's long fingers swooped down to pick it up but stopped short just before coming in contact. The hand curled and the Elf slowly rubbed his fingertips with his thumb in decision-pondering fashion. Less than a quarter of a moment later, he reached for a set of tongs hanging near the fireplace, lightly grunting with the effort.

Since they were ten feet away, Bombir took the hint and got them for him. BellJohn used the tool to grab the sword from the table, then examined it all over. After a sigh, he spoke.

"Stranger told me of this. I know not of its origins, though I suspect it to be very old. Its design is unlike anything I have ever seen—which I find fascinating—but great caution should be taken if you make the decision to proceed forth with this weapon, young Bombir. The one who carried it before you was no decent fellow—of that I am certain. Make absolutely sure it never falls into the hands of anyone you do not know or trust, and if at any time your mind's stability comes into question while it lies in your possession, rid yourself of it at once. I will conduct as much research as I am able on the subject and perhaps give you further information at a later time."

BellJohn went to offer the sword back but paused.

"I have one final inquiry before we move on," he said. "Has anyone else your group has laid hands on this weapon?"

"I don't think so," answered Bombir while trying to remember. "Oh yeah—just the lad."

The Elf glanced at the lad, then back to Bombir.

"I see. Here you are then."

Bombir felt a wave of relief as the cool metal was placed back into his hands. He held it tight and returned to his seat just as Sally rose to take her turn.

"This is the only thing I've got that's interesting," she said, unsheathing her curved knife.

BellJohn's eyebrows went high as he turned it over in his hands. The ten-inch blade was polished to a mirror shine, and the ridged handle was wrought of silver and golden metals. Sally never thought much of the intricate craftmanship of the weapon since she'd had it forever, but the look on BellJohn's face told her it was a bit more than a run-of-the-mill bargain blade. The Elf's eyes darted up to meet hers.

"Where did you get this?" he asked with a hint of anticipation.

"My mom gave it to me," she replied. "Wanted me to have something for defense when I walked around town alone or went out to my uncle's shop."

"Do you know where *she* got it?"

"Yeah, she got it from her mother too. It was passed down from mother to daughter for a few generations, starting with my great-grandma Elsie. At least that's what mom told me a long time ago anyway."

BellJohn stared hard for a few moments, enough to make Sally look away in discomfort.

"Has anyone told you what *this* says?" he asked her, pointing to something etched into the small crossguard.

"I didn't know there was anything written on it," she

said, eyes back on him. "I thought those were just squiggly lines."

"There are certainly words here," he replied. "It is written in Elfish—a lesser-known form of Elvish—and only a small number of Elves ever spoke it, myself included. It reads, 'Slicerator: Blade of Elsyrial'."

Sally nodded slowly as the suspense rose to ever-thickening levels, and BellJohn continued.

"Elsyrial was an Elf maiden who once lived here in Drivenrail. She stood out amongst the other ladies with her fiery and unruly nature, and though beautiful, it was the traits of wild defiance that caused her to become the focus of many a young Elfman's affections. Not that she was evil mind you, just that she did not care for the ways in which Elves have always traditionally done things. All advances by her lovestruck admirers were rejected, and eventually she began leaving the city, looking for thrills to have, adventures to go on, and fights to get into—"

"I can relate to that!" the lad rudely interrupted.

BellJohn narrowed his eyes at him, then kept the story going.

"I pleaded with her to join the guards or even the army if it was excitement or combat she craved, but she found those to be uninteresting. She desired to partake in risky and perilous deeds, and to do them alone whenever she saw fit. One day, she climbed far up into the mountains and challenged the atrocious Ek-Heglarak to a one-on-one duel. That vile creature was one of the last Ogres in Skiddle Earth, and amongst the most ferocious to ever live. In the ruins of an old Citadel near the top of Mount Vismel she fought him, armed with nothing more than this blade. She'd conquered many terrible creatures before, but gravely underestimated this particular foe.

"After getting badly hurt and worn down, she attempted to escape, but Heglarak bounded through trees and over stones in pursuit. She thought she'd lost him when she came limping back into the city, but the Ogre had been lured right in behind her. Three guards were quickly killed in the beast's raging onslaught, and only when a dozen warriors made their way to the area was Heglarak defeated. Ironically, it was Elsyrial herself who had regained her strength and returned to make the killing blow.

"I had a long talk with her once she'd recovered, and we agreed it would be best if she left Drivenrail. I never saw her again, but I heard she traveled west, setting up a place for herself not far from the town you now live in. Decades, or even centuries passed, and a day came when captain Elfelfius arrived home from a pursuit that led his company out that direction. He told me he'd spoken to her, and that she'd finally settled down, married a human man, and even had a daughter. The man's name escapes me at the moment. Jel... Jelly-something?"

Sally's eyes lit up. "Jallentine Kergrave," she said. "He died well before I was born, but that was my great-grandfather's name."

"Ah, well, I was on the right track," said BellJohn. "At any rate—you might know this yourself—but after her husband's death, Elsyrial left Vim Valley. It is not known to us in which direction she traveled or if she is even still amongst the living."

"I don't know either," said Sally. "Of course, I assumed she was long dead. I'd never heard she was an Elf or... immortal or anything. I think her name is written next to my great-grandfather's on a headstone with the same date of death for each."

"How unusual," said BellJohn. "We may never know what became of her. But at least now you are equipped with new information of your family. Not the least being the fact that you are indeed at least one-eighth Elf."

Everyone in the room's jaws dropped—all except for Randolf. He had simply raised his eyebrows slightly. Just after that, Stranger came back from his 'errands' and took a seat.

"What did I miss?" he asked.

Randolf leaned over and put his whispery lips within a quarter inch of Stranger's ear to bring him up to speed on their discussions.

Sally suddenly felt odd, as if she no longer knew herself. "What does this mean exactly?" she asked.

BellJohn took a sip of tea while he thought of a response, then said, "Though the situation is fairly uncommon, it is known that the Elven traits tend to drop off considerably with anyone past half. At one-eighth, I would expect you to have slight enhancements to agility, dexterity, and longevity, which could add a possible hundred years or so to your lifespan. But that's only a guess, of course."

"Wow, well... that's a lot to take in," she replied.

The lad once more broke a moment of silence in the room as he loudly said, "So, she's slightly an Elf, huh? That's super cool—I mean it really is—and we'll have to discuss it a bit more soon, but is it *MY* turn yet?"

BellJohn handed Slicerator back with a seated bow as he grilled up the lad with his disapproving gaze, then Sally returned to her chair. The lad gave her a friendly nod and a thumbs up as he made his way over to show off his sword, but almost projectile vomited when, out of his eye's corner, he noticed Bowman put his hand on Sally's shoulder. He tried to ignore it and remained awkwardly tense as he unsheathed his weapon.

"This—is the Super-Deluxo-Saber," he announced merrily.

BellJohn took it in his hands and began his meticulous inspection. "I have heard some rumors about this sword," he stated. "May I ask what material it is made of?"

"I was thinking you'd tell *me*," said the lad. "I heard a loud boom one evening that shook my house, and I go out back to find my toolshed blown to bits. When I searched for the cause, I discovered a huge chunk of rock or metal jammed into the ground. With a crap-ton of effort, I dragged it up outta there and immediately realized it was very thin and long like a knife.

I'd been needing an orange peeler—since I'd worn out my last one a few days before that. I was tired of buying a new one every month too, so I was hoping this stuff would be a little stronger. Just so happened that a big piece of it was barely hanging on and easily snapped off with a few kicks. Ended up being almost exactly the shape of a hammer, which was oddly convenient, so I used it to try and flatten out some of the rougher spots of the main chunk. When that didn't work—"

"Okay," said BellJohn, "so that you are aware, I do not have any idea as to what sort of metal this is myself. If it fell from the heavens, it could be absolutely anything. I was planning next to ask of how you shaped it, and I suppose you are already beginning to tell me of that, so do go ahead."

The lad blinked a few times, then kept going. "I asked some blacksmiths, but they wanted all kinds of stinking money. So, I snuck into a place at night during a thunderstorm, stuck the material over one of those forgey-furnace things, and used the hammer all night long to get the design I was looking for—which took about twenty-five storms until it was finished enough for me. Sure, it came out a little large, a bit crooked, and still rough in places, but it'll peel an orange in a flat second when it's not cleaving a regular sword in two."

BellJohn nodded several times, thinking hard. "I was told this weapon not only cut through the bones of a Wazgall, but actually *destroyed* one that had enhanced itself to a greater level of power. Is this true?"

"Sure is," replied the lad. "Didn't work so well at first, but after Stranger showed me some advanced sword techniques and I'd become desperate enough to try them, I was able to get the Saber to cut right through those boney freaks."

"Astounding," said BellJohn. "Normally, weapons that have been forged with the magic of Elves or higher-level beings must be used to strike down one of their kind—like Sally's Slicerator was able to. This is a very special and powerful weapon that is impossibly unique. I must say it looks more like a potato peeler than orange, but if it works for you, then by all means, keep it well. You've certainly struck gold with this one."

"You figured out what it's made of then?" asked the lad.

BellJohn chuckled. "Oh no, that's just a saying. I meant this was a very fortunate find, and even more so that you were able to mold such an incredibly strong material into roughly the shape you desired. Thank you for showing me this, and many thanks to all of you. It has been a long while since I've sat down to view and appraise such rare and wondrous artifacts. I am retiring to my chambers for the evening. I will see you all tomorrow. Goodnight."

The Elf then rose and made his way toward the door. He took a quick look back and noticed something while the lad fumbled to sheath his sword. It was another blade strapped to his side.

"Excuse me," said BellJohn while turning back around, "but may I ask what *that* sword is? I see it has some strange markings and appears to be quite old."

"Oh, this thing?" said the lad with a laugh. "It's a piece of crap I bought from a traveling salesman. It was dirt cheap and barely holding together. I only got it because I lost the Saber for a while until Jim found it for me."

BellJohn walked over to the lad with curiosity on his face. "Would you mind if I took a look at it?"

"Go right ahead," answered the lad as he pulled it from the strap holding it to his side and handed it over.

BellJohn's expression changed from interest to perplexion as he turned the little sword over in his hands. At one point, he viewed the blade so closely that the lad feared he would cut his eyeball on it. The Elf's gaze continued down to the handle, where at first nothing seemed to be found. He began poking and pulling at various parts, and now the lad was deciding which trash can to throw it in once the weapon had been broken from the Elf Lord's excessive fiddling.

'CLICK!'

Part of the handle did a half turn, then was slid upward to a new position.

"There are markings hidden underneath this moving piece," said BellJohn. "It seems to be positively ancient— even more so than myself I dare say. I may need some assistance in deciphering the symbols. Give me a moment to fetch one of my translating codices."

He carefully placed the sword on a table by the door, as if he was concerned the lad would run off with it if given back. The Elf hurried out of the room, and soon he was barging back in with a hint of uncharacteristic gracelessness. The lad thought he may have even heard a bell faintly jingle. Randolf joined in for a second opinion at one point, and the two went over the scroll for a terribly high amount of minutes. The lad's boredom eventually began to flare up as the oldsters mumbled and pointed back and forth between paper and sword.

Just before getting a chance to whine, the lad heard BellJohn call out, "Here we are!"

The lad leaned in with excitement.

"The symbols carved here translate to a single word: Shiftcicle."

"What the crap does that mean, and why was it hidden?" asked the lad with a touch of disappointment.

"I'm quite unsure," said BellJohn. "I must go through more of my texts and see if I can find any references to such a name. However, now that I look once more, I see there is some sort of button in this area as well."

He pushed on it a few times, adding more force with each press, but it would not budge.

"Seems to be—"

"Well, I'm gettin' tired," blurted out Bobill. "I'll see you all in the morning."

Each inhabitant of the room either nodded or said goodnight to the Gabbin as he yawned and made his way out of the room. Then, they went back to the matter at hand. After BellJohn was sure he could go on without further interruption, he continued.

"It seems to be stuck. Allow me to just...." He trailed off and pulled a small pocketknife from somewhere in his robe, then inserted the incredibly thin tip of the blade down beside the button's edge.

The knife was carefully worked up and down, then side to side. A tiny 'kerk' was heard, and the Elf put his knife away with a bit of a grin. "Let us make another attempt," he said. BellJohn's big, beautiful thumb dropped one last time to the shining metal button. It gave way and clicked in smoothly.

'Whrrr!'

Immediately, the sword began to hum, and less than a second later, a faint glow could be seen all over it. Thin lines of etchings covering the handle and the blade were cycling and strobing through every color imaginable, sparkling like a star. This happened for all of five seconds before the humming ceased and a sound like the release of steam issued forth with a 'Psssss!'. The light quickly faded out, and the sword returned to its normal, uninteresting state.

BellJohn's eyes darted up to meet the lad's.

"I cannot even begin to give an explanation for what just took place," he said. "But this artifact is likely far more valuable than you could imagine. Don't go tossing it in the refuse bin just yet. As I said, I will do some more reading on this sword as well as Bombir's and see if I can find anything. Which of course will have to wait until at least the morning, for the deep night will soon be upon us."

He handed the weapon back to the lad and stood.

"Truly this time—I bid you all a good night."

With that, he was gone. It wasn't long before the room emptied out and all the rest headed to their own quarters for the night.

***

The lad remembered his promise to Bobill as he threw himself into bed. So, he grabbed the green book from the nightstand, cracked it open, and rolled onto his back. He found the first chapter and read the words to himself in a low whisper.

"There once was a man who lived under a pile of mud." The lad chuckled at this. "His name was Bobill Gabbin. He didn't care for adventures or anything of such—"

The book suddenly dropped on the lad's face, and his arms crashed lifelessly to the surface of the bed. Then, he began to snore.

Chapter 24:
Fate of the Fingerbelt

"So, did you get 'half that sucker read' like you claimed you would?" Bobill asked the lad while eating their late-as-usual breakfast.

"Not really half..." replied the lad. "I did read some though. About your hooouuussse... and about how you didn't really care for adventuuuures.... All that stuff."

Bobill leaned in with a stern look, his eyes growing harder by the moment with a guilt-strickening fire. The accusatory pupils ripped into the lad's soul for what seemed like twenty-seven seconds. The lad looked around in discomfort, unsure of how to respond. Suddenly, the harsh face faded away into one of smiles and laughter.

"I'm only joking," he said. "I know you had a late night. I was up late myself. I'm sure you'll find time today."

"Right. I'll get to it after I finish eating, actually."

Bobill nodded, and the two ate their last bits of food.

"Off to read then," said the lad.

He walked toward the exit of the Dining Hall and nearly slammed into Sally, who was wearing a fairly modest swimming outfit and had a towel draped over one shoulder.

"Guess where I'm headed!" she exclaimed. "Wanna join? Bombir ate too much, so he's on the can for the foreseeable future, and Bowman said he had to repair a hole in his hat."

The lad gulped so hard that Elves outside probably heard it, then he began to sweat.

"I... uhh," he mumbled.

The ill-timed situation came at him like viper fangs to his windpipe. He was torn between a refreshing dip with his agreeable lady-friend and hours of reading geezer memoirs in a stuffy old room. Though, truth be told, the room wasn't stuffy at all.

"Go on, the lad," Bobill called from across the room. "The book can wait."

The lad sighed and looked down at the floor, shoulders relaxing.

"I'd like to," he said to Sally, keeping his voice low. "But I promised my unclecousin I'd read some of his book so we could discuss it before he dies of old age. I keep getting distracted and forgetting, so I should get started as soon as possible."

"Well, okay," she answered. "But you *could* always bring the book outside. I'll probably even listen if you read it out loud."

"Okay!" the lad practically screamed.

He ran upstairs, swiped the book from the spot on the floor it had fallen to after he'd passed out the night before, and walked outside with Sally to the pool. While she switched between swimming, floating, and sitting on the rocks, the lad managed to read a few more sentences. They would laugh about some of the things Bobill had written, then go off into a long conversation that may or may not have been related to what was read. After a while, however, the lad ended up playing around and somehow fell into the pool with the book in his hand.

Bobill was furious to say the least, but eventually admitted it was one of eight copies, and *that* particular version was missing the whole second chapter anyway. The lad was somewhat forgiven and handed a replacement copy which he spent the rest of the evening reading with renewed focus.

He read about annoying Dorks that ate everything in sight; his unclecousin's fears of leaving town for the first time; how he was nearly eaten by Trolls but saved by Randolf at the last possible second; the part just after, when he and his group found some priceless swords; his stay in Drivenrail that mostly consisted of sleeping in that closet; Giants throwing rocks; telling riddles in a cave with a weird creature.... That was it! That's where he found the ring. The lad paid extra special attention to every word in this chapter but, unfortunately, learned very little he didn't already know.

Next, the lad read about Bobill's reunion with the still-irritating Dorks, then their time at the house of Neebo the apeman and his secret backyard filled with dinosaurs.

"Dinosaurs?" thought the lad. *"Most of Ron Bomblethorpe's claims were more convincing than that."*

Now, he wasn't sure how much truth stretching was contained within those pages. Regardless, he continued reading into the night, finally deciding to take a break not long after the group had lost a member to the unforgiving forest of Kirkwoods. He'd read half the book. Before going to sleep the next night, the whole thing had been read in its entirety.

***

Bobill was all grins as he sat in the library with the lad discussing his book. He had to assure his nephewcousin that it was all there and all true more than once, though the lad was still quite skeptical.

"I can't believe you guys hand built a boat just to get to the other side of a river!" said the lad. "We did nearly the same thing on our own adventure, except ours was probably built worse and traveled much farther. And those snakehorses?! We saw one in the jungle! This crazy guy used it to pull us in his wagon to Debris."

There was plenty of talk, but an awkward aversion to a particular topic hung heavily over the room. The ring and its powers were mentioned in detail within those pages, and Bobill knew the lad would have read of it. However, the lad began to realize that *not* bringing it up might give rise to even more suspicion than if they talked about it.

"Shame about that neat ring though," said the lad nervously.

"Yes, it is," replied Bobill. "I spent so much time and nearly all of my money looking for it. But I feel like being out here away from that place for a while and taking my months-long nap has cured me of my desire. It was an interesting trinket, but nothing more. There are far more important things in the world to enjoy or worry about."

The lad nodded for a long time, staring blankly at a shelf of old books and not knowing what to say. Just then, Melleniel stepped into the room.

"Excuse me, Bobill," she said. "I think I may have damaged my violin. Would you mind coming over to the workshop and taking a look at it?"

She held the completely shattered instrument up for him to see. It looked as though it had been thrown against a wall and stomped on multiple times.

"Why certainly," answered Bobill. "Want to come along, the lad?"

The lad panicked—he knew it was almost time for the secret meeting.

"Uhhh... you go ahead. I have to... uhh... poop."

Bobill frowned at the lad's vulgarity as he rose to follow Melleniel.

"Didn't need to know all *that*—but alright then. I'll see you later."

The lad sank into his chair with relief, then he heard a sound.

"Psst! PSSST!!"

"Shut up! I know it's you!" he raspily yell-whispered while punching the secret pocket in which the ring resided.

"The lad!"

He suddenly noticed the sound was coming from a door to his right. He looked over to see several people piled into the doorway.

"Is he gone?" asked Stranger.

The lad nodded, then BellJohn rushed into the room and pulled a hidden lever that slid a bookcase out of the way to reveal a secretive stairway. Everyone filed in and descended the steps which came to an end in a large, dark, round room that looked to be carved out of stone. BellJohn snapped his fingers and torches flicked on all the way around them, then he pulled another lever to close the bookcase upstairs.

"Sit wherever you like," he said to everyone. "Just not in that extra-tall chair with the cushion."

As he found a place to plant his backside, the lad took note of the folks that BellJohn had spoken of before. There was a youngish human lady in chain armor that looked to be a bit taller and more muscular than him, with thick braids of black and blonde hair streaming out from under a partial helmet. Next was an Elf guy dressed quite unlike the Drivenrailians, his golden-brown locks swooping upward from each side of his head like the wings of an air beast in liftoff. A couple of generic Dorks, that appeared exactly how one would expect them to, stood just behind the Elf, and following them at a mid-range distance—was some other thing.

Once all were seated, BellJohn announced each attendant for introduction. He started with himself, then moved clockwise around the room.

"As all of you most likely know, I am BellJohn, Lord of this Elf city called Drivenrail." The Elf outstretched a hand, and with it, motioned to his left. "This is the Wizard some call Randolf the Bronze. He is known to many as a powerful wielder of magics and a friendly helper to those in need."

Randolf raised his eyebrows and stared at no one in particular while nodding with approval, though less so than if his highly mysterious ways had been mentioned. BellJohn then moved on.

"Here is the one called Stranger. He is a mighty protector that has served the people of Skiddle Earth for decades by wandering throughout the land and fighting back the evil darknesses which prey upon the innocent. For the sake of honest transparency, I must reveal that he is also the greatest king of our time—the ruler of Silver City in the east. There, they call him King Flaragrin the Righteous, which is his true name. Any further details of this will have to come willingly from Stranger himself."

By this time, at least five people in the room were slid to their seat's edge with mouths and eyes widened to near injury-inducing levels. Stranger—or Flaragrin—folded his hands in his lap and gave a humble, seated bow to everyone. When all had calmed down a bit, BellJohn proceeded once more.

"Next, we have young BombirThin. I have heard he is a

loyal companion to his friends despite the hardships of their journey here, and even single-handedly saved the entire group from a vicious Wazgall attack.

"His best friend is sat beside him—the lad, son of the dad from the town of Hometown to the west. He is the most recent finder and keeper of the object we will soon be discussing today. This young man is but a month shy of eighteen years, and within only the past few weeks or so has accomplished many harrowing feats. While sailing in a boat he'd built with the help of his friends, he fought and defeated the Dread Pirate Johnathew Kreatch who had been terrorizing western waters for over two dozen years, while simultaneously killing the giant aquatic beast known as the Unmerciful Sea Monster.

"Soon after, he scaled a mile-high gate and found himself in a desperate fight to the death against the mysterious and long-forgotten Crimson Pim. This servant of evil was one of several known as the Crimson Guard who were set in place long ages ago to prevent comings and goings at certain locations. Pim was their captain, and known to be the mightiest, the last, and the most elusive of them all. The eradication of this powerful foe is no small matter, and his questionable magic blade now rests somewhat safely in the hands of our own BombirThin, who used it to great effectiveness in aforementioned encounters. But going back now to the lad—he also braved illness, a perilous jungle, an assassin in the night, a pursuit by Ringwafers, mountain climbing, and finally, an epic battle against the legendary Mimson Moe and a Super Wazgall.

"All of this began with a simple vacation that turned

into a dangerous quest. With the help of his friends, and by fortunate chance and/or great skill, he has come here to us with an artifact which could change the course of history. But before we speak of that, we will move along with introductions."

The Elf applied a generous coating to his lips from a stick of balm, cleared his throat, then continued yet again.

"To his right is the lad's friend, Sally. She is quickly becoming a great warrior in her own right, and I believe this will only escalate with the newfound knowledge of lineage she has obtained. She is eighth-blood Elf, and has been wielding her great-grandmother's unknowingly Elven blade for years—even cutting down a Wazgall in a one-on-one duel and surviving a devastating wound in the process.

"To her right is her cousin, Cave-Man Jim. He joined late in the journey but has been essential in aiding his companions to their destination.

"Next to him is the skillful archer, Bowman Slim. He has been a voice of reason and maturity to the slightly younger rest of the group and has saved them from peril on multiple occasions."

The lad frowned a bit at the implications of that last sentence but shook it off as BellJohn moved on to the unknowns in the room.

"Our next guest is Breylamere Sleetsquire. She is the daughter of Guyler Sleetsquire, High Chieftain of Katheltwine Village to the east. She is an accomplished swordmaiden, and has fought in many battles against

Porks, evil Men, and various other unspeakable enemies which dwell near that area."

"That's darn friggin right, Johnny," she said disrespectfully.

BellJohn either didn't hear it or pretended not to.

"Moving on, we have Prince Melongrass, son of Fendrudel, King of the KirkElves. His mastery over bow and arrows is second to—" BellJohn cut himself off, glancing to Bowman and quickly away again. "Well... he's quite good with them—I'll attest to that.

"To his right is Limgee the Dork, followed by his father, Lorky. The two hail from the old kingdom under the Razorfied Mountains, but have since moved on to other, more above-ground lands of their kin."

Father and son stood and took a bow, then BellJohn announced the final member: a dripping, brown mass of goo with strangely human eyes near the rounded, headlike top.

"Lastly, here beside me, we have Murkamel Brownslap. He is one of the unfortunately low number of Mudlers left in Skiddle Earth, and is the grandson of their king, whose name is unpronounceable in the common language. He has traveled all the way from the deep marshes of Siltsenberg to join us today."

Something resembling a hand poked forth from the pile of mud and waved at everyone.

"Now that we are all acquainted with one another," said BellJohn, "let us quickly move on to the matter at hand, and the reason for our gathering. As we know, The Ring of the Time has been found by the lad on his journeys. This ring was made by the Dark King Rauson in ancient days, to be the most valuable piece of wearable adornment the world has ever known. It is powerful as well, having the ability to turn the wearer unseeable among other various effects.

"The thing of most concern is its tendency to corrupt one's mind. The desire to keep it for oneself can and has caused many to attack their own friends and family after simply touching or even seeing it for a moment, and few are able to withstand the temptation. Another issue arises when others aren't fully consumed by it, and the worth and value alone will send one running to the nearest shop for quick cash. The ring moves itself around in this way and is always growing closer to Rauson reclaiming it.

"The evil one was thought dead for millennia, but recent scouting and expert guessing have drawn the conclusion that he is simply in a weakened state. Due to the massive power used in its creation—followed by Rauson's defeat and the loss of the ring's twin—the energy contained inside this tiny metal band is his only hope of returning to his former might. There is so much history involved in this artifact that I could sit here for days and speak of it. Not to mention the other rings he crafted, and the remaining few that still move about the world in the shadows, decaying and destroying all things left in their wake. But, alas, we have no time for such things.

"Rauson's armies are growing and reaching out farther than they have in ages trying to locate the ring, for they know someone in these lands now carries it. The ring must be gotten rid of, certainly, but there is no place to hide it where it cannot be found, and no strength or magic formidable enough to defend it. All Rauson needs is time, and he *will* take it back."

"Okay," the lad piped in, "what exactly are we supposed to do with it then exactly?" His face flushed with embarrassment upon realizing he'd used the same word twice.

BellJohn's gaze fell upon him as he gave a response.

"It has to be completely annihilated, just like its counterpart, The Ring of the Phone, was. There is not a known power that can accomplish this deed in all the world... save for one: Mount Zoom, the place of the ring's birth. There is an anomalous force imbued upon the churning waters beneath that mountain. This force goes beyond any wieldable magic and sends the water's temperature into negative trillions of degrees. It will instantly icify anything that touches it into nonexistence."

"Always thought that story was made up," chimed in Bowman, who was leaning forward with his elbows on his knees.

"It is very real," replied BellJohn. "It lies in the heart of the lands of Dormor—the dwelling place of Rauson, his armies, and many other terrible beings."

"Hah!" snorted Breylamere. "No one can enter those lands! The impenetrable walls surrounding it are at least a hundred feet high and a quarter as thick. The only gate is guarded by thousands of evil creatures twenty-four hours a day and it would only get worse if someone managed to get past them. It is said that dark things live there which haven't been seen since the dawn of days, and your most horrifying nightmares would be laughable in comparison to them."

"Did you hear what Lord BellJohn said of our climbing a gate that was one mile tall?" Sally asked her. "I can't speak on the monsters, but the wall doesn't sound like too much of an issue."

"Yeah," answered Breylamere, "you certainly *can't* speak on the monsters. That whole multi-thousand-foot gate climb sounds like a load either way to me, little girl, but even if it is somehow true, I can swear to you, this is different. There are poison spikes, razor wire, and all sorts of other traps covering those walls—you wouldn't make ten feet up the side."

Sally nodded dumbly and stayed silent but was burning with rage at this girl's tone and remarks. She folded her arms and looked at the floor, trying to think about something else so as not to cause a scene.

The lad began to go off but was drowned out by another voice.

"What about the sky?" asked Bombir suddenly. "Could someone fly in and drop it through the top of the mountain? I've heard tales of a few folks in history that have created flying machines."

"Simple scouting missions have been attempted that way," said Randolf. "None have survived getting so much as a distant look from above. The enemy has more than enough winged beasts to keep the sky under control.

Besides, the mountain has no opening on its peak. As far as is known, the only way to the waters is a small cave nearly halfway up. Even that could have been heavily sealed in the centuries since it was last seen."

BellJohn piped in once again. "Breylamere is sadly correct. It is practically impossible to gain entry. But many here have displayed exceptional capabilities in a vast number of skills. Perhaps if a group was formed and they traveled to the walls, a way in could possibly be found. It's foolish, incredibly dangerous, and likely to fail—but I see no other option. If we do nothing, Rauson's armies could be tearing our lands apart within the year searching for the ring. Most of the Wazgalls were defeated, but they can and will return with greater strength, and worse things still."

All fell silent, and no argument could be thought of, aside from one.

"Well, who's going then?" asked the lad. "You and your Elf armies? Cuz I'm not going on any crazy suicide mission."

BellJohn sighed. "I'm afraid we cannot," he said. "My people are known and watched, and are unable to stray far from this place, especially to the west any farther than the Whitewoods. Our power and magics drain with the increasing strength of Dormor, and we would be of little use at the gates of that land. In addition, there are none in this city that could withstand the draw of the ring, and many would fight each other, try to keep it for themselves, or just simply give it to Rauson. That risk cannot be taken. This group I have gathered here however, possesses the perfect combination of arts to have a chance of succeeding.

The mission must be surreptitious in nature, and the group must not present itself as a threatening presence moving across the lands."

The lad raised his hand, but BellJohn continued.

"I can have scouts move ahead of you and warriors to your sides up until a certain point, but from then on, the company will have to continue on their own. Do you have a question?"

The lad put down his hand and responded. "What in the heck does *'syrup-tissues'* mean?" He emphasized the word by crossing his eyes and making a gesture with his fingers indicating quotation.

BellJohn gave a partial frown.

"It means secret, stealthy. You must travel unseen as much as possible and try not to come in contact with anyone you do not fully trust. I need volunteers from this room, and they would have to leave by tomorrow morning at least. Things are moving quickly, and haste must be taken. Who will carry the ring, and who will guard its carrier?"

The lad stood to his feet immediately and spoke in a serious tone. "I'm not going anywhere but home, and I'm going to save everyone else here the trouble of going for me."

He made his way to the very center of the circle, pulled forth the ring from his pocket, tossed it on the solid stone coffee table before him, and drew out the Super-Deluxo-Saber. There were a few gasps in the room as the lad backed up, then broke into a run. He jumped high in the air and brought the mighty blade down. It contacted the ring, shoving it straight through the stone and into the floor with a tremendous 'CRACK!' and a hail of rocky fragments. The lad lifted his sword and felt around in the stony wreckage below for the accursed circle.

After a minute or so, he found it. It was completely unharmed. Not the slightest blemish could be found on it, and thankfully for him, that was also true of his blade.

"Well, wow," he said.

Then he thought of all the things BellJohn, Randolf and Stranger had told him. He had no reason to doubt their words. His mind went to the future—of more Wazgalls and other dark creatures swarming the lands. He imagined them pouring into Hometown, then killing or enslaving his friends and his only family member, Bobill. He didn't want to believe this was really happening, but the choice had to be made.

"I guess..." he said. "I guess I'll do it. I've managed to not go crazy or kill anyone over this thing so far."

"Which is why I have believed from the beginning that you should be the one to carry it," said BellJohn, with nods of agreement from Randolf and Flaragrin.

"Aside from Bobill, I don't think anyone has remained sane as long as you have with it in pocket," said Flaragrin. "Even he became somewhat desperate and hostile over it eventually. There is no way it could be so much as mentioned to him now, much less shown."

"I'd like help, but I'd rather my friends not go," said the lad. "They've already gone through too much and taken some bad wounds. I won't have them risk their lives. Most of them still have parents waiting at home too."

"The lad has spoken," stated BellJohn loudly. "Who will join him in this quest to save the world?"

Slowly, every person in the room raised their hand—except for BellJohn and Lorky. With the former already having given his reasons and the latter explaining how he was too old and fat to go on secret missions.

The lad turned to his friends. "Guys, I can't let you—"

"It is their choice alone," BellJohn interrupted. "They can turn back whenever they want, and their families will be updated on their outing's extension. In the meantime, I will try to think of something to tell Bobill. It's a shame I had that closet bricked up. Prepare yourselves to leave by noon tomorrow. A great feast will be had tonight, and a spectacular send-off is ready for you upon your departure. For now, I have things to which I must attend. I commend you all for your bravery. Good day."

The Elf got up and threw the switch for the secret door, then everyone climbed the stairs back out into the library.

***

The lad spent the rest of the evening trying to convince his friends to just go home, but they wouldn't hear of it. They all agreed there was no way they were letting him go alone. At dinner, Bobill talked with the lad about some changes to plans he had.

"Lord BellJohn told me you young ones were headed home tomorrow," he said. "But he asked me to stay here a while longer and help him with some problems. The cook got sick for the first time in his three-thousand-year life, and they asked me to stand in for a while. I made this whole dinner myself as a matter of fact.

"Not only that, but it turns out the entire Elven marching band accidentally walked off a bridge and broke all their instruments. So, I was asked to help repair those since I have some skill in that particular area. I did want to accompany you on the way back to Hometown, but I suppose I'll have to meet up with you in a week or so and we can talk about our journeys some more."

"I'd like that," said the lad.

It was getting late and there were still a few things to do before leaving the next day, so the lad said an abnormally long goodnight to his unclecousin, and even found himself hugging the guy.

"Goodnight, Bobill."

"Goodnight, the lad."

***

Early the next morning, the lad was showering up and trying to keep himself in a good mood. He'd been telling himself that he and his friends were simply going on another adventure, and they'd be back in no time. Maybe the world would even be a safer place afterward for reasons he wouldn't let his mind wander into.

When he'd finished, he jumped out of the shower and

wrapped himself in the thick, soft, Elvish towel from the rack, then grabbed another. The bathroom door was ajar, so he kicked it open with his bare foot to go and retrieve the clothes he'd be wearing for the day. He walked out with his head down as he furiously rubbed the second towel at his soaked hair and broke into a song he'd read recently.

"We crossed the lands and defeated the dragon,

we did it ourselves with some help from a Gabbin!

Nearly eaten by dinos and Trolls,

an Elf and an Ape served us buttercake rolls!

Through forest green and over bridges brown,

we sailed 'cross a river and came to—AAAHHHH!!!"

The lad had lifted his head towel and screamed at the top of his lungs when he saw BellJohn standing before him with arms crossed. He quickly wrapped the extra towel around his chest and belly while grabbing the lower one with an iron grip.

"What the heck?!" he cried.

"Excuse me," said BellJohn. "I thought you'd still be asleep, so I came in to wake you up. I'll step out while you dress, but then I have something to show you."

The Elf walked out, pulling the door closed behind. When the lad was sure it was safe, he quickly threw his clothes on and called for him to re-enter.

"What is it?" the lad asked with heart still pounding as he brushed his melon-shaped hair.

"Where is your small sword?" asked BellJohn. "I found some more texts on it late last night and I believe I've discovered how it works."

The lad hurried to get the sword and returned to the Elf.

"So, how's it work then?" he asked.

"Untwist the mechanism like I showed you before, if you remember how."

The lad fidgeted with the handle until it popped open, revealing the mysterious button.

"Now, press the button once, hold the sword out, and yell 'holy shift!'"

The lad stared at BellJohn like he was crazy, but the Elf insisted. The button was pressed, and the lad shouted the ridiculous line. Aside from the same sounds and lights as before, nothing happened.

Before he could protest, BellJohn said, "Wait! Try it one more time, but with the Super-Deluxo-Saber in your left hand."

The lad shook his head, then picked up the Saber and tried again.

"Holy shift!" yelled the lad.

Unbelievably, the Saber vanished from sight.

"Wha—what happened!? Where's my friggin sword?!"

BellJohn smiled, then said, "Say it one more time, but without pressing the button."

Though confused, panicked, and annoyed, the lad obeyed.

"Holy shift!"

The weight of his junk sword, Shiftcicle, changed dramatically. He almost feared to look down, but when he did, the Saber had taken Shiftcicle's place in his right hand.

"The sword can store another sword within itself with the press of a button," said BellJohn. "Then it can be shifted back to the other sword with only a phrase. It was designed to be lightweight with a much heavier weapon sealed inside. A wonderfully genius idea for those who needed to carry enormous blades to fight the giant monsters of ancient days."

"That's awesome!" said the lad. "Kinda sucks that I have to say those stupid words though."

BellJohn smiled. "Well, it just so happens that I also read about how to change that. You can record a phrase for calling and sheathing. Just long-press the button for five seconds while saying your calling phrase. After that, *double*-press and hold again to record one for sheathing. You can make them either the same word or two different ones—whatever you like, as long as you can say it in less than five seconds."

The whole crazy process actually worked. The lad decided on 'Saber!' to call the Saber and 'Unshift!' to bring back Shiftcicle. He had to be at least holding the handle when the phrases were uttered, and once the preferred words were saved, the button's only use was to unbind the swords.

"I think this'll be really helpful," said the lad. "Thanks for going through all the trouble to figure it out."

"Not a problem," replied BellJohn. "Anything for the fellow that's about to save Skiddle Earth."

***

The entire group that would soon be leaving Drivenrail sat down to their last breakfast in safe comfort. Bobill was not present, and someone notified the lad that his unclecousin had stayed up unusually late and was still asleep. However, the lad and his friends were able to use this time to get to know their new traveling companions a bit better.

They told Breylamere, Limgee, Melongrass, and Murkamel of their town and some details of their journey to reach Drivenrail, and in turn, the four newcomers spoke a little of their own homes and past adventures. Though nobody really understood anything that came from the mouth of the Mudler. Breylamere did quite a bit of bragging and seemed to purposely compare her experiences with those of the lad's group, always adding something in to make it sound just a little more interesting. Randolf and Flaragrin stayed mostly quiet and simply listened to the others talk, which went on until just after eleven o'clock. The time for gathering everything needed for the quest had arrived.

The lad grabbed all the belongings he could comfortably carry from his room, then headed out into the hall. He gave Bobill's door a few knocks, but there was no answer. He sighed and joined his friends and companions as they made their way outside to a large patio facing the eastern gate of the city.

"We need to just leave before I start having second thoughts," said Bombir.

"I told you to stay here or go home, Bom," said the lad. "You still can."

But Bombir shook his head hard and straightened himself up.

"We're sticking with you till the end," said Sally.

Bowman nodded with approval.

"All of my magic and mysterious skills will be at your side the whole time," said Randolf.

"And I'll be there with Silvorkiel to guard you with my life and to continue your sword training whenever possible," said Flaragrin.

Limgee joined in as well. "My axe will hew the heads of anything that dare come within a thousand strides of our company! You can be sure of it."

Melongrass had been the quietest of the bunch, but he spoke up then too. "I see you have a skilled archer already, but one more can't hurt. I've had a few thousand years of practice myself, so between Bowman and I, swords may not even be necessary."

Murkamel made some bubbling and burping noises, and the lad pretended that it was helpful.

Lastly, Breylamere threw in her words of motivation.

"I've seen plenty of combat pretty close to that craphole we're headed towards. Been in more than a few battles in my life too, young as I am, and I can promise you that I haven't died even once. I've got your back, kid."

"Yeah, we'll see," replied the lad. "But you should really try dropping that tough-talk nonsense. I considered asking BellJohn to remove you from the group after the way you treated Sally. Don't know how we're supposed to work together when we've got members trying to start crap over every little thing."

The lad caught an implicating glance from Bowman, then added, "I have to admit, it's something I've been struggling with myself throughout this trip. I'm really trying to put it behind me now, so we definitely don't need any more of it."

Breylamere's mouth quivered, and she looked as if she'd burst into profane screeches at any moment. Instead, she relaxed her shoulders and sighed.

"Yeah, I guess so," she mumbled. I'll... see what I can do. Sorry, everyone. Sorry, Sally." She gave a pathetic shrug to Sally, who kind-of nodded in response, then she looked back to the lad. "This quest could end up being the most important thing anyone has ever done—I know that. I'll try not to let my stupid mouth ruin it, alright?

The lad looked at her a moment, gave a firm nod, and the two shook hands.

"You guys can call me Breyla by the way," she said in a somewhat more pleasant tone, "as my friends back home do. My sword is with you. Let's get this done."

The lad was actually smiling as BellJohn approached.

"You are all ready to go I see," said the Elf Lord. "My nephew and my niece have put together a little song to see you off. I must warn that this younger generation's music is somewhat different from our traditional tunes. But I hope it can give you encouragement and perhaps even some light entertainment."

The group looked to an upper level of the patio which was concealed by a huge velvety curtain. It suddenly split in the middle and quickly drew back to either side, revealing several Elves with strange instruments and dark clothing.

"Those are what we call 'electric guitars'," whispered BellJohn to the lad. "If you can believe it, Bobill was the one who showed us how to make them. The lead singer is my nephew, Athloswin, and the lead guitarist is my niece, Aerifin, who Flaragrin was attempting to go out on a date with when he was claiming to be 'running errands'. I'm not too keen on their relationship—she's only eighteen hundred years old for goodness' sake. Anyway, their friends make up the rest of the band. I'll be quiet now."

A few members of the lad's group jumped slightly when fire erupted from multiple spots on the stage. Mist rolled forth and lights of various color beamed out from behind the band like concentrated rays of sun. Through some Elf magic, huge square boxes with circular shapes on their fronts seemed to project the sound of the instruments far louder than any there could have expected.

Aerifin slammed her hand across the strings of her

guitar and let a deep, rumbling growl ring out. The note held long and steady as thunderous drums pounded twice, causing the lad's very clothes to swish back from the sound alone. The drum was followed by a continuous 'tap-tap-tap' of a metallic-sounding cymbal and another strum of the guitar. The drums hit again, thrice this time and even louder now. Towers of fire exploded upward along with each hit of the deep drum.

After a few cycles of this, the guitar rang out until it faded to silence. The lad almost thought it was over, but all at once, the fire, the beams of light, the thrashing drums, and the shredding guitar roared back to life. The gravelly, slamming tune ripped through the air for a short time, then Athloswin pushed back his black hair and stepped up to a small cone-shaped object mounted on top of a thin pole. Evidently, it served to enhance his voice to the levels of the other instruments, and the lad was shocked when his shrill cries echoed across the city.

"Whooooaaaa, yeaaahhh!!!" screamed the Elf before he backed up and let the music continue to pound.

A moment later, he leaned in once more and began to bellow out the lyrics with his powerful vocals.

The Lad and the Ring

'Go forth the lad, you've passed the test,
it's time to journey, it's time to quest!
With friends to your left and more on your right,
all evil will flee in the wake of your light!
Scale the mountain and cross the field,
nothing can stand against the Saber you wield!
There may be marshes and caves so black,
but Wizards and Kings have got your back!

Go forth, go forth!!
To the land Dormor!!
Go forth, go forth!!
And find a back door!!
Go forth, go forth!!
We say and we sing!!
Go forth, go forth!!
And all heck you will bring!!

Go forth the lad, under dark clouds that form,
vanquish your foes and pierce through the storm!
Slice up the Troll and stab that Pork,
fight alongside Elf, Man, and Dork!
Push on through to the Dark King's lair,
while we sing forever of your melon-shaped hair!
Stay the course, fight with all you're worth,
shatter the darkness and save Skiddle Earth!

Go forth, go forth!!
And defeat King Rauson!!
Go forth, go forth!!
Don't turn back, carry on!!

Go forth, go forth!!
Get rid of that thing!!
Go forth, go forth!!
Destroy that cursed ring!!

GO FORTH, GO FORTH, GO FOORRRRRTH!!!
YEAAHH!!!'

The guitars rang out one long final note, then came to a sudden halt as the drums quickly made three last booms. The stage went dark, and mist rolled out. Then a few moments later the curtains closed.

"I told them not to use specific terms!" croaked BellJohn with irritation.

"Eh, I don't think anyone else heard it," said the lad. "But I have to say, that was pretty dang cool."

BellJohn let out a puff of air and regained his composure.

"Are you all ready?" he asked.

Everyone in the group gave a nod, a thumbs up, or said 'yeah'.

"Right this way then."

As they followed the Elf, he turned and motioned for the lad to come up beside him.

"I nearly forgot about this," he hastily whispered while reaching into one of his robe pockets and pulling out a tiny black bag of velvet. "It is not the time or place to discuss it, so I've written instructions and placed them inside as well."

He leaned closer and pressed the bag firmly into the lad's palm, forcing his fingers to close around it. "No one can know about this, and it is only to be used in emergencies, so please be sure to keep it hidden. Don't go and get too excited though—I wish I could offer more—this was simply a last-minute idea that may prove to be of some use in certain situations. You may fall back in line and tell them I said to remember to practice better hygiene if they ask."

The lad frowned, shoved the bag in his pocket, then slowed to walk with his friends once more. Within a few minutes, they came to a closed gate within an archway that led out of the city. Elfelfius and Melleniel stood guard to either side and bowed low as the group arrived, then, they turned and threw the gate doors open.

"May all goodness go along with you," said BellJohn after stepping aside to clear the way. "This is no simple task, and again I must offer my most sincere praise and admiration for accepting it. If anyone can get it done, I believe it is this group of heroes. Farewell to you all."

The lad gave a slow and serious nod to the Elf. "Thank you for your hospitality, Lord BellJohn. We'll be back soon."

With that, the lad turned to face the dark tunnel of trees ahead of him. He took in a deep breath and his left foot broke free from the ground. Upward it rose until it crested its highest point, then it began to fall back down toward the dirt in completion of the very first step of the long and perilous journey.

END OF PART 1

Many hundreds of leagues away in the dark wastes called Dormor, ever-watchful eyes and mostly attentive ears were set firmly upon the head of a wicked and terrible king; one who knew well of the discoverance of a certain endlessly curving, wearable artifact. He had been secretly at work for ages, building his forces and preparing a full-scale attack on Skiddle Earth. Some of his evil servants had fallen already, but more were on their way. The king would stop at nothing to get that rounded piece of magic metal out of filthy and unworthy hands.

With a grim nod and the thrusting forth of his pointed finger, another truly menacing figure clad in dark brown armor responded with a reverent bow. It then turned away, climbing upon a great horned beast of unrelenting horror. The creature's massive gray wings unfurled, and with only a few mighty beats, it rose into the ominous thunderclouds with frightening speed.

'Riding over silent skies;

lost in vengeful echoed sighs.'

About the Author

Johann Balthasar Knörtzer is a bearded fellow who authorizes allegedly humorous, readable content. The only thing he loves more than being mysterious, is bragging about how mysterious he is.

Thank you so much for reading.

If you haven't already, please check out my social media for updates.

@johannknortzer
on Facebook & Instagram
or visit:

https://www.mythicbookspublications.com/johann

**ALSO BY
JOHANN**

Mythic
Books